Peter Mews was born in 1961. He is the author of *Maritime*. He lives in Melbourne.

BRIGHT PLANET

PETER MEWS

PICADOR
Pan Macmillan Australia

First published 2004 in Picador by Pan Macmillan Australia Pty Limited
St Martins Tower, 31 Market Street, Sydney

National Library of Australia Cataloguing in Publication Data:

Mews, Peter, 1961–.
Bright planet.

ISBN 0 330 36458 8 (pbk.)

1. Explorers – Australia – Fiction. I. Title

A823.3

Typeset by Midland Typesetters, Maryborough, Victoria
Printed by McPherson's Printing Group, Maryborough, Victoria

Papers used by Pan Macmillan Australia Pty Ltd are natural, recyclable products
made from wood grown in sustainable forests. The manufacturing processes
conform to the environmental regulations of the country of origin.

To my Father

It is a great pity to be without hashish at any time, indeed.

ALEXANDER TROCCHI

All the washing in the world would not render them two degrees less black than an African Negro. At some of our first interviews we had several droll instances of their mistaking the Africans we brought with us for their own countrymen.

WATKIN TENCH

MAY 24TH, 1842.

Now am I dead? Now that the birds are strewn on the plains below. Now that the river has dried and the fauna bakes on its banks.

FROM THE DIARY OF QUIET GILES, ESQ.

Day Zero

On the evening of the fifth of January a meeting of the Royal
Geographical Society took place in their rooms at the Raleigh
Club in St James's. It had been a cold day and the members
stamped their boots and stood about a blazing fireplace in the
foyer, warming their hands and exchanging pleasantries. A
string quartet had been installed in the farthest corner of the
room, where, beneath the canopies of two potted palm trees,
they played a somewhat too lively arrangement of Mozart's
Fifth. Sir John Barrow, for one, wished the quartet had been
stationed even further away, and he encouraged his companions to follow him through to the dining room.

Although this was not a scheduled Society Meeting, usual
protocol was followed and business was delayed until after the
meal. The men were seated at the central dining table,
beneath the heaviest chandelier. There was a menu at each
place, which the diners eagerly examined over an aperitif. The
fare was not unusually exotic but sufficiently uncommon to
satisfy their taste. Tunisian bean soup was served with Dead
Sea bread, followed by Hudson Bay venison and devilled
ham, accompanied as always by English peas and parsnip.

They drank an excellent Bordeaux from 1829, while on the sideboard several carafes were breathing.

Sir John Barrow presided over the meeting, the presence of the Society's President, Viscount Goderich, notwithstanding. The Fellows were meeting to discuss an application forwarded to Barrow by another member, Harmonious Giles, also present. In all, nine Fellows of the Royal Geographical Society were in attendance, a relatively small quorum, but many of the Society's members were absent for years at a time, exploring the different points of the globe. At this moment, for instance, Franklin was rather out of his depth in Hobart Town, fulfilling the post of Governor of Van Diemen's Land, while it was believed James Ross was somewhere inside the Antarctic Circle. Those members in the Raleigh Club, enjoying the warm wine and assorted cheeses, paid tribute to their fellow adventurers with a toast to Captain Ross and his polar expedition.

'He deserves a peerage if he reaches the pole,' said Beaufort.

'And the Founder's Medal, I dare say,' Viscount Goderich agreed.

'We can't just hand out medals,' countered George Back, whose own Arctic contributions had been thus far largely unrewarded.

'They knighted you,' said Croker, his wizened face taking on a sneer.

'But not you,' replied George Back, 'Secretary Croker.'

John Wilson Croker was universally acknowledged to be among the vilest of men, but he was unused to such direct effrontery.

'That may be a comment you regret, sir,' Croker hissed.

'Gentlemen!' Sir John Barrow called the meeting to order.

Barrow began proceedings with a formal welcome to Mr Huxley and Admiral Lacey, both recently returned from the Southern Hemisphere, then moved on to business. Sir John Barrow was seventy-six years old, nearing the end of his influence, but able still to impress his wish upon the Admiralty, as represented by several faces at the table.

'As you are aware, gentlemen,' Barrow lowered his voice, 'New Holland is a continent to the south as large as Europe, yet it is represented on our maps as a blank. We have circumnavigated its edges. Nothing more. The whole continent is, nominally, under our control, yet we occupy only the southeast corner. It is a perverse notion indeed to imagine that France will keep her hands off this prize, simply because we have sailed around its edges.'

'But, Sir John, did you not direct a settlement at Port Essington to protect us from the north?' asked Frederick Beechey.

'I have seen Port Essington with my own eyes,' Mr Huxley growled. 'It has become a byword for discomfort. En route to nowhere but itself, six thousand miles from Sydney from whence comes every supply, it will never succeed due to its ludicrous location.'

Barrow took these comments graciously, rubbing his rather handsome nose before resuming.

'There are settlements along the east coast, but to the north, Melville Island and Port Essington represent the sum of our achievement. We have made no inroads to the west apart from Captain Stirling's outpost and King William

Sound. Of the country's interior we know almost nothing.'

Barrow's dark neckerchief framed a formidable jaw. He sat very upright and spoke in serious tones.

'My point is this, gentlemen. I have reason to believe some intelligence regarding Captain Jules d'Urville and the Astrolabe. In addition to his mission to the South Pole – which, by the way, will be in every way surpassed by our own Captain Ross – d'Urville has been given leave to explore the coasts of Australia for suitable sites.'

Sir John took a sip of water.

'This is serious indeed,' said John Wilson Croker, whose attitude to foreigners was as fierce as Barrow's.

'An atrocious development,' said Francis Beaufort, his red cheeks reddening with indignation. Beaufort sat uneasily anyway, due to his kidney stone.

'There is no impediment to France, or for that matter Holland, taking up vast stretches of the country,' commented Mr Giles. 'We must act swiftly to thwart them. The country must be opened up, mapped, and the rich lands found.'

'Thank you, Mr Giles.' Barrow resumed control. 'Let me come to your application. It is your assertion – is it not?' Mr Giles nodded – 'that there is a river in the Port Phillip District of New South Wales which runs inland.'

'There are reports,' replied Mr Giles, his jowls working over his immaculate collar, 'several, unrelated reports that this is so. The course of the river runs away from the sea. We believe a branch of the river flows into Port Phillip Bay. It is proposed we begin an expedition at this point and follow the river inland.'

'I am very interested,' remarked Barrow to the rest of the

Fellows, 'to know your opinions.'

The walls of the Raleigh Club were lined with thick regency paper. Harmonious Giles followed the pattern with his eyes then directed his gaze at a sickly rubber tree. In pressing his case for this expedition to the Antipodes he was adhering to his own father's enduring advice, viz., lie with detail and deceive only in good faith. He could not look at the other Fellows while they weighed the information. Harmonious Giles had no doubt the mission was worthwhile, that was not at issue, it was the intelligence about the Astrolabe that remained somewhat vaguer than he had suggested. It may be that d'Urville was merely instructed to call in at Hobart Town on his way to the South Pacific.

The table was cleared and coffee served. A water pipe appeared, heavily adorned with gold plate and golden thread. A liveried manservant packed a mixture of tobacco into the wide bowl of the Turkish hookah. He passed it to George Back, who held the pipe to his mouth while the manservant lit the bowl.

'I am in favour,' Croker was the first to respond. 'I suggest we consider a closer exploration of the north-west also. The French cannot be allowed a foothold.'

'It makes sense,' agreed Admiral Lacey, whose gout caused him to wince as he spoke, giving an impression of a more heartfelt interest than he actually held.

'Mr Giles is correct. The country must be opened up,' said Francis Beaufort. 'Sooner rather than later.'

'There may be an Inland Sea!' Harmonious Giles was unable to contain his enthusiasm. 'Who knows what riches might be found?' He smoothed the white wisps on his pate, smiling now.

'Viscount Goderich? What say you?' Barrow asked.

'I cannot reason against it,' the President replied.

Beechey and Back nodded their agreement, and the Secretary asked if a show of hands was required.

'I don't think so,' Barrow said smoothly. 'Furthermore, I am sure the Admiralty will authorise the expedition without delay.'

'I have just the man, Sir John,' said Admiral Lacey, still animated by the gout. 'Elijah Blood! We'll send Elijah Blood. Cad's been seducing my daughter!'

'And may I put forward my son for the position of Scientist?' Harmonious Giles looked over the rim of his spectacles at Sir John Barrow. 'He is well travelled in Africa and is a first rate botanist – educated in Vienna.'

'What is his name?' asked Mr Huxley.

'Quiet Giles,' he replied. 'Esquire.'

' Never heard of him,' said Huxley, accepting the hookah from Frederick Beechey.

Ship's Log

H.	K.	F.	Courses.	Winds.	Remarks, &c.
1	3	4	SW	N.	Ship departed Plymouth after
2	3	5	..	N.	noon. She had a sentimental
2	4	4	..	NE.	farewell. Several Members of
					the Royal Geographical Society
					inspected the ship and presented
					us with their blessing. Mr Giles
					Senior, father of the Botanist to
					this expedition, gave a memorable
					speech. Some of the crew and
					many passengers expressed their
					misgivings at leaving England's
					fair shore.
					Strong winds and spring rain
					descended as we reached the
					open water.

Day One

Bright Planet berthed at Bareheep. 1842.

The barque creaked against the jetty and for a moment the air was still. Shouts rang up from the makeshift wharf. From the ship's railing the replies came, thin and scared. The antipodean air took their breath away. Already the dock men, bare-chested, red-skinned, were loudly asking for a passenger list, and a description of their persons, hoping to recognise a name. The ship's doctor identified himself and reeled off the particulars in his baritone. Behind him, Captain Elijah doubled over in a cramp, and his heaving could be heard in the pauses between announcements. The doctor would not let the vomiting interrupt him; he simply raised his voice. The men on the wharf cheered as the Angliss family was announced, from Dundee. On deck the Angliss girls smiled beneath their parasols.

A gangplank was raised to *Bright Planet*'s quarterdeck, and the dock men swarmed aboard. The foreman, a huge Scot with sunburnt forehead, marched up to the Captain who was still wiping his face with a spotted kerchief. He introduced himself.

'Angus Brut at your service, sir. What livestock are you carrying, m'lord?'

Not a frightening question in itself, but the beads kept appearing on Elijah Blood's forehead.

'Five goats, two dozen chickens, a pair of hogs, if they've survived.'

'You didnae bring my sheepies, then?'

A guilty tremor crossed the Captain's jowl. 'I'm afraid not, Mr Brut. We have nae sheepies.'

Angus took the news badly.

'I wouldnae complain, 'cept the food we get here is nae good, m'lord. Aye, by Christ, it is fuckt. I prefer to eat a dog to a kangaroo. Most of us scrounge for mushrooms and hope to catch a wee swan. We cannae afford Mrs Howe's game pies.'

'There is no mutton in the colony?' the Captain asked.

'These ones are special.'

Around them the crew was busy, rushing back and forth along the decks, coiling the ropes, and stowing the nautical items. The stevedores began unloading the ship, dragging crates and tea chests along the wharf. Their language, an arcane series of shouted oaths, was already foreign to their countrymen on board *Bright Planet*.

The paying passengers alighted, an even dozen. The expedition members followed: Giles, Cormac, and Angel, each with a small rucksack. A dirt track led through the scrub, away from the wharf. There were no buildings in sight beyond a small shelter which marked the entrance to the path. Two horses were tied up here. Beneath them the ground was dust. They stirred it up with their hooves, and blew storms of it up with their snorts. A bullock and its dray were parked a short distance away. Clusters of grey trees were dotted over the hillocks to either side of the track. They were not tall trees, and they were grey. The small party moved slowly over the stones and the dirt. The sun beat down on their black clothes.

The explorers politely overtook the settlers, and led the way toward the township. It was a journey of two miles. Not difficult, they just followed the track. But the settlers were slow, walking in family groups, and stopping frequently to adjust their dress and set down their bags. Their legs were not used to the slink and roll of the land. Giles used these opportunities to examine his maps of Port Phillip and environs. The track they were following was, of course, a blank. A made-up road. Giles longed to see the river, the great stream that appeared at night in the dreams he had been manufacturing for six months. He longed to see the racing water, boiling away, so he had been reliably informed, unnaturally. The Royal Geographical Society of London had tabled a report compiled from the testimony of earlier visitors to the colony, that the river ran inland, that contrary to all natural laws, the river ran away from the sea. The implications were obvious. A river must needs empty into a larger body of water, a basin or a lake. And consequently, Mr Quiet Giles, the botanist, wanted to believe that upriver where the source should be, there was, rather, an undiscovered sea.

After they had been walking for about a mile, the un-mistakable sound of axes came ringing through the trees. Bellbirds chimed. Hammers struck. The landscape's voice was changing. Soon everything would change, the wild woodlands would succumb to the sawyers' tools, and the superior will of the settlers would be imposed on the terrain, strangling the cries of the landscape. But for now the sound of the sawyers in the distance brought relief to the party, for they had begun to wonder where their destination might lie.

Although the track was well defined, wheel-rutted, and hard underfoot, the scrub encroached still. It offered the party no horizons. Above them, the sky was a brilliant blue, but the light refracted harshly through the atmosphere, presenting their eyes with an adjacent reality. The settlers concentrated on their steps. The explorers looked from side to side, assessing the dense tea-tree scrub. Cormac and Angel were cousins, adventurers both, who had their own good reasons for being six months sail away from Hampstead Heath. And they fully intended to further distance themselves. Bareheep was only the start.

Giles permitted himself no thoughts for home. He was absorbed in the wildlife, which continued its own calls, blissful above the song of hammers that peppered the air. The sounds were rich but the colour had been drained from the fauna. Brown moths lifted in plumes from the tea tree, grey lizards sunned on pale rocks, and in the sky, so many black birds. The track climbed over a small rise, rounded a corner, and opened suddenly on a large clearing at the river's edge. Cormac and Angel stopped. Giles opened his mouth to speak, but was cut short by the excited cries from Kitty and Cecilia Adams as they came upon the scene.

Houses were dotted over the plain, the fields laid out with vegetables and criss-crossed with tracks. And, riverside, the mia-mias and campfires of the Aborigines were visible among the trees. The dusky natives stood in poses, gaunt figures in possum skin, watching the progress of the axe wielders and bullock drivers.

The sight proved too much for Kitty Adams, who swooned, but took time to make an oath against her husband's name. Across the river was the township of Bareheep.

A small jetty had been built at the water's edge, a launching place for river traffic. Here a man was beckoning the arrival party. He stood on the jetty beside a low barge, a battered craft with rope railings. In the centre of its flat tray was a pilot's house that looked too small to stand in. The barge driver ushered them aboard, and consulted each of them for a coin, before taking up his overlong pole and pushing off from the jetty. The river itself was brown and wide and flowed in the usual manner. Giles allowed himself the pleasure of trailing his hand in the water as the barge carried them across to the infant metropolis.

❦

Bright Planet eased against the wharf as the animals were led down the ramp, clattering and bleating, most of them taking the opportunity to evacuate themselves immediately upon landfall, fouling the wharf spectacularly. The goats and the hogs sniffed happily through the communal shit. The wharf hands kept their distance, returning to the ramp for the last of the ship's cargo. The crew lined the railings of the barque, laughing, and looking out across the foreign land. They waited there for Captain Elijah to appear; waiting for the signal that shore leave had begun. The Captain was aft, in his cabin, spewing again, racked with the convulsions. This was no seasickness, though the queasy roll of the ship in port did not help his tender middle. It seemed to the Captain rather more serious than that. According to his diagnosis, he was in love. The sheer incongruity of the idea had sent his body into paroxysms. He was convulsing like a cat. Down on all fours heaving, making a terrible sound.

When the waves subsided and Captain Elijah's frame shuddered for the last time, he was able to catch a breath. He leaned against his bunk, kicking away the bucket of bile with his boot. As his body recovered, drugging itself, he felt a brief moment of solace. He mopped his sweated brow with a long kerchief, then reached inside his unbuttoned jacket and produced a crumpled letter. The Captain sighed, then smoothed the letter along his outstretched thigh. It was not a long letter and he read it quickly. He had read it before.

Then came a knock at the cabin door.

'Aye,' said the Captain.

'Aye,' said the lieutenant.

Captain Elijah struggled to his feet, re-pocketed the letter, and passed a hand over his beard and chops. He followed Lieutenant Trimm along the passageway and down the stairs to the quarterdeck, where the crew had assembled. The Captain prepared to address his men.

The officers stood to his right, flanking the gangway. Each of them in a fresh shirt, with all the buttons done up. The crew stood three deep along the railing, at mock attention, giving mock salute to the pacing Captain before them. Elijah Blood was a naval man, from a naval family, and he liked to see some respect shown to the traditions, although *Bright Planet* was a civilian ship and he no longer had the heart for discipline. He needed a break.

'I wish to remind you,' he began, 'that we have not yet reached our destination. Bareheep is just a port of call. Refresh yourselves. Take advantage of the weather. And steer clear of the natives.'

His guts were still no good.

Of course, not all the crew were aboard.

A seaman named Edwin Robins had absconded. He wore blue speckled trousers and carried a pocketful of the passengers' jewellery. His departure from the ship had been disguised by the commotion of unloading crates and animals. He hurried up the wharf to the Bareheep track, thought briefly about untying one of the resting mares, then continued on foot through the low trees. Edwin carried a calico sack over his shoulders and marched in good time towards the town. Soon, he heard the party of settlers on the track ahead. He slowed his pace, travelling at a discreet distance. He stopped when they stopped, listened to their voices, and felt swallowed himself by the grey land. The voice of Charlotte Angliss soared particularly over the black sand, through the blue air toward him. Her song above the birds' song. And this caused him reverie.

The thoroughfares of Bareheep, though dignified with names, were unsurfaced. The grass turned to quagmire after rain, and hard, potted dustbowls in summer. And it was this baked clay the visitors trekked along in their search for lodgings that first night. They arrived at Fawkner's Hotel on the corner of Collins and Market streets. Most of the rooms in town had been taken by squatters from upriver and Gippsland, who were in town for one reason or another, selling meat and grain, buying stores, and testing the local porter.

William Angliss and his family were the only travellers from *Bright Planet* able to secure beds at Johnny Fawkner's hotel. The Adams family, Herbert, Kitty, and daughter Cecilia, were forced to wander further, Kitty's voice growing harsher and harsher in her husband's ear.

'I'm telling you, Herbert, I want a soft bed tonight, I want hot food, and I don't want you tasting any vino.' She strode ahead of him, dumped the suitcase she had been carrying, adjusted her headgear roughly, and commanded, 'Come along, Cecilia.'

Herbert collected the extra bag, and continued awkwardly in their wake. He was thirsty. He tasted bile in his throat. His mind was shutting down, tunnelling his gaze to the ground, and he concentrated on the dried mud streets. He stepped on grass where he could but his ankles felt as if they were already broken. He had had an unpleasant voyage, though currently he longed for nothing more than the sickly roll of the waves.

The Adams family was forced farther afield. They crossed street after street, with no pattern to their search. The dismay which Kitty Adams felt at the sight of each filthy accommodation sent them reeling off towards the next. The sun and the strain wore on Herbert Adams. By the time he edged through the doorway of the Governor Bourke Hotel the sweat had soaked through his clothes, and the proprietress, Kitty Carr, had to sit him down in the front room with a glass of water. Kitty Adams, meanwhile, demanded to be shown her room. Mrs Carr sent the barman, Huge Lowry, upstairs with the visitors' bags, while she took the opportunity to riffle through the coats of her guests. Herbert Adams watched her. He had the look of a man ruminating, sober like that in the wooden armchair, though Kitty Carr knew nothing could rouse him from this meditative state. When his wife returned downstairs to complain about the squalor of her room, he stared at her too, his eyes filmed over, pearly and green.

The remaining members of the arrival party lingered on Collins Street. The residents shuffled by, bullock drays swore past. Traders lined the street and clerks shouted from upstairs windows. Brokers went by on horseback. A young city, it had sprung from the riverside almost fully formed, and was already dulled by its commercial routine.

It lulled Quiet Giles and his companions into contemplation. The explorers were happy to soak up the street. But the settlers they had accompanied across the seas were agitated by these surroundings. They had arrived at the place of arrival.

Fred Napper and his son George, known more widely as Kid, took off at once. They asked directions from strangers, actually conversed with the draped maid as she hung her washing from a branch jutting out over Elizabeth Street, and zigzagged the grid up to the Lamb Inn. This hotel stood on the north side of Collins Street, and required the Nappers to negotiate the crossing of a fair stream that flowed the length of Elizabeth Street. Once inside, the men were pleased to find two bunks in Room 13, a pitcher of water, and a stone basin. Through a small window which Fred was unable to close, they both watched a band of chickens scrabbling through the dirt, and further, behind the building, a boy was brushing a horse.

The two bachelors, Croaker and Fitch from Dublin, did not concern themselves with accommodation. They found their way to the back bar of Johnny Fawkner's hotel and set about getting drunk. They looked at their surroundings, the low beamed roof, the mud floor, the bearded denizens, and did not feel so out of place. Croaker pulled a string purse out from beneath his shirt, emptied some coins on the bar, and called for mugs of ale. He kept calling until the coins were gone, then reached again for his purse. Fitch drank with him, glass for glass, and so did several of the bushmen, occupying their own shadowy corners of the room. It took several hours to empty Croaker's purse, and by this time it was dark outside. Two lamps were lit, by Fawkner himself, to break the gloom.

Giles had been left with Cormac and Angel on a city corner. The last settler, William Brazil, a man of colour, stood with them for a while before he too stumbled off into the hot grey afternoon.

Giles remained silent. His eyes roved over the buildings, the verandahs, the railings. He took in the faces that passed, the horseback riders, and the burnt stumps of trees that they dodged in the street. But his mind was on the river. His first look had been too brief, but the river had not struck him as imposing. The flow did not appear quick, either way, though it was wide enough.

❧

Edwin Robins found Bareheep by a circuitous route. He had followed the group of settlers along the black track, keeping them within earshot while he thought of a plan. When he heard the cries of excitement ahead he knew they were close to the settlement. He turned into the scrub and worked through the undergrowth towards the river. He could have gone the other way, uphill, and circled around the outpost. But he was operating blind. He had no concept of space or distance here.

The sky offered no clues. It was too far away. Besides, he was thirsty. Although this escape had been planned throughout the long voyage, Edwin had no reliable information about the land he now crossed and he made his decisions momentarily.

Edwin was protecting two ideals. The first was his freedom. He would elude authority at any price, and operate his own moral code. The second was the idea of Charlotte Angliss. A relatively new idea for him, but he suffered greatly these pangs of love. He had contrived throughout the journey to be near her whenever possible. He had cut off his ponytail immediately upon overhearing a disparaging comment that she had made to her mother, concerning two old salts she saw preening and combing out their hair. Edwin sat up high, perched in the rigging for hours while she parasolled on deck with her family. Twice she had looked up smiling and once they had spoken conversationally.

So this was all he took with him, along the tracks skirting Bareheep, his thoughts of Charlotte and a bag of stolen trinkets. He believed one or two of the watches he carried to be quite valuable.

At dusk he moved through the trees along the river, the pink light darkening in the leaves. He traversed a wide marsh of reeds to the water's edge. Here he drank, leaning over the bank and cupping the water to his mouth. It tasted of metal rust. The water was churned by some rocky falls, the river moving in eddies and pooling. Edwin thought of curling up and sleeping, as an animal might, in a hollow, or near a log.

Day One (Night)

They found him sleeping. Two boys poking him with their sticks and jumping back, little screamers. He was on his knees, quick to protect his bag of jewels, looking around sheepishly, his eyes unaccustomed to the gloom. The boys ran away laughing. Edwin got to his feet, turning his face to the sky, listening for other sounds. In ten minutes he would be able to see nothing at all. So he moved now, like a frightened man, through the trees.

This time there were men with the two boys. Their white teeth smiling.

'Whitefella pissed,' the boys laughed again.

Edwin swayed. He had stumbled into the clearing exactly like a drunken man.

He saw their teeth first, then the dark shapes of their bodies. They wore no clothes, yet their skin was covered.

'Christ!' Edwin swayed back. 'Indians!'

They turned around, beckoning him before slipping away through the trees. Edwin crunched through the leaves behind the native party, following their flashes of movement through the thinning grove. They came to a plain, and crossed it under a tricky moon. Edwin followed.

In the sheer night, cries of mirth carried from the township. The village was invisible to Edwin, even as he stood on a hilltop directly to the east. The Aboriginals were camped on the hill. A group of twenty. They lounged on the ground, chatting in groups, warmed by several fires. It was clear to Edwin they had already eaten. He stood apart and did not attempt to engage them in conversation. After a while he sat, his back to a big gum tree, and looked out above Bareheep, the city he could not see. He heard the occasional cry, laughter too, shouting and laughing, but for Edwin this was a false night, and these were the cries of ghosts. They reverberated through the dark, and seemed to swarm above him. Edwin shivered with a fear he had not imagined. He looked back to the campfires but could no longer see the natives. His senses were failing. The night cries were closer as he peered into the blackness, certain there was movement in the trees above him. He looked to the stars, to their reassuring assembly of light, but the sky too was black. Clouds had moved in over the land and Edwin dared not move.

Downstairs at Fawkner's Hotel on that first evening William Angliss insisted upon a toast. He urged the publican to pour out a tot for each of the assembled patrons, and to pour one for himself. Johnny Fawkner, though a teetotaller, obliged. He poured himself a short one from a bottle he kept above the bar.

'To your health,' the wiry publican proposed to the newcomer, and downed the contents of his glass in a swallow. It was cold tea of course, though he charged for rum.

'To the Johnny Raw,' laughed the bar.

Croaker and Fitch, itching bachelors both, roused themselves for the toast, to toss back another stale rum before resuming their stupor. They took refuge in the familiarity of the ale room, the smells and the shouts, and the whispered language of the pioneers. Neither Croaker nor Fitch had found themselves equipped for landfall. They had merely succumbed, operating on dull instinct, and quickly became background action, senseless. Johnny Fawkner kept his eye on them, but had decided to delay their ejection. An uncommon beneficence on his part.

Fawkner's natural malignance surfaced soon enough when a roaming party of *Bright Planet*'s crew arrived. They had been touring the town in the dark, their clothes soiled badly from the various falls they had taken in the mud streets. The only lamps burning in Bareheep were those marking its public houses, so the boys from the boat had stumbled from one saloon to another. The sailors were used to foreign ports, familiar too with misunderstandings and resentful foreigners, although they had not encountered Johnny Fawkner before. He warned them that their first drink would be their last if they did not quieten their calls for harlots and sauce. He poured five tots of rum for the sailors and held his hand up for silence. Basin, the foretopman, was the first to taste the treacle.

'Do you make this yourself, then?' he asked Fawkner. The sailors roared.

Fawkner responded with a brick. He flung it lazily upwards from behind the bar, hoping to break the sailor's nose.

❧

Quiet Giles returned to the ship alone. He did not want to be caught on the roads after dark, and he had hurried along the black track to the wharf, with the sun already twisted along the horizon.

He found the wharf deserted and *Bright Planet* strangely silhouetted against the dim Australian sky. The waters of the bay were still, streaks of moonlight mirrored in its glass. Several ships were anchored further out, their masts standing stark like gallows over the black water. The planks creaked beneath him as Giles climbed aboard, but there were not enough sounds. He found no one on deck, so moved aft towards the cabins. He hesitated on the steps down to the gun deck, then turned back towards the Captain's dining room. Giles knocked but heard nothing from within. He eased the door open, and tilted his head to peer inside. A coffee pot and an empty bottle on the table; a fruit cake opened but barely touched. The door to the Captain's quarters stood ajar. Giles was hardly breathing, his body cocked forward across the threshold, trying to identify the sounds issuing from the Captain's room. Whimpering?

Mr Quiet Giles cleared his throat. There was a great rustling and rearrangement from within before Captain Elijah appeared, wiping his face with a long kerchief. He did not look well. His skin was blotched and his bleary eyes still wet from weeping.

'Ah! Giles,' the Captain tried to say. 'I'm glad you're here.'

'Is everything all right?' asked Giles.

'The ship is empty.' The Captain paused, for effect, cocking a red eye at the botanist, 'I'm afraid I have let the ghouls in.'

Giles frowned. Already fearing that his companions on the journey were mentally weak, and too easily deranged, he decided to ignore Captain Elijah's appearance, and proceeded rather stiffly to deliver his report.

'I have spent the afternoon looking over the settlement,' he said. 'Most interesting. The inhabitants have built themselves a remarkable city – it is as though they have torn it right out of the landscape. As if it were merely waiting to be uncovered.'

'I do not wish to remain here long,' the Captain replied, recovering his tone. 'I have not enjoyed this landfall.' Here he whispered, 'It has given me the oddest sensations, you know how superstitious I am.' Another pause, for thinking. 'God knows what sorts of birds are flying around.'

'Crows, sir,' Giles replied. Although strictly he need not address the Captain so formally, it made him feel purposeful.

'Tomorrow we'll sail upriver to the township, and refit at once.'

'I'll bid good night then,' said Giles, softly, and he backed out of the cabin's doorway. He hurried down to his own cabin.

The sailors were not discouraged by the mayhem in Fawkner's Hotel. The flying brick had indeed accounted for Basin, the foretopman, his blood congealing through his hair, but after several minutes of insults and recriminations, the sailors were on the street again. The four of them stood outside Fawkner's doorway with the lamplight washing over Basin's prone figure.

'You've kilt him, you mad cunt.'

'Let it go, lads. I need a drink.' This from Basin himself.

They took it in turns to drag him along the night streets.

Fawkner watched them go before turning back inside to accommodate William Angliss, who had watched the whole performance with dismay. Fawkner put his arm around the Scotsman and steered him towards the small dining room.

'Are you hungry, sir? I could have some eggs made up.'

Mr Angliss declined.

Johnny Fawkner was not discouraged – he showed his guest the library, a quiet room for 'mentel stimulation' with ratty leather chairs and piles of English and colonial news-papers. A sight for sore eyes, thought William, his spirits somewhat eased. He made his excuses to the publican and climbed the thin stairs to his room. His wife was waiting there, undressed, her blood close to the skin, flickering under the lamplight.

It took the sailors half an hour to cover the two blocks to the Governor Bourke Hotel.

Here Kitty Carr was twirling her dresses across the saloon floor, keeping alive her undoubted talent for theatre. The sailors, the *Bright Planet* boys, were welcomed inside despite their looks. Kitty Carr had an eye for a shilling. She plumped up her bosom as she spoke to them, rearranging ruffles, and flapping, letting in some air, knowing as well as anyone how milky her skin remained.

'There'll be no billiards tonight – I apologise for that – but your boat has dumped a dead man in my lap.' Kitty gestured through to the billiard room where poor Herbert Adams was now laid out on the green-top table, surrounded on three sides by interested onlookers, the ale foaming in mugs. Alone at the head of the billiard table sat Kitty Adams, Herbert's wife. She grieved with long, intricate curses, drawn out of her in evil, sticky breaths.

Mr Giles's assistants, Cormac and Angel, were there table-side, addicted by science to the sight of death, and leering vainly over the clammy form. There was a history between these two, medical boys both, a history of procurement and gothic practices in the streets north of Mary LeBone. They found themselves nostalgic here in the colonies, with yet another body on a slab before them. But that old business on the Heath, the bad business that had set them on this global flee, was still fresh enough, at least in Cormac's mind, to force the flush of guilt over his already sunburnt features.

❧

Quiet Giles banged clumsily down the corridor to his cabin, a small room with bed and chest and table, and closed the door behind him. He removed his coat and flung off his boots with some vigour before striking a match for extra candles. His cabin began to glow. In the yellow light his face looked briefly young, but as he contrived to position his legs beneath his writing table, the contortions of his torso were mimicked by his facial expressions. He propped himself awkwardly up and unplugged a jug of wine. He was an ungainly man.

Giles pulled a volume from the table drawer, a leather tome, handsome enough, but the makers had skimped on the papers, the corners of which were already stiffening. He wiped a nib and opened his book.

The

Most Remarkable Year of

THE LIFE

of

QUIET GILES ESQ, MEMBER RHS

CONTAINING AN ACCOUNT OF

HIS VOYAGE TO THE INTERIOR OF TERRA AUSTRALIS

and the other extraordinary events which happened to him

IN AUSTRALIA

WRITTEN BY HIMSELF

1842

It was finely drawn, this frontispiece, and Giles lingered over it before turning the thickish pages.

16 MAY 1841
The ship had been ready for two months before the Captain stepped unsteadily aboard this morning.

It is now the middle of May in the year of our Lord.

Elijah Blood is the Captain's name. His late arrival explained by the onset of a malaria. His skin is still yellow. His beard is thin.

MADEIRA, MAY 30
The wind changing to E.S.E.

We weighed anchor and stood to sea.

JUNE 4
The ship is too small. Only 95 feet long and 15 wide. A barque the navy did not care for and speedily decommissioned. A coffin for sure. It has only four guns.

It was clear these early entries could do with some work.

JULY 29
We left Madeira more than 8 weeks hence, past the dismal clusters of rocks – the Deserters and the Salvages – and on to Tenerife. We lay off for ten days in Santa Cruz re provisioning – a town full of beggars and immodest women whose rosaries proved no charm against pox and the clap. The markets afforded fresh meat, neither plentiful nor good, and vegetables are scarce on the island as are fish, though poultry abounds. The ship was loaded with pumpkins, onions and

goats. Pipes of dry wine well priced – brandy was also a cheap article.

The two naturalists accompanying us on the voyage – Cormac and Angel – who had thus way provided no signs of their ability, restored some of my faith by forming parties to attempt the climb of the legendary peak of Tenerife.

The passage to Rio in the Brazils was very hot and subject to heavy rains, and the boat sluggish through the long nights of stifling heat and soaking rains. During the day, at the Captain's insistence, health measures were diligently performed. There were frequent explosions of gunpowder and liberal use of oil of tar – these were preventatives against impure air.

The weather more pleasant at the equator – five weeks out of Tenerife – and shipboard awnings were spread on deck to accommodate the balmy weather in the lower latitudes. Beneath this shade passengers were able to pass the afternoons in discourse and light attire. At the end of eight weeks we have arrived at Rio. Here the nymphs are rumoured to throw nosegays at strangers they fancy for an assignation and the entire crew has been roaming the streets of the port without sleep for three days.

We must buy sugar rum port wine rice tapioca tobacco wood hogs and poultry corn flour vegetables and fruit yams and coconuts oranges and limes.

Giles found his blank page and began a new entry. He scraped the nib across the sheet in an untidy hand, trying to maintain a formality in his notations, for he was still conscious that his audience would indeed be the community of science. His ruminations were interrupted by the return to the ship of various members of the crew, the lucky ones, presumably, who had found the way back in the dark. Giles heard the specific arrival of his assistants who lodged in the next cabin, and whose rhythmic muffles and curses continued for too long to ignore. He thumped the cabin wall.

The Captain in his cabin was sufficiently restored to make his own entry in the log. How he feared these antipodes, these far-aways, but he logged the departure of his passengers and confined his remarks to ship facts. Captain Elijah was weary, his beard stained as red as his bloodshot eyes by the wine he had spilled.

Ship's Log

H.	*K.*	*F.*	*Courses.*	*Winds.*	*Remarks,&c.*
1	3	4	N.b.E	S.	Mod't breezes and pleasant Wea'r
2	3	5	..	..	Saw a smoak on the shore. (twelve indians trading for knives – treated kindly) Sorrento.
2	4	4	..	..	The place was already marked on the Admiralty charts.
					Noon: Docked at Port Phillip without incident.
					i. All passengers disembarked but no Customs
					ii. All livestock unloaded and losses recorded.

Day Two

Edwin opened his eyes to an early light. He looked up through the eucalyptus leaves, glad of the blue sky and the song of birds beyond.

His limbs were stiff and his back sore from sleeping on the earth, so he lay still for some time, watching the shapes in the tree above him and the gentle sway the breeze made. There were black things hanging from the branches of the big gum, heavy pods or dark fruits rearranging themselves. Edwin concentrated on the forms, realising as he got to his knees that the tree was dripping with bats, returned from their skirmishes of the night, and now pendent, hung up in their hundreds. Edwin scrambled away on hands and knees. The ground beneath the tree was littered with sparrows' beaks, for as anyone knows, the demon bat eats the head, skull and all, of its prey, but will not touch the beak.

Edwin scampered, emitting little whimpers as he ran; unused to wildlife, he sought the comfort of the natives' camp. He reached the spot, the hilltop where they had feasted the night before, but the fires were out, and the tribe was gone, the sun still barely risen above the township below.

He looked down over the colony, thinking of Charlotte, but with no idea, or plan, to see him through his first day of freedom.

❦

Captain Elijah Blood also woke, but he had not forgotten his circumstance, his despair had not dissipated, and his nausea remained. He had slept in his boots, and he swung them down onto the cabin floor – but he moved too quickly, draining the blood from his head; taking in gasps of stale air, he vomited a stream of rhubarb-coloured bile over the buckles of his boots.

'Damn!' the Captain cried, and wiped his mouth with his sleeve. He reached for the wooden pail of water he kept in his room, and began ladling it over his head.

On deck, the crew were relaxing, consuming some remaining rum after breakfast. Quiet Giles patrolled the deck, disapproving of the sailors' antics; but lacking the power to reprimand, he merely scowled at them and waited for Captain Elijah to appear.

❦

Edwin Robins imagined the city. The horses and the carts. The commerce of the day beginning, the shout of activity in the streets, and breakfast in a thousand houses. He had not eaten for a day, but hunger would not move him from his perch. He was a criminal now, as before, and he needed to plan. He watched the township carefully, deciphering its rhythms, looking for patterns in the criss-cross of its streets. Drays moved up the hill toward his coign, but veered away to the north, the trees too dense for traffic.

Closer to the action, on the same road, a man and a bullock worked without luck at a badly positioned stump. A huge tree it must have been. Edwin watched as the town expanded. Shops opened and the traffic increased. Packs of men emerged into the bright day. Edwin pulled out his purse to re-examine his booty. Two watches on good chains, some brooches, a ring set with blue stones that shone brilliantly back as he turned it in his hand. There were other items too, baubles or jewels. Edwin's father, Godwin Robins, had shown him once, producing a handful of glamour from his stripy breeches, how to tell the stones apart, but the information was lost now in Edwin's memory, erased by the closing remarks his father had made.

'Jewels is always better'n cash.' By which Edwin knew what he must do. He had to get rid of the pretty stuff, buy some clothes and cut his hair, and more than that, change his name and disappear.

But his mouth was so parched.

Wary now of trees, he skirted the hillside looking for a track down to the river flat. The ground he walked was warming up, and he was careful with his feet on the black sand which worked its way easily inside his canvas shoes. The low grasses and scrub swiped his legs as he passed, scratching his skin, and causing him to imagine snake attacks and lizard frills. But it was the ants that got to him, as soon as he stopped to survey the path below. Edwin brushed at the first sting – it felt like a March fly – but yelped at the second, which was inside his shoe. He looked down to discover his feet covered in red and black creepers. The ants were bigger than he had seen before, more businesslike, climbing with their front pincers raised. They looked back at him before embedding those poisonous tongs in his already scarlet legs. He tried to be quiet as he ran, slapping at his heels, straight down the hillside towards the water. But he cared not if he exposed himself, his thirst too was gone. He cared only to bathe his mistreated toes in the wide stream. And when he arrived, still flailing, warding off any further natural incursions with his limbs, he dived straight in.

Once again he wished for a new uniform.

❦

Giles ate nothing. He too was examining his feet, shod as they were in calfskin boots. He did not plan to walk today.

As soon as the Captain emerged, Giles confronted him with his impatience.

'The tide is already well advanced, Captain, we shall lose it if we don't weigh shortly.' Giles approached the bridge. 'Furthermore, not all the crew are aboard.'

Captain Elijah raised an eyebrow. Having attained the bridge, he held firm with both hands on the railing.

'Sploon!' he bellowed loudly and suddenly, calling for his lieutenant. 'Cast off at once.'

'All hands.'

To Quiet Giles, who stood directly beneath him, he remarked again, 'I don't like this place.' And Giles noticed the bespattered buckles of the Captain's boots.

Slowly the ship turned. Moribund, the ship's doctor, joined Captain Elijah on the bridge. Together they watched the scenery slide by.

Mud flats and marshy ground lined the edge of the water. Where the river opened upon the bay a large sandbar had formed, and Captain Elijah was forced to navigate around it, before entering the river. Yarra Yarra. Quiet Giles took the opportunity to mark their entrance by repeating the river's name to all within hearing. He felt the breeze on his face and closed his eyes in pleasure. Cormac and Angel surprised him by their appearance on deck, sporting bruises and the raking marks of fingernails. And surprised him again with their exclamations at the sight of daisy yams on the shore.

The mouth was easily deep enough. The crew took the ship at a leisurely pace. There were nine men working the boat, following the low orders the mate echoed across the deck. The Captain had charts of the bay and the river estuary, but he barely glanced at them, navigating by eye up the wide brown stream. The surface of the river told him all he needed to know, where the channels were, and where the snags lay underwater. He muttered to himself much of this time, scanning the water from bank to bank, briefly raising his voice to his mate to begin the relay of a command.

The ship's doctor joined Giles on the deck below. They had come maybe three miles upstream, and here already another river entered, wider at its mouth than the first. The ship came around, dragging its stern wide, and, raising an extra sail, they breached the new water.

Moribund leaned into Giles.

'Mr Giles,' he said, 'I think you'll find *this* is the Yarra Yarra.'

And then he gave his customary snort, preceding an unexpectedly high-pitched gale of laughter. Giles was polite enough to accede, turning his gaze over the swamplands bordering the river. The first birds were arriving. Plover, snipe, geese. Cormorants, teal, so many ducks and water-fowl that Giles was pleased to recognise. He pointed them out so gaily at first that Moribund thought he was singing a schoolyard song. But Giles's tone sombred as the tally of names mounted. These birds were commonly known in Europe and Africa, the swamp scene could have been plucked from any number of locales on the Mediterranean. This would make dull reading indeed.

The vistas did not improve on the glide upriver, though the views were not unpleasant. The lands looked quite rich, plains stretching gently away, thinly wooded with honey-suckle and she-oak. If not for the huge red gums lining the southern banks, Mr Quiet Giles feared that he would be announcing the discovery of some countryside in a valley near Cirencester. As *Bright Planet* rounded each bend he expected the scenery to unfold more reasonably. But the landscape approaching Bareheep consisted of a succession of gentle hills and dales. There were indeed some enchant-ing spots.

Giles noted, as the morning progressed, that the weather was too warm, that his eyes were not adjusting well to the light. He waited for the animals to appear. On the poop deck Captain Elijah was smiling, but Sploon and Lieutenant

Trimm both saw the streams of sweat running down the Captain's neck. His pores were just opening up. The men noticed this, and they exchanged a glance.

As they neared the fledgling city, the swamplands resumed to the south, but on the right the ground was higher. The animals did of course appear, several sheep carcasses floated stiffly past starboard, their feet in the air. Moribund he was by name, but the doctor had the grace not to point these out to Giles, fearing no doubt that the botanist could only bear so much disappointment. The river curved around a prominent hill covered with grasses and she-oaks, and Bareheep was revealed anew: a grid of rude streets, shanties, low verandahs. Here and there a stone house. The crew watched in silence, their ship sidling by, until the city seemed to shrug its bones, smoke appeared, and figures began waving from the shore. The buildings beyond the wharf grew suddenly more imposing, and a string of grander facades sloped up a pleasant thoroughfare. On board *Bright Planet*, someone was laughing.

Quiet Giles, though, was beside himself with disappointment. Surely he had not imagined the hot dun landscape of the day before, the desolate feeling of the alien land? The settlement too seemed different, or rather, more familiar.

'Take note, Mr Angel, of the flora surrounding the town, and if you will be so kind, report back. Please reassure me that there are such things as native grasses, strange flowering plants, even lichen and moss that we have not seen before. In short, I want an unknown species.'

This was no small task for Angel, as most grasses and flowering plants were unknown to him. He had been able to convince Mr Giles during their interview in Deptford of his botanical ability, but he knew nothing more than could be found in the pamphlets he had swotted during the hot coach ride from Cheapside.

'And you, Mr Cormac, will spend the afternoon making drawings. I want Bareheep from that hillside,' Giles was pointing. 'And I want a view of the river, including those falls.'

Giles pointed again, past the ships that lay moored ahead of them, in a natural basin that formed beneath a rocky falls stepped into the river.

'And pray God,' he said to no one, 'there is a way past those rocks.'

❦

Edwin dried himself in the morning sun. He lay on the river bank, still breathless from the panic that had so engulfed him. He had woken to a surprising world, unnatural surely, but he had not thought he would be so afraid. Nor feel so ashamed. He chided himself, and for a few minutes let the warmth of the sun bathe his thoughts.

He had dived into a shallow part of the river and sunk his hands into mud on the river's bottom, sparking further fears, and he broke the surface spluttering. His shoes sank in the mud, as he stood waist deep in the water, looking around and blowing hard. He reached down to remove them from his feet, threw them onto the bank, then unstrung his trousers before hurling them too. He groaned as he did so, a cry really, unable to fathom such poor luck.

His jewels! He lurched back to the bank, the mud sucking at his every step, the river reeds striping his legs with weals as he scrambled up the shore. Edwin was sobbing as he reached his trousers, sobbing with relief as he fondled the pink purse still tied to his trouser pocket. He bundled everything inside his wet shirt and stowed the parcel between two rocks. The stones were safe, and he crawled back to the river's edge and slipped forlornly into the water.

The swim, his thrashing about, had done him good. He lay now with his clothes drying, and one eye squinting against the sun. Downstream, there was activity on the water. He was still a mile or so from the township, but he could hear voices carrying upriver, and inland he caught fragments of a song the sawyers had begun.

He collected his clothes, and dressed again, though they were still very damp. He followed the river back towards Bareheep in search of a crossing, until he rounded a bend that allowed him a point of vantage of the wharf, and the river traffic that had roused him. Beneath him a pile of heavy rocks had tumbled across the river, forming a noisy falls. And the sound was soothing. Two large ships were moored in the lagoon that formed below the falls, and many smaller craft, skiffs and rowboats were parked nearer the wharf. Punts ran back and forth, and a merchantman was unloading at the dock. All in all, a reassuring scene.

Edwin's clothes were dried stiff on his limbs. He had scratches on his face, and his hair was aghast, having dried in blond peaks, but he blended in well enough with the crowd that had gathered outside the Customs House. Here were sailors of all types, merchants waiting for their barrels, and gangs of loitering young men. All of whom were watched over by a ruddy-faced constable, all belly and flamboyant chops, stationed discreetly near the entrance to a busy thoroughfare, but whose red waistcoat shone out like a beacon nevertheless. Edwin kept his eye on this portly agent as he moved through the crowd.

He recognised his ship, *Bright Planet*, coasting past on the river, saw the figures waving on deck, and all around him cries went up. Edwin turned on his heel, worked back towards the Customs House and, out of view of the constable, he scurried away up an unnamed street, quickly finding himself in a large market square. The stall holders held up their cabbages and pears for Edwin to inspect and he took the time to laugh in their faces, but his immediate problem was clothing. And money, for he needed coins before food.

Edwin smoothed his hair as best he could, adopted a swagger, and brazened it through the jeweller's door. The clanging of a bell immediately unnerved him, and his first words for the day were a stammered 'Good morning, sir!', spoken loudly.

From a seat behind the counter a bald-pated man removed his glasses and did not reply.

'I have some items to sell. Family items.'

Still nothing from the waistcoat.

'A watch,' Edwin said, producing his bag of jewels,

knotted tightly to the waistband of his breeches, 'and a bit of this and that.'

His fingers struggled with the knot. So much that his lungs began to constrict, emitting little nervous laughs, and firing his cheeks. The string was not giving way, and Edwin's broad-bitten nails could gain no purchase. The jeweller smoothed his strip moustache and hummed. He hummed in a way Edwin did not like. He tore at the string again.

'Would you have a knife, sir? A blade or a dagger I could use?'

The jeweller refused to engage. He replaced his glasses slowly. He had slow movements for everything. He opened a drawer with a long sigh, the maple soughing against its own grain, to reveal a tray of tools, delicate supplies, picks and pliers and polishers.

The knife was sharp enough. Edwin felt it with his thumb. The jeweller stood back now as the young sailor sliced his purse over the glass counter. He held position for a moment, arm raised, fingers gripping the horned blade, then the clatter of pearls, and the soft descent of fine chain, the clatter of rubies. Of course the watches fell heavily. Cracking the glass in fact, the jeweller's glass.

'I'll not give you nothing for them, you foul thief!' The force of the small man's anger surprised Edwin, the quivering brows, the short teeth. He had a spiteful look.

'What about this?' Edwin held up the blue ring, the sapphires, blue even in the air between them. 'It must be worth a few coins.' He held the dagger in his other hand. Though still he had not understood the plot, the jeweller was unhappy with the scenario.

'Pah!' said the waistcoat, but he reached for the ring. He turned it in the light, then slid it onto his pinkie finger, and admired it there from several angles.

'Belong to a fat lady, did it?'

'I will not hear a word against her,' protested Edwin. 'Not me old mum.'

The sun came into the room hot, late-morning bright. It glinted against the stash of items on the counter, the gold, and the tiny down covering the jeweller's pate. He smiled for the first time, a blunt smile more suited to a bigger man.

'I'll take the jewels,' he said, 'and I shall furnish the Chief Constable with your description. You won't be hard to find, you look like a thief.' The jeweller laughed. 'I'll tell him to look for the tow-haired sailor, and he'll find you in someone's garden stealing taters.'

The jeweller was a small man, surely, but he contained a lot of blood. To Edwin's horror, most of it seemed to be pulsing out through his waistcoat. Things happened quickly. Edwin saved the watches and tore the blue ring, agate or whatever, right off the jeweller's hand. He left the blade in pools of dark and sticky blood on the counter and turned for the door. The bell clanged again and he was back on the street, stuffing the trinkets and timepieces into his pocket as he ran. Passers-by, shoppers and dray drivers, looked on, noting his features and the way he grimaced as he ran. Already the events were receding, but Edwin was replaying them in his mind, too dismayed to think ahead.

The jeweller had finished his speech, maintained his pleasant tone and slowly replaced his glasses. He blinked, smirked again and squealed when Edwin Robins reached over and stuck him, stuck him like a pig. Edwin could still feel the tingling in his hand, he'd brought it down so hard it must have split the ribs of the little man. The bell on the jeweller's door rang again and Edwin took one look back, only to see the red waistcoat stagger out amidst a chorus of cries from the onlookers, one arm raised in protest, before pitching forward onto the hard dust.

❧

Bright Planet was anchored in the river alongside two big three-masters, *Hindsight* and *Forethought*, the two largest ships in port. Reluctantly, for his guts were still no good, Captain Elijah climbed to the prow of the ship's dinghy. He installed himself in the cramped space and closed his eyes while Trimm rowed gracelessly across the pond. He opened them, not even alarmed, when Trimm banged the dinghy against the jetty posts by way of braking.

The Captain set foot on land at last, as unsteady now as he had been seven months earlier, jumping from his Plymouth hostel bed and crumpling to the floor. The leering gaps in the Bareheep dock forced him to grip Lieutenant Trimm's arm rather too tightly.

Up on the wooden wharf, Captain Elijah smoothed out his coats, aware that his arrival was being noticed, both officially and unofficially. The official reception came in the plump form of the Customs Master, Badgery, who hailed him with one arm raised, from the steps outside the Customs House. There was a certain pomp in the greeting.

The Captain carried his box of documents in his right

hand, mopped his brow with his left. He saw the constable in his waistcoat. He saw the barrow boys. He saw three gentlemen foppishly feign laughter over a joke at his own expense. In several places money changed hands. The Captain's trousers chafed in the heat, the water coming out of his person was quite remarkable. Once again he dabbed at his cheeks. He trailed Lieutenant Trimm gratefully through the crowd, the port scene.

At the edge of the throng he saw the gangs of idle young gentlemen in their threes and in their fours. They saw the Captain and he saw the city behind them, traffic and stalls. He did not like the look of this place. He said as much to Lieutenant Trimm as he shook Mr Badgery's hand and looked up at the white stone walls of the Customs House.

Badgery noted everything down, names and dates, scrawling them with a nasty quill while the ship's Captain waited. Captain Elijah sat on a hard wooden chair, with his boots spread wide apart, one arm cocked on his knee. He held his temper, checked even the mildest hint of his impatience, for he needed this man, this oddly hirsute outpost official, and the money and promissory notes he would shortly be doling out. He whiled his time examining minutely the walls of the chamber, the oak desk before him and the miraculous sproutings on Badgery's forearms. When these arms eventually reached under the desk for the strongbox, the Captain held back a smile. Badgery unlocked the box and removed a roll of notes. He peeled off several bills, talking low as he had been all this time, his arithmetic apparently benefiting from the incantations of numbers.

Captain Elijah secured the money inside his coat and slowly folded the promissory notes that Badgery had so elaborately signed. These were his ticket of leave; he could begin restocking the ship for the expedition, and as he quit the company of the Customs Master he was pleased to note that he had conducted the whole transaction without uttering a word to the strange beastly man. In the lobby, however, Badgery's offsider was lurking.

'Monsieur Le Souef,' cried the redhead, 'Customs Inspector.'

The Captain halted, visibly dismayed.

'What is it?'

'A consideration,' replied Le Souef, bowing slightly, 'I will require a consideration.'

'What for?'

The Captain glared down at the man but the wretch was grinning back.

'It will save me having to search your ship, mate, it'll save you a lot of time.'

The Captain unpacked his roll of notes and peeled one off for the inspector.

Outside again with the air thin and hot and the pain in his ears returning, Captain Elijah instructed Trimm to locate the missing crewmembers, who had slipped away from the docks and dispersed once again into the metropolis. It was midday and the Captain was pleased to note that the prickly air was causing all around to break out sweating underneath their woollens. Elijah wiped his face, red kerchief, and then set off himself to find Doctor Moribund, who had been summoned to the Governor Bourke Hotel to attend the body of Herbert Adams, and, it was possible to imagine, to give the widow succour.

❦

Quiet Giles spent the afternoon in the library at Fawkner's Hotel.

A profound melancholy had descended upon his features. It was a gloomy room. The two glass-fronted book cases, the two worn leather uprights and the fraying *chaise-longue* were afforded no light from the small, south-facing window. Giles glanced through the yellowing stack of newspaper beside his chair. He had already read the London papers six months before, read them as he always had, in the bay window of his Kensington home with a shapely pot of tea and a rack of warm toast, so it was with a poignant humour that he was forced now to peruse the local dailies.

The *Herald* contained little more than personals and land sales listings, though the front story expressed outrage at the inconvenience suffered by the patrons of the Governor Bourke Hotel the previous evening, being forced to share the bar with a corpse stretched out on the billiard table. The *Patriot*, on the other hand, was openly salacious, devoting keen paragraphs to the *Divers Acts of violence and ribaldry* that Fate and Fortune had recently visited upon the slatternly streets of Bareheep. Giles read these with interest. Although dismayed by his own curiosity, he reasoned that the study of civilisation was, or could easily be, Science. The *Gazette* he looked at last, put off by its Byzantine typeface and the rather oafish patriotic tribalism it trumpeted. But a particular piece attracted his attention: a lengthy list of complaints by women concerning a local squatter had been fashioned into an envious tale touting the exploits of an erotic maniac.

But for most of the afternoon Giles slumped rather stiffly in his library chair, gazing at the shelves. His eyes were lidded in the gloom, and though he was not sleeping he did not look up when one of Fawkner's daughters brought him a tray of cakes and ale. She spoke softly to him, a surprising whisper that registered slowly in the swirl of his private thoughts, but was enough to rouse him from his brown study.

Giles turned to watch the girl go, dimly aware of the fatuous expression on his reddening face. The Fawkner girl, Sarah Jane, was a complete sauce, the type of Beer Street dancer he had sometimes glanced at when he found himself in that corner of London. But typically Quiet Giles was sexually shy and he had remained faithful to his wife. The last weeks of the voyage, from the Cape to Hobart Town, had tested him sorely. The weather had been pleasant and the ship had simmered with the variously unsatisfied lusts of the voyagers. Again in the library Giles was affected.

Meanwhile, outside the town limits, Giles's two scientific assistants were cruising the countryside. Cormac pencilled sketches of the Bareheep variations while his cousin reclined on the hillside. Their collecting had not gone well. Angel had insisted upon staying in the shade while the sun was high, and then confounded them both by producing a wrap of opium to pass the time.

'I will just tell him there was nothing I did not recognise,' Angel reasoned as he lay back on the leaves.

'It all looks strange to me,' replied Cormac. 'Strange trees, strange lawn . . . The light is too dry.'

His drawings were good. They showed the city's grid of clean facades, drawn from above, nestled between three hills. He drew the river idling past, its banks lined with high trees, and all of this beneath such large skies, which made everything seem low.

'I'll put some grass in a bag,' said Angel.

Angel closed his eyes to the late afternoon light, flares of which danced inside his eyelids, and lay still, with the air moving across his face. He used his knapsack like a pillow. Cormac licked the tip of a pencil with his tongue. The sun began its last descent, and in the weakening light Cormac could see the detail in the colour of the trees. In the hillside the layers of rock darkened and hued. The beasts were in the sky, lifting from their trees into the blue air, and with their black wings beating they followed the course of the river away from the sun. Suddenly, too, the sound of birds ceased.

Cormac packed away his sketchbook, unnerved by the quick malevolence of the evening. Beneath them now, in a clearing on the hillside, a herd of strange animals had appeared, a group of thirty or more large grey kangaroos.

'Jesus, Angel! Will you lookit them!'

Angel opened his eyes.

'Oh! Cousin, will you lookit them!'

In unison the animals lifted their heads to watch the two men; they remained perfectly fixed, profiled, though Cormac noticed one or two continuing to chew.

'Do you recognise those, Angel? Seen a few of 'em on the Heath?'

'Shhh, Mac! You'll scare them away.'

Though they were off anyway. Cormac and Angel watched the animals bound through the long grass and quickly disappear.

❧

On the corner of Market Street, outside the hotel, an organ grinder competed with a trio of violins for the attentions of the early evening crowd. The chance of these musicians scoring a coin from the passing strollers was actually increased by their discord, and indeed Quiet Giles felt in his pocket as he passed them on his way out of Fawkner's Hotel. It was after seven, darkness arriving, and he wanted to make it back to the boat.

Giles found a man at the dock who could row him out to *Bright Planet*. The man was drunk and missing teeth, and Giles was not drunk but paranoid. The onset of night was giving him horror. It was a familiar torment. Giles stilled his own teeth as he palmed the gob his money. The boatman did not own a dinghy but he borrowed a canoe for the jagged journey across the river, and Giles ascended the ropes with his trousers quite wet, much to the amusement of Basin the foretopman, who was nursing his head on deck.

'Feeling better, Basin?'

'Quite, sir, though the wound still bleeds somewhat,' he said, touching his temple.

Even in the link light Giles could see the man's fingers were wet.

'Come to my room, Basin. I'll sew it up for you.'

Giles forced the shipman to kneel while he cut away some black hair from the area of the deep pink gash. Giles held a thin candle close to the man's head, accidentally dripping some white wax over his shining cheek.

'Careful!' cried Basin.

Giles held firm, this time pouring spirits liberally over the area of the fleshy wound.

'Bite this.' Giles handed him a biting stick, and, with one hand pushing the lips of skin together, began to sew.

When it was over, when the screaming finished and they could once again hear the carousing sounds of Bareheep across the water, Basin turned a flushed face to Giles and thanked the scientist. Giles dismissed him and paused for a moment of reflection after the cabin door had closed, before opening his diary with a flourish of the wrist.

NOVEMBER 7

The rough weather has passed, but we are in the midst of a great swell and remain at the mercy of the waves. The ship itself is overcome with nausea. Below decks the stench is so great that many of the crew stay on deck night and day, wrapping themselves in the rigging to sleep. No one can eat. Moribund has visited the paying passengers.

This was not what Giles wanted to read. He searched

through the early entries, trying to recapture his state of mind. This first night on the river was agitating him, this time of night reminding him of his wife, something about the sudden dark that made him think of her silken quim.

Giles was still greatly disturbed, too, by the letter that had reached him at Plymouth before their departure. His wife had written audacious things, seated provocatively at her dressing table in Kensington, with a wanton use of ink, audacious things for Giles to carry with him, to fret over, to spoil his calm at all times.

June 16 Santa Cruz

No activity on board. I have remained at my hot desk all day, the air in the cabins does not move and at times I rush to open the door, fearing that I have already breathed each breath twice and the atmosphere will soon be poison. I have written three letters to Mary and deemed none fit to post. I must not chastise, but she must be warned of the dangers.

It is clear she suffers from clitorisme – the act in which women substitute, perforce by a kind of artifice, the pleasures which are reserved for love between the two sexes. It is for women the same thing that masturbation is for men. Our last union was not easy. Her frantic movements dislodging my member too early. My seed spurted over her whiteness while she continued apace. How large her bud had grown! The constant attention sees it gorged and ripe, surely the size of my thumb. It is only now I can see the signs.

Clitorisme points to the collapse of social order, for such women do not masturbate alone, they are addicts, sunken and debauched slaves. Do not let me imagine the seemly drawing rooms where all etiquette is abandoned, where the women engage in their crimes against nature.

He stopped reading. He shook his head as if to clear it, and then took up his quill. The candles had burned low and the light was flickering, but the sounds had returned. Giles could hear the voices now, the songs that carried across the river to his cabin, the raucous clamour of Mollies in their rooms, an argument rising and falling, and the swift crack of a leg breaking on the waterfront. He could hear Elijah Blood coughing in his room, a keening impatient sound, and Giles thought the Captain must be drinking.

Captain Elijah had certainly tried a couple of tots, but had spent most of the evening prone on his bunk, hoping to ease the desperate pressure in his lungs. At least the river mooring allowed him a still berth. His stomach felt better, but he could not sleep without the pitch and the roll of the sea.

Eventually he rose, pissed long into a bucket, then took the three steps to his desk. He sat up at his table long enough to record an entry in the log.

Ship's Log

H.	*K.*	*F.*	*Courses.*	*Winds.*	*Remarks,&c.*
1	3	4		S.	Took Bright Planet upriver. Easy
2	3	5	..	..	draught at every sounding.
2	4	4	..	..	Moored below the falls.
					Met Customs and recd £29 for
					each emigrant embarked.
					Trimm in charge of shore activity.

Day Three

Captain Elijah was a ladies' man.

The Admiralty wives had secured his rise through the ranks. As a young man his looks had been so dashing, so faint-inducing, that his reputation preceded him to ports far across the globe. There had been an incident in Gibraltar that delayed his rise from lieutenant to Captain, and forced him to cool his heels in Plymouth for six months. He had been obliged to await the retirement of the offended admiral before the Naval Office could be persuaded to give him his own command.

Captain Elijah Blood became himself at age thirty-three. A time when he still loved the sea, the adventure and the prizes. Each new command brought him closer to joy, and on the waves, with the wind square in his face, the crew shouting their song, the beauty was in the black beard of his being. This was before Clara Lacey of course, before he knew the terror of that love which changes.

It was Clara's letter he carried, and he read it again this morning, holding his breath against the rolling nausea he felt. He did not vomit though, he survived the crisis with a bout of hot sweating, and was actually hungry by the time he reached deck. Again most of the crew were absent. Trimm and Sploon were smoking on the poop while Mr Giles walked thoughtfully forward and aft, hands behind his back.

Captain Elijah approached Giles, ignoring a call from Sploon, and surprised both of them with a bassoony greeting.

'Good morning, Mr Giles! Do I startle you from your thoughts? 'Tis no weather for such countenance.'

'Good morning, Captain. I cannot break the habit of walking the decks, though there appears land on both sides. Permit me to say you look well this morning, sir.'

'Yes, Giles, I slept somewhat last night and suffered only a few shivers this morning. Will you accompany me ashore? I dare say I feel like some eggs.'

Captain Elijah did not wait for an answer, bellowing immediately for Trimm to unfasten a dinghy.

Ashore for only the second time, Elijah took Giles by the arm. Together they skirted the porters and parrots on the quayside, the dapper youths, the quick crowd that formed, money transactions, agents, errands. In Market Street the stalls were up, the shops were open, a milliner, a chandler, shipping broker's office, and certainly an undertaker. Here a coffin was being built for Herbert Adams. It stood on a trestle in the street; a young man with flaxen hair, in dunga-rees, was planing the edges and the shavings had collected around his feet. Arm in arm, the two ship's men climbed the hill to Collins Street. Here they turned right, seeking a room with coffee and newspapers and general ambience.

Collins Street was broad and almost elegant. There were stylish buildings to one side, views from the other, but there were no shade trees, only a few obstinate stumps of the local variety. The Captain walked more steadily here. He swallowed a mouthful of bile that rose suddenly as the promenade spread before them, but spat the second mouthful into the dried mud at his feet. Giles gave him a consoling look, mid-sentence, as he absorbed the anthropology of the early city scene.

'You can see for yourself the grand frontages and colonnades are facade, the dirt shows through,' Giles concluded.

'It remains a false city, you might say, the mock centre,' enjoined Captain Blood, 'of a *faux* civilisation.'

'Yes!' cried Giles.

'Mock Victorian!' cried the Captain and they roared, laughing.

They walked a long block down Collins to Elizabeth Street. Here their progress was halted by a somewhat unpleasant watercourse which flowed the length of Elizabeth Street to the river. They followed the line of the creek north looking for a simple crossing, Giles again noting the two-storey houses on either side of the street, the privies of which were connected to cesspits that fed, by mistake or design, into the creek before them, itself feeding into the Yarra Yarra, from which the drinking water was of course pumped. Giles kept these observations to himself, mindful that the Captain was seeking breakfast. They forded the shitty creek with the aid of jumping stones, strategically positioned by some helpful mason, and continued the path up Collins Street to the door of Overton's, where the smell of baked bread was so enticing. Citizens from all over were milling around this shop, munching buns in the street and stowing loaves in their carry-alls. The Captain refused to queue for bread and he led a reluctant Giles onward. At the next corner, beneath a sign depicting native women arms akimbo, they found a coffee-house run by a certain William Nicholson, who roasted and ground his own beans, and was quick to acquaint the two newcomers with the one-horsepower steam engine he employed for the purpose. A lank boy stood beside the coffee machine, sweating damply into his apron. He allowed the quick grope of his employer's hand to go unacknowledged. The aromas inside Nicholson's coffee-house brightened the travellers' humour and, pleasantly, their window table afforded them a good view of the wide street. The proprietor made small talk as he produced his steaming blend.

'I read about you fellows in the *Herald* this morning.' He set down their gold-rimmed cups. 'I thought you must be adventurers the moment you walked in.'

Captain Blood and Quiet Giles blushed, or Giles did, for the Captain's face had already flushed superbly, the coffee searing the roof of his mouth and burning all the way down. Nicholson smiled, and spoke walking away.

'I see most of the explorers, stopping in here for a coffee on their way through.'

'May I see the newspaper?' asked Giles.

As soon as it was produced, Quiet Giles eagerly opened the broadsheet. The Captain nursed the shredded skin on the roof of his mouth. William Nicholson leaned over the botanist's shoulder to read aloud an article that recalled the arrival of Count Strzelecki – the enterprising pedestrian naturalist – who had arrived in Bareheep with his friends and *compagnons de voyage* two years before. He found a 'scruffy gimcrack town' of six thousand people, mostly young, male and free for all sport. Nicholson took pains to point out Strzelecki's own eccentric behaviour. This information was by way of an aside, to counterpoint the patently marvellous city the explorers enjoyed today.

Giles was confused at the intrusion. He lifted his eyes from the already yellow newspaper, and saw that Nicholson was in fact hoping to read the whole piece, despite the discomfort of craning his neck somewhat. Giles set the broadsheet down and gazed sagely through the picture window until the proprietor withdrew. Nicholson's breakfast entertainment comprised the preamble to an item in the *Port Phillip Herald*. The newspaper also included a nice paragraph trumpeting details of the *Bright Planet* expedition launch, but Giles was able to read that for himself.

They spent a large part of the morning at the window table. Traffic was heavy outside. Collins Street was lined with cabs, and horse feed was blowing all over from loose bags and boxes. Nicholson sent for the boy's mother with the elaborate breakfast orders of the newcomers. The Captain got chops and eggs. As did Giles. But there was brown sauce and toast, though not in a toast rack, and not the best toast. Behind them the coffee drinkers came and went, the boy fuelled the boiler of the roasting machine, and the smell of roasting coffee, heavy and intoxicating, enlivened the room.

In good humour, Giles refused a third cup. He folded the newspaper and glanced at the Captain, who was engaged in monosyllabic conversation with Nicholson's boy. The boy's eyes were rimmed red, as rheumy as the Captain's, pleading, pitiful.

'Please!' the boy implored.

'No,' said the Captain, his beard wet around his mouth from making the sound.

'Sir . . . ?' Giles interrupted.

Outside again, they took their bearings.

Collins Street sloped up to the east, the loamy thoroughfare pitted with stumps and choked with bullock drays. The bullock drivers swore impatiently at the passers-by, the horsemen and the smart boys who lined the street smoking. The cause of the commotion was quickly clear. The front dray was pitched forward, and its bullock, sad-eyed, was down on all fours refusing to move. The driver, face to face with the animal and driven himself by the taunts of his fellows, was laying into the beast, first his fists then his feet. His blows were ineffectual and the shouts continued from behind.

'Give her the tail twister! That'll wake her up!'

This advice brought a cheer from the quickly assembled crowd. Giles and the Captain lingered too, watching the plumes of dust rise from the bullock's black hide with each blow. Soon enough the driver tired and walked around to the rear of the animal. The sweat was pouring from beneath the driver's felt hat. He was a wiry little man, the muscles showed through his shirt as he grabbed the bullock's tail, which humorous appendage stiffened and flicked in his hands. He twisted the tail hard, then twisted it sharply again. The crack rang out in the street and the animal bellowed. A great groan from the crowd preceded the cheer as the bullock rose to its feet, shaking its head from side to side and flinging drool onto one or two of the nearest smart boys. It stood there swaying, sick at the thought of its own snapped tail askew in the air behind it. The driver resumed his station and the traffic continued, Giles and the Captain heading back up Collins Street in the manner of a stroll.

Fawkner's Hotel was misshapen, a two-storey, whitewashed brick fort, with a quaint pyramidal roof, like an umbrella opening. The building occupied an imposing corner above the marketplace, overlooking Customs House and the Yarra Yarra. On the south bank of the river could be seen horse riders skirting the swamplands. Inside the hotel were two drinking bars, a dining room, smoking room, and library. Refuge enough for the overheated inhabitants of Bareheep.

The two ship's men sat uneasily in Fawkner's library, unable to lean back comfortably in the leather uprights as they conversed with the proprietor, whose savagery was only thinly concealed by a tailored suit and an undeniably handsome tie.

'It seems to me, gentlemen, that the upper reaches of the river, though as yet unexplored, will be found to be tributaries which feed yet another river system. Thus can be explained the unnatural direction of the flow.'

'Quite so,' said Captain Elijah Blood. 'The whole expedition is misguided.'

Giles regarded the Captain queerly.

'It is our object,' he responded, 'to follow the guidelines of the Royal Geographical Society and to discover the truth of the matter.' Giles paused. 'We seek such knowledge in order to dispel myth-making and uninformed public opinion about the interior of this continent.'

The other two men, in turn, regarded Giles.

'Have you been upriver yourself, Mr Fawkner?' asked the Captain.

'Only as far as Poison Hill, where the Scotsmen do their boiling down. That will be far enough for me. Beyond there only Fools go. Squatters and natives. And a fine mess they make, from all accounts.'

Fawkner took his leave – he had better business to attend – and immediately Giles rang the bell for service, having no space in his mind for doubting. When Sarah Jane Fawkner appeared he asked her for lemonade and biscuits and, after a quizzical pause, rum. She too regarded Giles oddly, but completed the transaction with a sarsaparilla smile.

The afternoon light slanted into the room, shining off the stains on Captain Elijah's boots, lightening the rum in his glass, and heating the crotch of his woollens. He downed the glass and poured another, then tilted his head in a listening attitude while his companion talked.

'Observe and deduce!' Giles was saying. 'That's how I was taught. Observe and deduce.'

The Captain's head tilted further as Quiet Giles recalled his boyhood years at Lyme Regis, the birds' eggs and the animal bones, three rows of preserving jars under his bedroom window, and his disapproving mother spilling the skulls outside, burying them with a sermon.

Captain Elijah was already dreaming, nostalgic and sick for the women he no longer knew. Gorgeous and stupid daughters, irascible wives quick with their fingers, creamy angels lounging at the wharf. These women he had loved or allowed himself to waste. Nothing consoling, however taut the skin, in the folds of memory.

The two science officers, Cormac and Angel, reported in late, arriving at Fawkner's just as Giles's head was nodding for sleep in the library. His book had spilled open on his dark lap, and one hand rested loose, half curled, on the page. Giles breathed through his open mouth while his eyes fluttered beneath a black fringe of hair. An observer would note the twitching in his cheeks, the falling hair, the open mouth, and be able to deduce a certain state of mind within.

Cormac and Angel, the sandy, tow-haired blonds, observed as much. They shuffled together through the low door to the library. Angel cleared his throat, hemming and hawing, while Giles roused himself.

'At last!' he cried. 'Progress at last.'

He beckoned the two youths into the library, offering

them the rather pretty love seat, which they eventually took, so that Cormac faced Mr Giles but Angel could not but sit at right angles to his companion. Giles regarded the cousins, front-on and profile, raising his brows at one then the other.

'Well?' he asked eventually. 'What have you got to report?'

Cormac looked around the room, crossed and uncrossed his legs.

'Is the Captain all right?' he asked, inclining his head toward the supine commander, whose arms hung limply over those of the uncomfortable chair, his face awash with sweat, and who was making a considerable noise of snoring.

'I guess,' replied Giles.

Cormac began his report.

Their scientific inquiry may not have been thorough, but he presented the results clearly and appeased Giles somewhat with his lively manner.

'We have scoured the surrounds to the west and north of the metropolis, finding undulations of a pleasant scale and one or two outposts on the better slopes where gardens have replaced the natural flora. Two miles to the north there is a suburban settlement where many Irish have built themselves inferior dwellings. They call this place Newtown.' He paused to assess the botanist's reaction.

Unsmiling.

'Some of the houses weren't too bad,' remarked Angel, as if this concession might sway the mood.

'We saw a large group of kangaroos,' Cormac continued hopefully.

'Show the drawings,' said Angel helpfully.

To Giles's surprise the sketches were good, the views captured a strangeness, an antipodes of landscape that he had hoped for. His patrols of the city streets had dulled his sense of their exotic location. Giles had seen only that industry abounded – there were sawmills, metal foundries, tanneries, fellmongeries, and boiling-down works at the river. The streets looked English, the newspapers read like English newspapers, the Insolvency Court was full – to all appearances it was an English town. But Cormac had captured something else with his drawings, the pretty town nothing but a weak fracture in the scenery. The view across the river to the south showed the swamps and the dense scrub stretching for miles.

'The air, as you will have noticed, is swarming with crows,' Cormac continued. 'Cawing from one end of the day to the other.'

Giles nodded, shuffling through the drawings.

'There's empty bottles scattered for miles,' chimed Angel. 'Bottles all over.'

Giles examined the sketches made to the west. The valley was obviously a beauty spot, with picnic grounds marked with cairns and a lake labelled in Cormac's neat hand, *Saltwater Lagoon*. He turned over the sheet and baulked at a languid depiction of a shirtless Angel, in repose and smoking, but passed over it without comment. He glanced at his two assistants propped up in their chair. Neither returned his gaze. They were taken instead by the ghastliness of their Captain's appearance. His face had broken out in hives, angry welts on his neck and cheeks. He was awash with sweat and, all in all, Giles conceded, did not look well.

❦

To the west of the city was Saltwater Lagoon, beauty spot and hunting ground. The land sloping down to the blue lake was purple with pigface in full bloom and the air was filled with the mingled odours of purple lilies and Myrnong flowers. Deafened by the noisy birds above him, Edwin Robins stumbled into this miasma of vapours. The crows appeared over Flagstaff Hill and the local birds started screaming, particularly the elusive spur-winged plover, but curlews too, and the water birds began to run, ducks, ibises and blue cranes in numbers.

Edwin stumbled again. His pursuers were gaining on him easily, their horses fast through the grass.

The two riders were followed at some distance by Chief Constable Wright, on foot and heaving. His large frame shuddering forward on his too-short legs. By the time he reached the lagoon Edwin was cowering on the violet earth, circled by the Whelan brothers, whose identical beards hid identical sneers.

'He's ours, chief,' said Murray Whelan. 'He tried to take off wiv me bruvver's 'orse.'

'No,' breathed the ample policeman, 'I'll take him in.'

❦

As evening fell, Giles found himself alone on deck. He admired the purple sky and the low clouds sweeping the pink from the horizon. Taking just a moment to breathe, Giles looked down at the black water of the river. He resolved to shave his moustache the next morning, and began preparing his thoughts before retiring to his cabin and the blank pages of his diary. He had arranged a bed at Fawkner's for Captain Elijah, leaving Cormac and Angel there to tend his alarming symptoms, and downstairs he bade a good night to Fawkner's sweet daughter. She had smiled and looked down. He felt a flush between them, and bowed too, smoothing his chops with one hand as he departed.

Now Giles installed himself at his desk, cramping his knees against the cabin wall. He delayed opening his diary. Instead he drew a blank sheet from his leather folder and began a letter to Mary with a sentimental greeting. He wanted to convey to her the dread loneliness that had overcome him since their arrival at this secluded city. He tried to make his words plain, but the page soon filled with exclamations. Giles feared that Mary, replete from her frequent salons, must regard him as a parsimonious husband. She had every right to exclude him, deport and exile him thus. He signed off with a flurry, her anchoretic lover.

Giles moved within his cabin like a monkey in a cage, clambering over shelves and riffling through his trunks. He was hungry, so he fixed himself a snack from his private larder. A decent plate of Brazilian sausage spread with fine chutney from Shepherd's Walk. Then he unpacked his copy of Labillardière's book of Australian flora, opening it at the

Swainsona formosa once again, the first plant in the collection, the first example of which was smuggled back to Kew in the pockets of the pirate William Dampier. The drawings pleased Giles, page after page of exotica and improbable colours. He pulled out his other *Florilegia*: Ferdinand Bauer's sketches, Dampier's *New Voyage*, and Robert Brown's *Prodromus*. He laid these open on his desk, piled atop each other, each drawing obscuring part of another. Settled thus, he produced his coloured inks, arranging the little bottles in a line before dipping his finest brush into the violet vial. Giles proceeded to colour in the petals of a *Trachymene billardiera* he had copied, though this was of course a yellow plant.

He started drinking well before the men began returning to the boat, rowed out to the middle of the river in gangs. He heard them clambering up the hull ropes, and he heard the deep splash when one of them dropped, followed shortly by another, great peals of laughter, snorting, someone spewing over the side. Giles did not leave his cabin, did not let their antics disturb him; he had taken out the laudanum tonight. There he remained, absorbed in the drawings, tracing out the patterns of an Angophora leaf.

Captain Elijah woke from his fever shortly after nine o'clock. He woke to a dark room, ravenously hungry. His limbs felt light. The welts on his skin were gone. He felt rested. For a moment he felt his old self, an optimistic wave of lust, and he planted his socks on the floor. He felt around for his boots, then he lit the kerosene lamp. Everything normal. By the time he got downstairs, however, the dizziness had arrived, and he sat down quickly on the bottom step, where he passed a few minutes before Fawkner found him.

'Feeling better, Captain Blood?'

'Christ! I thought I was a goner,' he muttered.

'Feel like some porridge now? Cold mutton? What's your fancy?' Fawkner was chewing on something himself while he spoke. A blade of meat so obviously dry it had collected in shreds through all the cavities in his mouth.

'Do you have a shot of rum?' asked the Captain, hungry for the second time that day.

He let the sinewy proprietor lead him to the kitchen, finding the family seated there, gathered at a big table over supper. The girls looked up at the Captain, big-boned girls with wide eyes. He managed a swagger as he took his seat, with a nod to each of the ladies.

So while Johnny Fawkner poured out a tot of reasonable rum everyone smiled, including Captain Elijah, who was trying out some charm, and even so the silence was not uncomfortable. Captain Elijah had come to fear conversation, the awkward intimacy of a fresh acquaintance; he no longer desired to know the details of other people's lives. He was merely passing through, enduring the series of situations that made up his journey.

'Your men from the ship have gone,' Fawkner informed him.

'Strange buggers,' muttered Mrs Fawkner, sawing off a hank of mutton from her plate.

'They thought you might spend the night here,' continued Fawkner. 'Of course, you are welcome to stay.'

The Captain sipped his rum, and then sipped his beard, before announcing to his hosts that he was recovered, quite, so much that he felt like a stroll in the evening air, still warm after all.

'It is too dark to go roaming, Captain.' This from Mrs Fawkner, whose opinion was echoed around the table in grave nods. 'You'll do an injury for certain.'

'Nonsense!' cried the Captain, adopting pomp. 'You are too kind. I must thank you for caring for me. Too kind.' He smiled benevolently at the family and wiped his eyes as he rose from the table.

The Captain found the night air black and bracing, the great draughts sharp in his lungs but invigorating nonetheless. He strained to listen for sounds in the dark; for a moment he could hear nothing above the noise of his own blood rushing. He walked assuredly east, retracing the steps from his morning stroll along Collins Street. His mind had come alive, rejuvenated by the attack of illness, and was now calmly, excitedly, sorting through the possibilities. The way was lit by the occasional glow of lamps from upstairs windows, but he lacked a destination. He turned north at the Elizabeth Street stream, fording the water confidently in his boots, and slipped into unfamiliar streets. He passed no one, but the city was no longer silent.

Bursts of raucous talk were peppering the air, guiding the Captain's progress. He was assaulted by the fetid rhyme of urine and blood, fresh manure and decomposition. He cut down alleys, paths so dark he had to feel his way along wooden walls, behind which he heard coughing and low moans, hard whispered words. The blood in his veins so thick and thrilling that the Captain's throat constricted, and when he came at last to Lonsdale Street his breathing was so laboured and his face so flushed that the first two ladies he encountered gasped in alarm. The street was awash with revellers, spilling out of doorways and some sprawled in the hard mud; the few lamps there were gave off a purple haze, a carnival air.

Figures emerged into the light, arm in arm, painted or drunk, and skipped past the Captain, who was standing now on the wooden porch of the Governor Bourke Hotel, his breath rasping through his beard.

Captain Elijah had been operating on instinct. He had made no coherent decisions all evening, having been propelled through Bareheep by his own racing blood and heavy glands, but he stole a moment here, while his pulse slowed, to reflect on the situation. There had been rain and the street was turning to mud. He needed a drink, something to thin his blood – he reasoned there must be too little flowing through his frame and it was causing all kinds of dizziness.

So he sidled through the doors of Kitty Carr's hotel, adjusting his clothes self-consciously under the gaze of Kitty herself and the two jacks who perched beside her at the bar.

'Rum, Captain?' Kitty asked. 'Let me buy you a drink.'

❦

By 7 pm Monsieur Rotin, the ship's cook, had abandoned his galley, never to return. He clambered down the starboard ropes to the last dinghy and rowed himself across the darkening water to the dock. M. Rotin was prepared to take his chances in the far-flung metropolis. Anything to avoid the prospect of further advances from the ship's mate, Jerker Jenkin. He had taken several items from the stores and he began drinking from an earthenware jar after only a few strokes of the oars. His subsequent zigzag progress was witnessed by Dr Moribund on the poop. Moribund gave it no mind. The sun was low in the west and he was glad to be alone on the ship again.

Not far away, holed-up in his cabin, the shy botanist was thinking the same thing. *Bright Planet*'s crew had all returned to the township as soon as they could.

It was odd however, thought the doctor, that no one was left on watch, but it was also clear that the chain of command had broken down somewhat over the last days. The attractions of port had lured Moribund too. He had spent the afternoon in the company of the new widow Kitty Adams, overseeing her grief, comforting her with slow words and clutching her soft bosom to his chest. These ministrations had left her weak, so the doctor removed her shoes, unlaced her corset and encouraged her to the cushions on the best bed in the Governor Bourke Hotel. There she lay, keening silently while Moribund cooed above her, kissing her hands and her hair, trailing his own hands over her.

'There, there,' he had said.

'Yairs, yairs,' she said. 'Yairs!'

Now Moribund produced one of his favourite pipes. The

walnut bowl was rimmed with gold and the stem inlaid with mother-of-pearl. He felt in his waistcoat pocket and unwrapped a light bronze wedge of hashish, from which he rolled a ball the size of a peppercorn. He packed the pipe with a thumbnail and crouched out of the wind to light it.

He patrolled the poop as the sky reddened above the collection of boats at anchor, and gazed across the river to the south where three men on horseback were taking the air. The smoke from Moribund's pipe billowed away, colouring the breeze a particular purple, reminding him again of his afternoon house call and Kitty Adams' stupendous feats of abandon. This is the way the doctor's oblivion began.

Meanwhile, in his cabin, Giles heard the rain begin outside, sudden rain, arriving in a squall, the sound all around him. He tasted the laudanum, reflecting almost at once on the nature of his own bliss. He lay back on his bunk, drowsy and sleepless; he let the waking dreams begin. The city streets of Bareheep, already catalogued so neatly, seemed in Giles's memory to be overgrown. Refuse had been dumped everywhere and animal carcasses were upturned in the road. The river too was boiling with sheep and horses caught up in the deluge. Such scenes were not new to Giles. His opium dreams were always conflicted. Thus he could see the patterns of treachery in nature, the extravagance with which science was thwarted. Giles knew that his senses were deranged, of course, but only in this manner could the journey continue. The lakeside walk, the afternoon jaunt.

Dr Moribund . . . He too was prone in his own cabin, naked but for his socks. His bunk creaked beneath him as he writhed. The kind of hirsute agony the doctor endured was not merely imagined. It was constructed lividly from his black room, dark so that he could be blind to the creatures that tormented his skin. Fleas ran through his hair, jumping in their hundreds from his pillow to nest there. Tiny spiders curled in his groin, stinging his bald scrotum. Moribund screamed with delight.

Giles wondered at the sounds. The ship was alive with hallucination. He raised himself from his bed and momentarily removed the hot images from his mind's eye. Candlelight and shadows. He manoeuvred himself to his desk, a comic move that the awkward botanist had mastered. His wicker wine case, purchased that very afternoon, was still open on the desk, eleven quarts of opium prepared and corked. The twelfth bottle was in use and though he was already in vivid conference with the underworld Giles poured another draught. After another brief dream he packed the case away and brought out his diary. The pages of his precious journal crumpled under his fingers, the words receded before his eyes, blurring and disappearing.

There was a line of lighted rooms along the second floor of the Governor Bourke Hotel. A reveller in the street could pause to gaze up and be rewarded with a shadow play, naked men and women cavorting and so on. Though no one looked up, there was too much fascination in the street.

Above the verandahs of Lonsdale Street, Captain Elijah's condition had improved. He had spent an hour downstairs in the billiard room drinking ale and swallowing herrings, a restorative he had not previously enjoyed. This night the fish slid down like salty snails. The Captain was entertained at billiards by Kitty and her jacks, Sir Thomas Fry and Aaron Greedy. A relaxing game, which Captain Elijah won easily, was followed by a wager and a much more competitive effort by Sir Thomas Fry. Sir Thomas was not a knight. His parents had christened him thus, not wishing to rely on his future achievements to gain himself the title. He had left Cheapside at fifteen and worked his passage to the colonies, turning excellent swindles in the ports Cape Town and Madras. He turned another one here for Kitty Carr, fleecing the Captain of coins.

But Kitty Carr stopped the games. Something in Captain Elijah's red-rimmed eyes, the old lady killer, moved her to protect him. She ushered him back to the lobby, to a divan flanked by potted palms. Here she ran her hand through the Captain's hair.

Kitty had been a procuress in Deptford and was not rid of her old habits in Bareheep. Upstairs, in several bedrooms, were women who looked to Kitty for every need. She dressed them, fed them, brushed their hair, and in the salon of their toilet, she advised them to marry the first raw johnny who came their way, as long as his purse was full. For their part the women, though not really interested in marriage, kept their bosoms powdered.

There were a lot of hangdog squatters in the front bar of the Governor Bourke Hotel. They drank long draughts of

Colonial Ale and rocked back in their cracked boots, always a hand in the pocket of their evening weeds. This was the show they'd been waiting for. They raised a cheer as the girls came down the stairs, sashay and shake, one after the other, Miss Ashley, Georgiana, barefoot on the tiles, Emily and Jane, dressed alike in lacy white, finally Charley, her name was Charlotte too.

They crossed the hall and moved colourfully through the bar, greeting the patrons. Kitty Carr called Charley over to the palms.

'Here is Captain Blood,' she said. 'I want you to look after him.'

'Yairs,' replied Charley. 'All right.'

Captain Elijah's blood was racing through his ears again. He was aware that he was giving the lass a foolish grin, but was unable to adjust his expression, and so followed the tall girl up the carpeted stairs with his glazed eyes and his right hand in hers. He watched her calves move up each step, tense and relax, then followed the line of her thigh to her hips which also moved, buttock, buttock.

Charley chatted. From the moment she closed the red room's door, draped her boa over the doorknob and turned to loosen the Captain's neck cloth, she had fluttered forth the words, providing the constant glib of conversation while she got rid of his boots and tore open his trousers to reveal his rather astonishing cock. This stopped her momentarily, a pause she used to clamp her lips around his empurpled knob and lavishly lick his balls, before rising miraculously out of her white dress to reveal her spectacular chest, her breasts heavy and firm over him. The Captain lay halfway on the bed in his open underwear, one leg bent in the air; he lay like a dog expecting trouble. Now Charley told him about the Italian licorice at Mrs Carroll's lolly shop, working her dress over her hips then flinging her blonde mane back with a sweep of her hand. The other hand cupped a breast, almost coyly, as she came towards him.

Captain Elijah flung his longjohns aside. He scrambled backwards up the bed to at least get a pillow before she clambered aboard with her yawning fanny and slammed herself down. She took his breath away, winded him slightly, then ground her hips so sweetly he could feel every part of her blonde yoni gripping him hard. Charley was an entertainer. She reached around to grab his balls and started singing a breathy tune, a number Captain Elijah did not know. The old man was about to break out laughing, the minx was so enchanting, but his main point of interest was turning Charley over, reversing so that he might roger her standing up, in his socks.

He greeted the widow on his way out.

'Why, good evening, Captain.'

'Mrs Adams!' Captain Elijah's flush was genuine. 'How nice to see you.'

The widow, also blushing, was in the company of Sir Thomas Fry and the dynamic Kitty Carr. They broke from their conspiratorial group; Kitty Carr moved to attend the fat policeman, Chief Constable Wright, who had only looked in for a nightcap, as he wilted at the knees and hit the ground mid-wail; Kitty Adams, though, was intent on

Captain Elijah. She was in excellent spirits, her lips glistened in the hotel light, her eyes beamed at the Captain.

'I was sorry to hear that you had suffered a misfortune,' he told her.

'Well, Herbert did.' Mrs Adams maintained her equable gaze. 'My husband.'

'Yes, of course. He never looked comfortable, mind . . .'

The widow smirked as the Captain tried not to complete the thought. He blushed, again his cherubic cheeks. Behind them Sir Thomas Fry was clearing the red balls from the billiard table to make way for the ailing Chief Constable.

Kitty Adams seized his hand for a moment.

'What do you make of this place, Captain?'

'The pub?' he asked.

'No,' she laughed. 'These antipodes.'

'Oh, marvellous,' he replied, and took advantage of the developing medical emergency to make a simple exit.

He loosened her grip and was away.

Captain Blood, who was not inexperienced with vice, was taken shy by the unabashed debauchery of Bareheep. He beat back towards the river, dodging the fast girls and the comrades. The dandies wore long coats and the thinnest beards. The air was heavy with their jeers and catcalls, the ground sticky underfoot. These denizens of the street were so vastly different to the daytime crowds, when there were so few women to be seen and those few were invariably, as they say, 'wrapped in a mantle of proper reserve'. The bushmen too were gone. As for the natives, Captain Elijah saw only one: a young male appeared at the door of the Caledonian Hotel, beneath two lamps lighting its name, he was there but a moment before the door opened and the boy was quickly slipped inside.

The many lanes running off Lonsdale Street were filled with fornicating couples, coves and petticoats roughing it in the shade. The stench of urine was everywhere. Outside each hotel, in the lamplight, musicians were camped, organ grinders and Germans, an African with a top hat holding a python in each hand. The Captain hurried past, stopping only to buy a snack from a man selling hot roasted potatoes, then sauntered home in the dark. He hitched a ride at the dock with a dinghy full of his own crew. One man rowed and the Captain led them all in a song:

> 'You ladies of lubricity
> That dwell in the bordello
> Ha-ha ha-ha, ha-ha ha-hee
> For I am that kind of fellow . . .'

Ship's Log

H.	*K.*	*F.*	*Courses.*	*Winds.*	*Remarks,&c.*
					scientific party ashore
	..		..		Lts Trimm & Sploon 2 days
					leave
	..		..		midshipmen and sailors all quiet
					Moribund unsighted
					Accomp'd Mr Giles through
					the new town. v. remarkable
					familiarity.
					Passed several chandlers and
					ships stores

Day Five

At 6 am, still dark, Giles awoke stiff from his bed, fearful at once for his sanity.

A rumbling whimper had woken him, it was his own voice protesting the unjust circumstance that found him cornered. In his sleep he had been screaming. His dreams, usually so sanguine, had lately turned loathsome. His pre-dawn imaginings were traversing a landscape of such disquiet that he had to quell the desire to scream again, restricting himself to a low moan and covering his eyes with his hands. An oneirological investigation into Giles's nightlife would reveal too much. He didn't try to comprehend the taunting giant clitoris, unwieldy in his wife's grip, or the enormous nipples of her companion, but rather let the images subside as he brought his feet to the floor.

The day stretched ahead. When he reached the air, the cool blue sky vast and reassuring, Giles was able to clear his mind. He was a reasonable man. He walked the deck in his usual manner, greeting those sailors who were not drunk and refusing to return the slurs of the others. He made his tour then returned to the poop deck. Here he found the cabin boy loitering.

'Young Bertram! How pleased I am to find you here.'

The boy did not reply, looked at his toes pushing through his canvas shoes.

'Fetch my razor and some soap. A bowl of hot water from the galley, there's a good lad.'

Young Bertram took his time. Time enough for Giles to have second thoughts. He had grown fond of his moustache, stroking it down with his fingers for the last time. In fact he had already delayed one day. It was clear however that in Bareheep gentlemen did not wear beards. Squatters were hairy as hell and were expected to be wild men; merchants wore trimmed moustaches and side whiskers, but professional men were viewed with suspicion if they chose to cover their features with facial hair, as if they also had a past to conceal. Giles had already had his hair cut, neatly barbered, with a short fringe. His hair was rather beautiful, its straight black bangs his most feminine feature. Giles was determined to follow fashion, he would not be judged other than a gentleman.

Bertram returned with his shaving kit and a bowl of water.

'Captain said I could go ashore today,' said the cabin boy as he handed Giles his razor. It was his way of saying farewell.

The water was cold. Giles lathered and scraped, rasping the razor through the follicles. He lathered again and scraped his face smooth. There was bleeding; Giles could see the pink in the water, but he had not thought to ask the boy to bring a mirror. All in all it was a reasonable job. The hair on his face was gone, though its shape remained on his pale upper lip, as if he might have painted it on. His cheeks were so brown.

❦

Oh! Gorgeous Day.

For the second morning in a row Edwin Robins woke to the sound of a padlock key. Only thin rays of sunlight, spearing through the cracks, lighted his windowless wooden cell. He crouched in the far corner and watched the door. It swung wide and Edwin shielded his eyes from the glare of harsh daylight. A figure fell through the door, silhouetted on the wet earth floor, then the daylight was gone, the padlock clasped, boots walking away.

The man, he was a boy really, swore heavily from the turf.

'Those bastards doan know,' he turned to Edwin with a wide smile, white teeth in a black face, 'but I'm not stopping here.'

The boy got to his feet and touched the ceiling, then took two steps back to reach the opposite wall. 'There's no damn room!' Again he smiled at his cellmate.

'Name of Pierre,' he said, brushing the dirt from his bare arms. He wore black worsted trousers and a buttoned check waistcoat, but no shirt, and no shoes to cover his dusty black feet. Edwin shook his hand.

'Edwin Robins,' he said. 'But I'm ditching that name. Call me Citizen Louis,' thereby invoking his grandfather's revolutionary name. Edwin was energised by the arrival of this smiling native, already plans were formulating in his mind. The future was once more available. Again he thought of Charlotte Angliss.

The watch house on the corner of Stephen and Little Collins streets was a brick building, still incomplete when Edwin Robins was inside – so overcrowded that he and Pierre found themselves in a weatherboard wing. They had no water, no trough to piss in, nothing to eat. They sat cross-legged in one corner of the cell, breaking splinters of wood off the wall with their fingernails, and collecting them in a pile against the rear wall. Their fingers were sore, spiked and bloody, but they were in good humour. Pierre was a lively youth, full of a contagious bravado which Edwin now adopted, as much out of wonder as hope. Edwin knew he deserved nothing. His rages were uncontrollable when they came, regrettable, but afterwards his demeanour was engaging, even charming. Pierre would not have cared. He treated them all the same – the Europeans, whose society he moved through, had imposed an unknowable structure of order over his childhood territories. Pierre was resolutely friendly, respectful of weapons and machines, but he felt morally able to reject the strange barbarisms of white law.

Their pile of splinters and sticks grew. Outside the walls they could hear the conversations of passers-by, the sound of horses clipping past, and the shouts of an irate shop-keeper further afield. Edwin relished these sounds now; he would be rejoining their throng. His cellmate, Pierre, produced his grin yet again, withdrawing a tinder box from the pocket of his waistcoat.

'Those fellows are too damn stupid,' he said. 'They took my shoes but let me keep the damn matches.' He paused, 'But Pierre doan need matches to make the fire hot.'

'I do,' Edwin told him. 'Citizen Louis lights the fire.' He took the tinder box from Pierre, and was instantly placated. He opened it with his smarting fingernails. Pierre crossed quickly to the door, he put his eye to the cracks, collapsing the slim vistas into a picture of the prison outside. The courtyard was empty. On one side a stone fence to the street, studded with shards of glass. The main building was closed off from the yard by a heavy iron gate. Pierre turned back to Edwin.

'Let the fire get hot. More sticks!' he cried. 'Damn!'

The fire took the kindling in a gulp, but burned long enough for Pierre to wrench a strip of wood from one of the house planks. The fire licked up the wall. They waited as long as they dared, half the rear wall was aflame. Edwin kicked at the wood with his canvas shoes, a plank split and fell away and the street flew in through the smoke. The planks fell into a lane at the back of the gaol. It was just dirt and daylight when they stepped through the fire. Pierre was on his knees at once, shovelling dirt with his hands to put out the fire. He flung it everywhere.

'Don't want those fellows to know we're gone,' he said.

They walked quickly, pretending not to walk quickly.

The smoke from the fire gave them away, a pall of grey that hung in the windless air over the gaol. A series of cries rang out behind the stone wall, but Edwin and Pierre had already turned east into Bourke Street, their studious gaits causing no alarm.

Ahead was a commotion of dust stirred up by a herd of parading cows. Dogs were arriving from every direction, mutts and strays, attracted by the incessant yap of the two cattle dogs that kept darting in at the heels of the herd. Pedestrians and shoppers gave way, pressing into doorways and lining up under the verandahs to wait for the animals to pass. The fugitives ambled past the bystanders towards the herd, which was about to break into a run, all the dogs barking, flashing in at their shins.

'Damn dogs,' said Pierre, and flung himself flat against a shopfront as the animals surged.

Edwin stood behind a verandah post, eyes shut, his eyebrows raised, assailed by the smells of hide and dust, the pounding of the air, the hooves on the ground. Then they were past, the boys were free.

Edwin was merely running away, but Pierre knew the way home. Moreover his people were everywhere. There were groups of Aborigines at every corner, older women and men, quite naked, who waved to Pierre or said a few words as the felons passed.

In Henry Milbourne's barber shop Captain Elijah Blood was still enjoying himself. The pleasant hour at Kitty Carr's, two nights previous, had revived him. He was operating in the world again, overseeing the days. The re-provisioning had begun, stores were mounting in a warehouse by the dock, but it would be a week before the expedition could begin. Already his day was a success, having secured a load of wood for half what he would have paid. With his face steaming under a hot towel, Captain Elijah heard the comments the barber made, but did not feel obliged to reply.

'I'm on stage this evening at the Theatre Royal,' the baritone informed the Captain. 'That's my true calling.'

Milbourne removed the towels and Captain Elijah was able to regard himself in the mirror while the baritone barber grabbed him by the jowls and forced his head back.

'D'you want to keep the beard, sir?' Henry Milbourne inquired. 'The seafaring look, eh!'

Captain Elijah remained mute.

A shining silver razor appeared in the barber's hand.

'I'll just clean it up a little, eh?'

Quiet Giles waited for Captain Blood in the library at Fawkner's Hotel. He had taken to reading the colonial papers each morning, as relaxing a ritual as any. Giles asked Fawkner's pretty daughter to prepare tea and toast for him. He went to pains to explain to her the shade of brown he preferred, between blonde and brunette, he liked his bread fleshy and he liked it served cool. It arrived golden and warm, but was served in a silver toast rack, cut beautifully; and he could wait for it to cool. The tea service was Wedgwood, quite nice thought Giles. He opened the *Patriot*.

The press were dissatisfied with the design of Bareheep, particularly the wide–narrow–wide alternation of streets. The narrow lanes were already slums, fetid with urban distemper.

A certain Robert Hoddle was to blame. Eager to provide wide streets with thorough ventilation from noxious vapours, Hoddle had pegged out the city with pretty avenues, ninety-nine feet wide. But he neglected to map out service lanes or rights-of-way, so just crammed them in at the last minute. Hoddle, it seems, was a lazy surveyor and 'not very particular' about measurements. Indeed, the chain he used was four or five inches longer than standard.

Sarah Jane Fawkner poked her head around the library door, her milky skin so clear.

'How do you like your toast, Mr Quiet?' She giggled.

'Excellent, Sarah.' Giles watched her disappear. 'What a beautiful d. . .'

The girl shrieked in the hallway, then laughed again.

Now Captain Elijah stood in the doorway, his hair cut and his beard perfumed. He wore a goatee, and it was quite clearly a source of alarm.

'Are we late?' asked the Captain.

Funerals were a matter of honour to him, part of his duty, but strictly speaking the man had been out of his charge when he died. Captain Elijah was there for Kitty's sake, dear widow, of whom he had grown fond during the voyage out. He sat with Quiet Giles in the third row at Scots Church in Collins Street. The air inside the church was cool, despite the midday sun beating down outside. The funeral of Herbert Adams had drawn a respectable crowd though he was known to so few in Bareheep. His fellow passengers on *Bright Planet* were there, most of them. Kitty Carr and Sir Thomas Fry sat alongside the widow and her daughter Cecilia, while perched immediately behind them were the twins, Emily and Jane. There were several other mourners in church, sobbers and sighers, whom the Captain did not recognise, including a group of native women camped on the floor near the pulpit.

The sermon was brief.

'We all die,' said the parson. 'We all shuffle off.'

He clearly knew little of the man they were mourning.

'Today we mark the passing of Herbert Adams, a brave traveller who died far from home. The new lands of Port Phillip will provide his rest.'

'Hallalooler!' cried the Aboriginal women.

Outside the church the mourners mingled. They gathered beneath the only tree, an old eucalyptus which Giles regarded with interest.

'Are there refreshments?' asked the Captain. He wore a black frock coat, lace collar and cuffs, with a blue necker-chief, and his newly revealed face was reddening.

Kitty Carr called them over. In the shade of the church awning a trestle table had been covered with white damask and laden with jugs of lemon cordial and sheep sandwiches.

'We're going to the theatre tonight,' announced Kitty Carr. 'Will you join us, Captain? Mr Giles?'

The two men exchanged a glance.

'That would be most agreeable,' Giles replied.

The Captain's new beard offered little protection from

the sun, it no longer covered his porcelain cheeks, and he was looking thirsty.

'That's settled then, you may call for us at 7 pm,' said Kitty. 'I believe you know the way, Captain.'

The Captain nodded, though he certainly did not. He was pouring himself a beaker of cordial. Adding a little rum from his smallest flask.

Moribund appeared with Cecilia Adams. She was a handsome young woman, skittish like a colt. He covered her hand with both of his, murmuring low words, though her green eyes darted from side to side, and she wasn't listening.

He turned to Giles.

'There's a show at the playhouse tonight. Might be lively.'

William Angliss approached Captain Elijah, his wife and daughter in train.

'Good day, sir!' He clapped the sea dog on the back.

'Do you not find these festers foul?' William Angliss was referring to the pestiferous airs which wafted throughout the streets of the city. The corner of Russell Street and Collins Street, where they stood, was particularly noxious. Animals that had died, or fowls, were sometimes piled there, until a city councillor spied such a heap and ordered a dray.

'Reminds me of home,' said Captain Elijah.

'Aye, and the cholera.'

'That's what this plaster is, on our shoes,' Giles pointed at a dusty blackness which coated all their boots. 'It's dry now, but when it rains that mud is black cholera.'

'Jesus!' said the Captain.

'I've bought some land a little out of town,' said William Angliss. 'We shall build a house there.' At this his daughter, Charlotte, rolled her eyes. Nor did her mother wish to live any closer to the native bush than they already were.

'Where is your land, Mr Angliss?' asked Giles.

'Newtown,' he replied. 'To the north.'

'I intend to take a look up there.'

'Oh, there's nothing there yet.'

❧

On the Eastern Hill they rested among the trees. This was the edge of town. There was traffic about, Edwin could see, and houses stretching up Brunswick Street to the north. But Pierre led him away, further into the wild forest.

'We'll be safe with my cousins,' he said. 'They stay in a good place.'

They tracked through undergrowth. Edwin was crunching the dry leaves beneath his feet, he could see no path. The distinct aroma of the trees took over. The undergrowth, ferny plants and spikers, camouflaged the earth. The forest let the fugitives pass, and the sky, glimpsed through the grey, ghostly canopy, was in order.

The alien wood was full of noise. Above the roar of insects was the chatter of small birds, and the harsher call of crows high in the trees. Everywhere the rustling of foliage, louder than his own sharp breaths, signalled the movement of fauna, but certain small odd sounds which surrounded their progress, these Edwin could not identify.

He had fallen behind Pierre, who had become increasingly silent, and was now appearing and disappearing from view.

'Where you at, brother?'

The voice came out of nowhere.

Here was a naked man in dungarees, facing Edwin with a spear. Asking him again.

'Where you at?'

Edwin looked around for Pierre.

Two more men arrived, sauntering out of nowhere, then another. In fact all around him eyes blinked. The trees were bathed in an iridescent light, and momentarily Edwin saw the forest in silence. But someone was laughing, like a laughing bird. Edwin recognised the clear peals.

'Damn good joke, that one.' Pierre's checked waistcoat appeared.

'These natives are friendly,' he said, clapping Edwin on the back. 'Here is Sneaky Pete and Prince Albert, and Colombo,' indicating the trio closest to Edwin. 'They think you lost.'

The wood thinned out and the party climbed a grassy hill. Edwin stuck close to Pierre. They didn't follow in single file, but rather traversed the hill in a sweep. On the lee bank the group gathered in a clearing. Someone made a fire. The rest of the men lay down in the lush grass, talking in their own language, adjusting their britches.

'Lunchtime,' Pierre told Edwin.

He thought everything was funny, chattering while Edwin kept his mouth shut.

He laughed at the goanna his cousins grilled, tearing a mouthful with his teeth.

'Tough bugger.'

Edwin needed Pierre, translator and guide, that much he knew. His brief time in the company of these native people had caused only alarm. But for the rest his head was empty. He lay back in the shady grass, resting with the others out of the midday heat.

They waited there, in the afternoon – maybe, Edwin supposed, for an animal to appear. Or for the quiet that took over their grove, as the minutes stretched. The birdsong had ceased and there was only the deep cool of the earth they lay upon, the sour taste of grass in his mouth. Up close there was only black soil and pale green shoots. Slowly though, like a long wave breaking, the summer intrudes, the insects start and the reptiles run; soon one of his lean companions stretches and speaks the quick language. But Edwin had already taken up residence in the silence.

❧

'Hold on, Giles,' said the Captain. 'I need a piss.'

He had stopped at the entrance to a laneway, where mud and urine had mingled to form dark streams running into the street. This lane, like any number of others in the city, had become a public convenience. Even as the Captain was buttoning his britches, two other men unhitched themselves at the wall, and urinated expressively.

'Fuck off, you great poof,' one man told Giles, who was loitering some feet away.

'Yes, fuck off, old boy,' said the other.

Giles and Captain Elijah resumed their walk back to the wharf. Their mood was not solemn in the least, neither thought the next thing of Herbert Adams' passing. Giles regarded the bills posted on walls, fences, any available space, advertising powder or oil or hardware or tea. Such posters were littered all over the streets, yellow letters dropped at a windy corner. He examined one that caught his heel. Moreover there were signs over every shop: boots, keys, spectacles, three-dimensional anchors and fish advertising nautical wares.

'Have you secured our supplies, Captain?'

'We're wooded and watered,' he answered. 'The carpenter has new tools. The animals will be a week, though. It will be a week at least.'

'I have given my assistants a list of supplies I need. Scientific material.'

'Where are those two?'

A load of wood for *Bright Planet* had been delivered by dray to the wharf, bay 13, below the Customs House. Here it remained. The stevedores refused to transfer the load to the ship. Lieutenant Trimm was overseeing the consignment, but was faced with a blank apology from the foreman. Trimm, red-faced, appealed to the Captain.

'There appears to be a snake, sir, in the woodpile.'

'Won't anyone kill it?' demanded Captain Elijah.

'Scared, sir.'

'What does it look like?' asked Giles quietly.

'It's black,' said Trimm. 'With a red belly.'

'What is it, Giles? Deadly?'

'Red-bellied black snake. Not deadly. Quick, though.'

'There's two of 'em,' the foreman told him.

The snake was in the timber, coiled beneath a pile of faggots. Trimm pointed it out, a very lustrous black, and Giles and Captain Elijah took one or two paces back.

'Has anyone got a stick?'

Trimm wore a gold-tipped cane as part of his livery, it dangled by his hip. He fidgeted with it nervously. The Captain gave Lieutenant Trimm his inquiring look.

'Oh! No, sir! It is my wand of office.'

'Will this do?' The foreman intervened, holding an iron spoke about four feet long.

Lieutenant Trimm poked about. He had removed several logs, endeavouring to make way for a clean swipe at the serpent, which had not bothered to move during Trimm's excavation. He was not confident, but he crouched and raised his arm, testing his swing. The staff was heavy and he knew the first blow had to break its back. Otherwise he didn't want to think. His fellows looked on, unconvinced.

Lieutenant Trimm smacked the snake once, very fast, very quick, flattening its back in four places into bloody pulp, coiled as it was, still.

'It didn'y even twitch,' said an onlooker, one of a small but interested crowd that had formed to watch the denouement.

Trimm leant back on his haunches.

'Oh! Christ!' he said, as the second snake appeared. It struck him on the wrist, whipping itself at him then wriggling away on its red belly. The crowd swore and stepped back. The sleek black creature headed for the water. It crossed the boards of the wharf, weaving past crates of cheese and tubs of tar, and slowed only to regard some caged fowls before propelling itself off the edge of the dock into the dark, fast-flowing water.

'Told ya there was two of 'em,' said the foreman.

There were two neat punctures. The skin surrounding the wound was yellowy white, and damp with sweat. Trimm's face was suddenly pale too, like poor marble, masked with moisture. Giles applied a tourniquet, having removed the lieutenant's brocade jacket and torn a strip off his shirt sleeve.

'Hold still,' he said. 'I'm going to release the venom.'

Lieutenant Trimm breathed in fast, sharp draughts, he couldn't get enough air. He nodded, falling back into Giles's arms.

'I'll do it,' said Captain Elijah, who had been hovering all this time, quite aghast at the turn of events. After all, he had given the order. He knelt beside the two men and put his mouth to the wound, while behind him the crowd remained respectful, offering one or two suggestions, but they were largely hushed by the drama unfolding before them.

'Ahoy! Mr Giles!'

The call came from Cormac or Angel, the happy cousins, who now entered the tableau on the back of a bullock dray laden with boxes and jars. They were eager to display their spoils to Mr Giles. They had bought all sorts of nets, fishing hooks, machines for catching insects, cases of bottles with ground stoppers to preserve animals in spirits, a telescope for looking under water: nearly all the scientist had requested. Giles cut them short.

'Ah, Cormac, young man, we could use your assistance.' Giles called him over. 'Have you any experience with snakebite?'

Captain Elijah made way for Mr Giles's assistant. He clambered to his feet, giving a reassuring pat to Lieutenant Trimm's already painful arm. Cormac got to his knees.

'Don't swallow any,' Giles warned him.

Now Cormac put his mouth to the wound. He tasted a sour mix of blood, spread his lips over the two punctures and drew in a sticky mouthful. He spat at once.

'Very good, Mr Cormac,' said Giles. 'Once more should do the job.'

'I'm not going to do it.' Cormac looked up, his mouth red, the blood staining his already brown teeth.

The evening was pleasant, cool but no breeze. Bourke Street was still full of strollers, soon to repair home for dinner, before donning their dark coats again for a grog at the Lamb Inn or the Highlander. A crowd built up outside the Theatre Royal, waiting for the doors to the shed to be opened. The *Bright Planet* party, Captain Blood, Mr Giles and Dr Moribund, accompanied by Kitty Carr and Kitty Adams, and her daughter trailing a few yards behind, arrived in good time. They chatted in the street for several minutes, politely greeting the patrons Kitty Carr brought before them. Names such as Spalding, Dunlop and Beaurepaire. Everyone shook hands.

Inside the theatre it became apparent that the audience was a mixed bunch. The stalls were filled with cheap larrikins and hairy bachelors. None of them kept to their seats and nearly all of them smoked; grey plumes went up all over the room. The circle was better dressed but the seats swayed dangerously under the weight of the spectators. While the lights were still up the audience amused themselves, those on the balcony spitting gleefully on the deadheads in the free seats, who, involved in their own skylarks, kept their hats on.

Once they were settled Kitty Carr held on to the Captain's hand, whispering something he didn't hear. The lamps went out and the stage was dark. The claqueurs went wild, hooting and setting off firecrackers. The Bareheep Players' production of *The Revenger's Tragedy* began. There was so much smoke produced by the furious pipes in the audience that much of the early action was hidden. In any case the play was a mess. The Captain's barber, Henry Milbourne, was the licentious Duke, and his spontaneous delivery of dialogue in song was roundly booed. When Fanny Cathcart appeared, playing the chaste Castiza, the house went up. She was beautiful indeed, porcelain-cheeked and raven-haired. She streaked about the stage to evade the merciless pursuit of her virtue by the Duke's son, played by a boy no better than a street Arab. So thought Kitty Carr, and the Captain agreed. There was a good amount of death in the end, and the curtain came down on a stage strewn with the bodies of *dramatis personae*.

The upper level of the theatre began to sway and shudder as the audience rose in a roar to resume their horseplay. Fists were flying in the pit below. Giles, unflustered, ushered the ladies down. Outside they dodged the waiting cabs, and strolled the clay streets back to the Governor Bourke Hotel, where the gentlemen bid a subdued goodnight to the ladies, then turned tail for the long walk back.

'Nothing like Sheridan, of course,' commented the Captain.

Giles was relieved to agree. The Captain's mood had deteriorated since Lieutenant Trimm's accident. And he had been silent for the last twenty minutes. It was only now, crossing the water in a dinghy, Moribund at the oars, that he chose to engage in discourse.

The doctor was disappointed that the evening had ended so abruptly. He would have happily joined the ladies for a nightcap, he was quite smitten with the widow after all, and her vixen daughter. Moribund pulled at the oars and the men continued in silence.

Lights from the ships shone prettily across the harbour. Not enough though for Moribund, who scraped the dinghy noisily against *Bright Planet* twice before the Captain grabbed a rope. He looked annoyed. Conversations from neighbouring vessels carried dreamily on the breeze as the three men climbed the rope ladder to the deck. Captain Elijah retired at once, asking that Moribund look in on

Lieutenant Trimm, and leaving Giles to take the air on the forecastle deck.

❧

Captain Elijah's quarters were situated at the ship's stern, but his blows could be heard as far aft as the crew's squat on the orlop deck. He was banging his fists against the cabin wall; the blows reverberated through the planks. Clara's letter was face down on the floor, opened for the first time in two days. When the fury passed, as suddenly as it came, he lay back on his bunk. He retrieved the letter from the floor. Clara Lacey's *billet-doux* had reached him the day they took the tide at Plymouth, it came with the morning coach. But it had lain unopened on the bureau in his dining room, along with some papers from Admiralty and other mail, until the ship was past the islands and under way. He began reading again, stroking his new beard for a moment, then holding his belly.

LONDON MAY 16
My Dearest Elijah,

   What have I done?

   If I could take it all back, I would. Nothing I said that night was true.

   It was the moon, the sherry, the strangeness of the surrounds. I will not marry that man.

   I shall rather make a shabby spinster than go through that charade.

   I am in a state you see, I know you are leaving because of me. You want to lose yourself in the waves, make an heroic passage, whatever it is that will punish me. But forgive me, my darling, I'm asking you to stay. Jump ship. Cancel the voyage. My father has given me a house on the Downs. We could languish there . . . Elijah, my love.

Could you see me again?

Captain Elijah paused here to vomit. He pulled his bucket close and retched painfully the brown muck the replacement cook, William Weed, had provided for supper. He would read no further. He wiped his lips then closed his eyes. But sleep did not come, he lay still while his body toiled and his head filled with imaginings. Of course he had replied to Clara, a stricken, frightened missive, posted from Tenerife, but no correspondence had reached him since.

❧

Quiet Giles was in a subdued mind. A pall had been passed over the evening. Normally the theatre was a most pleasant diversion, but tonight he had been unable to engage. The Captain was out of sorts and in no mood to talk; his assistants were noisy, were preoccupied with themselves and, in any case, subordinate; Moribund was far too lustful. Giles shied from his conversation. As for the ladies, the fine clothes and perfumed air, he found them agreeable of course, if a little diffident. He did not but remark a few polite things to young Cecilia Adams. Haughty thing.

These thoughts made up the bulk of his diary entry. He

was pleased with his style, however, and added an exclamation mark. He finished with a note about Lieutenant Trimm and the snakes, then uncorked his bottle and poured out a draught. Giles spent the next hour in private amusement, before falling asleep naked at the desk. His head rested on the open diary, his blank fringe obscuring an earlier entry to which he had been making some adjustments.

Ship's Log

H.	K.	F.	Courses.	Winds.	Remarks,&c.
					purchased sufficient wood at
			..	..	2 guineas per cwt
			..	..	livestock confirmed
					attended funeral of H.Adams
					(passenger)
					evening ashore
					NB: Bertram, the cabin boy, has
					absconded, rumoured to have
					joined M.Rotin,
					Lt Trimm inconvenienced by
					snakebite, and requires several
					days

Day Eight

Giles took his breakfast eggs at Fawkner's Hotel. They arrived, as usual, with chops and relish, and as usual the meal was too hearty for Giles. He murmured an apology to Sarah Jane Fawkner as she collected his plate.

'Don't worry, Mister Giles,' she said. 'I'll eat them.' She raised a chop to her mouth and tore at the dry meat in the centre, the best bit. She smiled at him, still chewing, and there was a little grease on her lips.

Giles lingered at the table for toast and coffee, but did not repair to the library this morning. He had an excursion planned, a walking tour of the surrounding country. Crumbs from his breakfast were sprinkled over his maps, and he had made marks with a pencil, but Giles had still not made up his mind about the tracks they would take. One could, after all, walk ten minutes in any direction and find wilderness.

At a quarter to ten his assistants, Cormac and Angel, arrived. Giles packed his maps away and stowed Gould's *Birds of Australia* in his satchel.

'You be careful, now,' said Sarah Jane Fawkner.

She gave him an apple in the hallway. A small hard Jonathan, which he weighed in his hand a moment, then he tucked that away too. They both blushed, and not for the first time Giles felt the hot tickle of wool trousers against his skin. She held her hands on her hips, and arched her shoulders as if she was about to laugh.

'She's definitely on for you, sir,' Cormac observed once they were outside.

Giles was not so sure. He had been duped by women before. Sarah Jane Fawkner was indeed giving him glimpses of her sweet nature and her varied charms, paying him special attentions. For the most part he was able to play his usual flattered man, but occasionally her looks were so lascivious as to make his member stand.

The bush began abruptly. They stood under the shade of a shop verandah in Lonsdale Street. The far side of the street was heavily treed. It was clear that they had reached the edge of town. There was a band of boys with brooms cleaning the roadway, guarding the lines, and sweeping storms of dirt into the trees. Two or three cottages had carved out squares of the bush, but for the most part this was an ancient forest.

Quiet Giles and his assistants stepped out from under the verandah. The two cousins carried packs laden with equipment and jars. Giles carried his books in his satchel. They strode evenly off, looking for a path through the trees, unwilling to just blunder in. Giles pulled out the map, but could not find a point of reference. Indeed, the wheel-rutted track they eventually took bore no relation to the markings on his map. They followed the track through the noisy trees, up and down hill, until it reached a more substantial road from the south. Giles's nose filled with the smell of horse shit. This road was too well travelled. The explorers, hearing the approach of a carriage, veered off into the bush. The trees had thinned out and the ground was level, their progress was hardly impeded, but Giles tried to keep the road in sight.

In this manner they were able to skirt the suburb of Newtown, passing through the long grass at the back of the new houses. They passed several children playing in the scrub, while closer to the cottages a black-haired woman was chopping wood. The children stopped their game to watch the explorers trample past.

Captain Elijah had been abroad all morning. He was now taking a tropical tour of the shops in Collins Street, hoping to complete his ship's requirements. Drawn in by the confectionery window, the Captain went through his lists in Overton's coffee house, enjoying a cup of tea and a slice, and glad to be out of the heat. He had been to the tannery, the fellmongers, the boiling-down works, nearly all the hot, stinking factories that lined the river to the west of Bareheep. As a result he had negotiated several tidy arrangements made good with Badgery's promissory notes. Captain Elijah could see the expedition turning a profit, especially afterwards, when he would secure a cargo for the return passage to Plymouth. Thinking about money often soothed him.

At the boiling-down works Captain Elijah had bought legs of mutton. Nearby he had acquired wheat and buckwheat to be milled on board, and great tubs of biscuit. Salt beef and bacon were plentiful and cheap, dried peas and beans less so. He had also returned to William Nicholson's store, seeking a good exchange on coffee. He arranged for all these, along with several barrels of malt for making spruce beer, to be transported to the dock. The Captain felt obliged to provide malt for the crew, for although there were plenty of lemons to combat the onset of scurvy, the men were unable to give up their daily habit of spruce beer. There was also a certain demand for spirits and wine, which he would have no trouble meeting. For Captain Elijah had two days ago secured a load of rum and brandy, plus three kegs of Colonial Ale, thanks to advice from Le Souef, the Customs agent, whom he had encountered at the racetrack on Saturday afternoon.

The Captain had recognised the unruly red hair. M. Le Souef was volubly cursing a grey nag as it was led away to the yards. The horse passed and Le Souef was soon happily engaging a track bookmaker. Le Souef was an inveterate speculator, and consequently a particularly zealous Customs inspector, for his speculations were invariably bad. The Captain kept his distance and studied the form, for he too was fond of a flutter. He bought a fizzy spider and added a little from his flask.

'What horse you on?' The agent had sidled up, taking Captain Elijah by stealth.

'Blowfly,' replied the Captain. 'Number 6.'

'Mmmm,' said Le Souef thoughtfully. 'So am I. Perhaps you'll bring me some luck.'

They watched the race together, mostly in silence, but when the horses entered the straight, they moved closer to the barrier and saw their number flash past on a black mare. Le Souef squealed. The mare won running away. Afterwards, in passing, asking after the ship's progress, Le Souef mentioned to Captain Elijah that he knew of some quantities of liquor for sale.

Upon this advice, the Captain had duly presented himself at the brickworks shortly before sunset on Saturday evening. The factory was really a wooden barn high on the left bank of the river, surrounded on three sides by lively stacks of bricks, and on the other side by a deep basin of earth, the ragged crater left by the quarrymen. There was a large convention of Bareheep citizens outside the barn. Many of the brick stacks had been employed as liquor stalls, with dozens of men lounging in various brick cubbies, tasting the new brandy.

'It's a regular thing,' Le Souef had assured him, taking the Captain's arm and steering him past several rowdy marines from another ship. These men had straightened their backs instinctively upon seeing Captain Blood.

'Ev'nin', Captain.'

'Evening, boys.'

Le Souef led him to his own stall, where a man in a broad-trimmed straw hat was pouring brandy into tumblers for two gentleman slopes. Le Souef, of course, touched nothing, mindful of his official responsibilities, but his straw-hatted man could arrange anything the Captain might require.

'Contraband,' Le Souef whispered as he left, making a comic move with his eye that may have been a tic.

Lieutenant Sploon cleared his throat.

'More tea, sir?'

Captain Elijah looked up from his notes. Lieutenant Sploon's portly frame stood before him, his arms laden with cake boxes and tins of fancy biscuits.

'Would you like me to order you a cake?'

'Sit down, Sploon.'

Captain Elijah had always thought Lieutenant Sploon had an unhappy look about him, and would not normally seek his company. Sploon, of course, thought the same about the Captain. But today, for reasons drilled into him during childhood and too distant now to remember, was a happy day for Captain Elijah. It was his birthday.

'It's my birthday,' he told Sploon. 'I'm thirty-eight.'

'Well, absolutely, sir, happy birthday!'

'Let's have some cake. Eh?' The Captain waved his hand at Mrs Overton, who was serving behind the counter. She waved back.

Sploon had been shopping with the table allowance Captain Elijah had provided for each of the officers. It was incumbent on the officers to find their own food and drink for the journey. Sploon had splurged it all on cakes and champagne. The least he could do was open one of his parcels. He chose a sponge with white icing, and presented it to his Captain.

'Could we have some candles, please,' Lieutenant Sploon demanded loudly. 'And cream.'

Captain Elijah was not surprised to hear Sploon express his doubts about the expedition. The lieutenant did not, in fact, expect to return. He was a superstitious man.

'We have a crew of thirteen. We weigh on the thirteenth. We might as well be sailing on a Friday.'

'There's no women aboard,' replied the Captain, consolingly. Though naturally he agreed with his portly companion. There was no lack of omens.

'Plenty of redheads in this town, too,' added Lieutenant Sploon.

Captain Elijah gathered his things, filing the papers into his pocketbook, returning his pencil to its slot. On his way out he bought four extra wheaten loaves from Mrs Overton, and some dark chocolate squares.

There were groups of Aborigines at the end of every street. To a casual observer they may have seemed to be merely loitering, occupying nuisance camps, but to someone with a keen eye there was structure to their behaviour. The occasional signal or shout was easily ignored by the mercantile surroundings, but the communications of the native people were in fact part of a systematic operation leading a party of cousins through the antagonistic streets of Bareheep. The party, which included Sneaky Pete and Prince Albert, carried in its midst various stores and items they knew the Europeans would be unhappy to find missing. Edwin Robins stood with Pierre, his guide, at the corner of Collins and Elizabeth streets.

Pierre held a pack of cards. Edwin was trying to keep his head down. He had already seen his ship's Captain walk unevenly past, followed by Lieutenant Sploon, not twenty yards behind him. Edwin was uncomfortable in the city surrounds; he expected a constable at any moment.

Pierre handed Edwin a playing card, the jack of clubs.

'You all look the same,' he said, patting his bowler hat, showing his white teeth. 'Not like me.'

'Fair enough,' said Edwin.

'Fair enuf,' said Pierre.

The raiding party had stolen through Bareheep by strategy. They crossed Elizabeth Street at the footbridge, and it was here that they were in most danger. The lower class of clowns often gathered at this muddy corner to watch for accidents, waiting for some unlucky citizen to sprain a limb, or a maid to take a tumble in the stream. But on the far corner Pierre now diverted this gallery's attention long enough for six Aboriginal men to cross the bridge unheeded, despite their faces being daubed and ochred, and the fact they were carrying several good crates of booty on their shoulders.

The party split into pairs and proceeded separately towards the East End. Occasionally a cry rose above the city's roar, an animal's call, and the raiders stopped where they were, just sat on the ground, forcing the traffic to go around them.

Meanwhile, Edwin and Pierre made a run for it. The deck of cards was strewn all over, and his bowler hat was trampled into the ground. One red-faced cringer had grabbed Edwin by the shirt, while the patsy lunged for Pierre. Both these boys could run, and indeed Pierre was away, but Edwin delayed his escape, preferring to break the cringer's jaw and stand over him for a moment, before setting off at a quick jog.

❧

Quiet Giles reclined beneath the shade of a large acacia tree, resting his feet while Cormac made some sketches. Angel had set off after an animal that Giles had seen, but it was a bad sighting and Giles held little hope for a capture. Giles wore his show boots, a pair of black Russians. They gave his gait a military jaunt. They were comfortable enough, but after an hour or so tended to blister his toes. They also tended to remind him of his wife, for Mary disliked to see him wear them.

They had collected many specimens of plants, mainly variations of Asian or African species. Giles would check them later against his books, but he had seen nothing new. For the moment he was pressing leaves between the tissue pages of a specimen book. He had bulbs too, flowers and seeds, and samples of several Proteaceae he admired.

'Couldn't find it, sir!' Angel returned out of breath.

Giles's feet still hurt.

'Never mind, Angel,' he said. 'What I want now are some insects. Take the nets and see what you can catch.'

'But, Mr Giles,' protested Angel. 'You know I can't stand flying things.'

'There'll be bugs on the ground,' said Giles. 'And don't forget the jars.'

The botanist leaned back against the tree. He took the apple from his bag and with a sense of abandon bit into it. A sour, crisp bite. Cormac looked up from his drawing and regarded Giles. His employer looked dreamy-eyed for a moment, then raised the apple to his lips again.

'Would you like a bite, Mr Cormac?'

The young man accepted the proffered fruit. He took a bite and handed it back, and did not express his surprise at the taste.

Cormac's drawings were beautiful. In particular, his repro-duction of the *Angophora floribunda*, which abounded in these forests, was stunning. Cormac had captured the yellow pods, like little bells, and the iridescent shades of its green foliage.

'Perfect!' cried Giles. 'These drawings will make excel-lent plates for my book. What do you think, Cormac? Might bring you fame.'

'All right,' he said uncertainly, working his thick lips over his graveyard teeth.

Giles moved back to his tree. Despite the blisters he was in good spirits, appreciating this outdoor recreation. He thought to engage his subordinate in idle chat.

'Why did you seek this expedition, Mr Cormac?' Giles asked. 'Was it for the science?'

'No, sir.' Cormac hesitated before continuing. 'There was some trouble at home.'

'Oh?'

But the young man declined to elaborate. Clearly the 'trouble' would reflect badly on himself. Cormac understood Giles well enough to know that his assessment of Angel's murderous activities on the Heath would not be favourable. Angel had coshed the man as usual, the dusk perambulator, and Cormac himself had riffled his waistcoat for a purse, but this dupe was dead. Angel had hit him too hard, cracking the temple.

The two cousins had then arrived with the corpse at Doctor Moribund's surgery, paying the cab driver with the dead man's cash.

'Jesus, boys!' Dr Moribund protested. 'Do you know who this is?'

'It is Sir John Suckling, the cricketer,' Angel replied. 'We marked him out.'

Cormac and Angel left the dead man in Moribund's care. No doubt he cut him up doing one of his experiments.

Now, Cormac thought, as he resumed his drawing, is no time to dredge up the past. What Mr Giles doesn't know won't hurt him. For, indeed, Cormac wished Giles no harm.

The quiet man with the book of birds open on his lap.

The scientist had retired into silence. He was bird-watching.

❧

Edwin Robins broke off a sprig of tobacco and crumbled it into the bowl of his pipe, pressing it down with his thumb and then sprinkling in some more. He leant back against a tree and smoked the pipe, away from the group, at the edge of the picnic grounds.

The tobacco was a prize from this, his first raid with Pierre and his cousins, who had made their escape without incident. Edwin himself had skulked the length of Little Bourke Street, past the shadowy houses and street vendors to Stephen Street, where Pierre was waiting. Their escape route took them past the gaol that had so briefly housed them, then up the hill to the edge of town, where a gang of stray dogs had gathered to pick through the gutters. Edwin and Pierre crossed the no man's land to the trees. The dogs followed.

The raiding party reassembled on the hill, one of the tribes' lunch spots. By the time Edwin arrived with Pierre the celebrations had begun, and the booty was spread out for their pleasure. There were a dozen men in all, some now dressed in wigs and fur. They had raided a gentleman's house in William Street, plundered his larder and his wardrobe. But this gentleman could only provide a very sticky lunch, jams and marmalades, a jar of lemon butter. Excellent lemon butter, according to Pierre, who let one of the dogs lick out the jar.

Prince Albert broke open a crate of champagne.

'Fizzy drink,' said Pierre with a grin.

He popped the first cork, laughing as the bubbles ran over his chin, then passed the bottles around. Edwin took a swig, puffed on his pipe, sat back satisfied.

Edwin was often quick to anger, always wary, but he found the company of these strangers relaxing. At times like this, when the work was done, and they were laughing on the hill, Edwin sensed a tranquillity of their souls. He was aware too that their time was short. The outskirts of Bareheep were visible from the hill, various industries had spread along the river bank. There were gaps in the forest where the market gardeners were attending to their plots. Here were the new lords of the soil.

The Governor's house was prefabricated by the Royal Engineers in Sydney, but the roof had been made the wrong size to fit the building. Consequently the house had very wide eaves extended at a far lower pitch than usual, giving it a sleepy appearance. It had been built at the top end of Collins Street where the loamy road outside was still pitted with stumps. The *Bright Planet* contingent arrived here shortly before sunset. Governor La Trobe opened the door himself. An elegant man, he giggled and ushered them inside.

Captain Elijah Blood, Lieutenant Sploon, Ship's Surgeon Moribund, and Mr Quiet Giles were presented one by one to the guests assembled in the reception room. La Trobe's wife, Sophie, guided them to the couches, before offering them sherry. There were several crystal decanters on the sideboard, a maid filling the glasses. A dozen guests were enjoying the vice-regal atmosphere and some polite banter. Giles recognised the Fawkners and

Mr William Angliss and his wife, but the other guests, a young widow surrounded by two bachelors and a pastor, he had not seen before.

He circled once, glass in hand, then perched on the arm of the handsome red couch. The gleeful Governor set upon him immediately.

'I was a rambler too, in my day,' said La Trobe. 'Mexico and North America.'

Giles, refreshed from his day's excursion, was glad of civilised company.

'Are you a naturalist, sir?' he asked.

'I am a continental man, I suppose, but science has been my great love. I should like to show you my collections, Mr Giles, before your expedition embarks.'

'I should be most interested, sir,' Giles replied, self-consciously smoothing his black hair. The Governor looked so immaculate.

Mrs La Trobe was a charming host. She stood by the side-board in her slim dress, a cream confection that could not defy the swell of her bosom. She called the guests through to the dining room, smiling serenely as the party trooped past. Although she detained Captain Elijah for a moment to brush some lint from his coat with her hand.

'You look like you've seen a ghost, Captain Blood.'

The Captain smiled weakly.

'We do have a resident ghoul,' she whispered. 'But I doubt he would appear so early.'

Simpson, a manservant in butler's livery, served the first

course and attended to the wine. The guests clinked their Waterford glasses. Too late they realised that the Governor, head bowed, was waiting to say grace. He made a touching prayer for the safety of all present, particularly the explorers whose journey would take them into the wilds of Australia Felix.

Giles found himself seated opposite John Fawkner, and separated from Governor La Trobe (who sat at the head) by the socially precocious Lydia Angliss. Captain Elijah was placed at the far end, closest to Mrs La Trobe. Moribund and Lieutenant Sploon were stationed together, doomed to pass the meal well within the range of William Angliss.

No one asked about the soup. Giles brought a spoonful to his lips.

'Sheep's head, I'd say,' ventured La Trobe, suppressing a snigger.

He immediately put his guests at their ease with his pleasant manner and his pretty smile.

'I wonder, my friends, which of us has eaten the most unlikely animal or fish. I can tell you that in Mexico I have been served a dish of flamingoes' tongues.'

An excellent conversation ensued. La Trobe listened to the responses from around the table. There were some surprises. Camel came up twice, and Captain Elijah had tasted bear as a lad, but Giles, of course, won with hippo.

'Tell me about your ghost, Mrs La Trobe.'

'Please call me Sophie, Captain.' Out of the corner of her eye she followed the progress of several bugs scuttling across the floor.

'Sophie, then.'

The Captain's life was full of mysteries between women, and again he was aflutter, overheating. She touched his arm, a conspiratorial gesture.

'My husband doesn't believe, of course, but. . .'

'What's that, my dear?' The Governor was blessed with excellent ears.

'Captain Blood is interested in our ghost, Charles.'

La Trobe dipped a crust in his soup.

'Is it Batman?' asked Fawkner.

'He wears a kerchief over his face,' replied Mrs La Trobe

'That's him!' Fawkner erupted. 'Batman always used to ride about the camp with his face covered. Hiding his catastrophic nose.'

'Venereal,' commented the Reverend Clow. His first word for the evening.

'People are dropping off like flies.'

The widow agreed, and the conversation turned to the colony.

It was the opinion of John Fawkner that Bareheep was indeed a venereal township filled with drunkenness and crime, meekly punished by floggings, stocks, and time in flimsy gaols. Already this summer there were epidemics of typhoid and dysentery. The water was no good; carried in carts from the river and sold for a few gallons a penny, it wasn't fit to make beer.

'Our neighbour, Mr Hodgson, was burgled this morning,

broad daylight!' declared Mrs Fawkner. 'They left him quite without clothes.'

'Yet another outrage!' decried Reverend Clow, who seemed about to say more. His roast mutton had just arrived, and for a moment it was unclear whether he was commenting on his plate or referring to the predicament of Mrs Fawkner's neighbour.

'The Indians must overcome their distrust of fixed abodes and sedentary habits,' opined Governor La Trobe.

After dinner the men did not retire. There were not enough rooms. The whole party was ushered back to the reception room, where port was served with some crumbly biscuits.

Mrs Stephens, charming widow, and the Governor's wife sat either side of Captain Elijah, emphasising their remarks by touching his forearm. The Captain was distracted by the shooting pains in his legs and arms. The others settled into various reclines and desultory talk.

Governor La Trobe guided Giles to a large filing chest. Here, in the drawers, he kept his butterflies, and the two enthusiasts enjoyed a lively conversation about their own ramblings. Giles only briefly discussed his West African tour, though, for he was still unable to shrug off the disappointment of that trek. Giles had acted on a last-minute whim of the Royal Society to follow Richard Landers on his quest to discover the true course of the Quorra River, Mungo Park's Niger. But he had been waylaid at Bussa by the ruler there, who refused permission for Giles and his porters to continue, and so was unable to catch up with the geographer. Secretly, Giles had been relieved. Mungo Park had perished here, so too Clapperton, and before him Captain Tuckey and Major Peddie. It seemed a suicide mission – though Landers had returned a hero, of course.

Dr Moribund joined them at the butterfly chest, clutching his second glass of port. He had offended Mr and Mrs Angliss, and the Reverend Clow, with an anatomical joke, and was now ready to start on the host. He waited for Giles to complete his entertaining description of a small moss in fructification, then forgot the joke. A short time later Lieutenant Sploon retrieved Dr Moribund from the red couch, where he was espousing the benefits of hashish to the appalled reverend.

'I alter my mood according to my need,' he said, as the ship's party made their farewells.

❧

Captain Elijah instructed Lieutenant Sploon to support Dr Moribund on the dark walk home. These two proceeded arm in arm, weaving considerably, but at least remaining on Collins Street. Giles and the Captain walked behind.

There had been an altercation outside the Melbourne Club. The ship's party stumbled upon two men and their seconds, immediately after a duel. Apparently one of the men was injured. He remained on the ground, but he shunned assistance. One of the seconds packed the pistols away. Such events, thought Giles, were the natural consequence of a town containing such a surfeit of single men.

Back on board *Bright Planet*, Captain Elijah barked at

Tom Collins, the sailor sleeping on watch, to remove the various crates scattered across the main deck and to store them below. These crates contained stores and victuals, and Captain Elijah had given specific instructions regarding their storage before he left for dinner. He delayed retiring now until Seaman Collins had woken two of his mates downstairs and together fulfilled their unpopular duty. The whole ship remained awake until it was done.

Giles was at his desk, detailing the day's activities in his diary and cataloguing some of his samples. Such work often made him homesick. He longed for a Royal Society dinner, in the company of his peers, where he might come forth with some dazzling observations about his discoveries. Picturing the scene, though, he reminded himself that in all probability Darwin would be there, with his fool's luck.

Giles took a night cap. He began reading over some recent entries, fresh nib in hand.

JANUARY 1, 1842
The new year dawned a glorious pink over the great southern continent which now fills our horizon. Mid morning, the ship sped through the heads into the wide sweep of Port Phillip Bay. In the waters we saw many dolphins. There was dense scrub over every hill. The Captain spied smoke on the eastern shore and insisted on stopping for a trade. This most pleasant morning was interrupted by Dr Moribund performing an operation on deck. The doctor removed a tooth from poor Thomson's head, using black pliers and a bulkhead. The

*midshipman was unconscious by the end, thankfully, blood
from the wound all over.*

*The ship docked at Sandridge. The passengers were dis-
embarked and I accompanied them overland to Bareheep...*

Giles wondered again how the city fathers could arrive at
such a name.

Ship's Log

H.	K.	F.	Courses.	Winds.	Remarks,&c.
					Captain & Crew: 13 souls
			..	..	1st Lt Trimm
			..	..	2nd Lt Sploon
					Surgeon Dr Albert Moribund
					First Mate 'Jerker' Jenkin
					M'shipmen; Thomson, Slink-letter, Forte
					Seamen; Basin, Wickham, De Louse, Collins.
					Carpenter; Wm Weed
					Scientifics: Giles + 2
					M.Rotin, ship's cook has deserted. Weed to take over the duties
					Bright Planet delegation entertained at Governor's residence
					Trimm no better

Day Thirteen

At last, the day had arrived. Quiet Giles made his last visit to Fawkner's Hotel for breakfast. He completed his eggs then decamped to the library for newspapers and coffee. There he read a smug report in the *Herald* describing scenes of riot and debauchery at the brickfields on the Yarra, where 250 gallons of spirits were sold each week. Sarah Jane brought in some coffee. She wore a white blouse over a long skirt, as pretty as ever.

Giles caught a glimpse of her bosom as she set down the tray, the milky skin beneath her clothes. He flustered when she caught him looking. But she was not offended. On the contrary, Sarah Jane seemed pleased. A flush was burning her plump cheeks. Giles watched in disbelief as she began unbuttoning her blouse. The curtains were open to the bright day outside, any passer-by could glance through the window and witness the unfolding drama of her skin.

He jumped up to draw the curtains, but Sarah Jane ardently pressed her mouth upon his. She drew Giles over to the love seat – she had hold of his member through his trousers – and climbed astride the chair. The girl was naked!

Her fine bottom in the air, delicious folds of pink nestled

amongst a tangle of black hair. This was too much. Giles found his prick in his hand, gorged with blood, and was quite overtaken with the ferocity with which he entered her. She looked back at Giles over her shoulder, and he spent at once.

But Sarah Jane had not had her fill. She quickly revived his prick with her mouth, then leaving it glistening between them, she lay back on the love seat and pressed his head between her loving thighs so that he might gamahuche her. A feat he performed with gusto. Soon though he was back inside her sweet portals, and with what enthusiasm, what fiery upheavings did Sarah Jane greet the piercing thrusts of his dart of love. She cried out as Giles fell across her bosom, and felt his hot sperm commingling with her own spendings.

Sarah Jane was quickly dressed. She buttoned her blouse, smoothed her hair, while Giles returned his intromittent organ to his trousers.

The hangings on Flagstaff Hill were set for Saturday afternoon in order to attract the largest possible crowd for the event. The townsfolk arrived early with blankets and picnic baskets and plenty of community cheer. The hilltop offered a pleasant view of the fledgling town rising up from the banks of the swollen river, and beyond, to the south, ships were visible on the bay, making their way in and out of the heads. Here, hillside, there was merriment throughout the early afternoon as the young population enjoyed their best meal of the week. The lucky ones chewed contentedly on hanks of pork, while the majority consumed double portions of damper and re-boiled shanks of sheep.

All but the youngest drank champagne, for these days were special. Numerous but still special.

Governor Gipps had been heard to complain during his visit that the whole country for miles, for dozens of miles, was strewed with champagne bottles. Indeed even the boundaries of the town were marked out with cairns of the same.

The Angliss family, still new to Bareheep, remained the subject of much attention and mirth. It was their first picnic in the bush. Their first hanging likewise. They wore their finest clothes and camped apart from the general throng, preferring to absorb the proceedings from a distance. But Bareheep was fascinated with the Anglisses precisely because of this aloofness, or more precisely because of the two Angliss girls, their fine figures, their rose-tinted cheeks. Women were rare in the town, and young unmarried women simply unknown.

William Angliss stood upright throughout, nodding to new acquaintances between slugs of tea from his silver flask. Groups of men sauntered by, doffing their black hats to the ladies who sipped champagne beneath their parasols.

They were nestled between two fallen logs, seated on a blanket they had lain out over the ground. Behind them the thin forest began, and from that wilderness came the cries of unknown creatures. It was warm and the flies were incessant, and from beneath the ladies' rug, trains of insects emerged. Ants of all kinds grazed upon the picnic and supped from the sticky tumblers.

The crowd strolled easily over the hillside, an air of festivity about them. The city was but a few years old, yet already it had its traditions and conventions. A definite strata existed among the social classes, transplanted directly from the British Isles, and though there was a lack of genuine aristocracy, there was a surfeit of pretenders, William Angliss among them.

Edwin was in the trees.

He watched the hangman check his noose. He watched a constable patrolling. Elsewhere there were games, sack races and catch the greasy pig. Edwin watched Charlotte Angliss and her family. She sat with her sister, Anne, on a picnic rug, eating cup cakes with icing. Their parents were standing some distance away, engaged in conversation with an officious-looking red-haired man. A pastor was nearby, dabbing his forehead with an handkerchief. Edwin watched as the young pastor approached the Angliss girls. After an exchange of pleasantries Charlotte's younger sister got up from her picnic. She walked over to the clergyman, opened her parasol, and offered it to him.

Edwin moved closer.

He stood at the edge of the trees, still wearing his sailor's garb, quite visible if anyone cared to look. Charlotte lay on her back, one arm covering her eyes from the sun. He had been stalking her for days. Now he called her name.

'Who's there?' She lifted her head.

'Pretty Charlotte,' called Edwin again, closer this time.

'Why, if it isn't Edwin Robins!' She smiled. 'Have you been hiding?'

He stepped towards the fallen logs. He needed to impress upon her the urgency of his situation. *Bright Planet* was leaving at two o'clock, and he had determined to be aboard. Two days ago Edwin had overheard De Louse and Wickham, two of his old shipmates, bemoaning their impending fates as they passed his corner. The information had set him thinking. It was his most effective escape plan, no one would be looking for a stowaway on that fey vessel.

'Come for a walk, sweet Charlotte,' he said. 'I'll hold your umbrella.'

Charlotte Angliss was in her teens. The affections of men were still mysterious to her, forbidden and exciting. She had noticed Edwin's attentions towards her throughout the long voyage, always watching, always blushing, and she had not objected. Nor did she object now, though he was dressed like a ragamuffin and obviously needed a bath.

The deflowering was simple and swift. She had no words to express her confusion. She worried at the state of her clothes on the forest floor. She was the cleanest girl he had ever known, he marvelled, but close up there is no such thing as beauty. With his face in her neck Charlotte saw Edwin for the first time, all pores and hairs, shuddering as he impregnated her with his seed.

Charlotte put her skirts in order and restored her blouse. Edwin walked with her to the edge of the clearing. Charlotte wondered if she had the ability to walk the remaining yards to the picnic grounds, or would shame and guilt strike her down in a swoon. She did not like the wild. It was an outrage, of course, but in many ways it was, after so many fumblings, such a relief. When Edwin said he would return, the light shifted across Charlotte's face, and the sound she made, a kind of pleading, echoed through the trees. The silence that followed embraced them where they stood.

Bright Planet was tied up at the wharf, loaded and ready. The animals were aboard, chickens and goats and dogs. Captain Elijah had met with Mr Badgery at Customs House in the morning for another silent exchange of signatures and paperwork. He had returned to the ship to find Moribund waiting for him in the great cabin.

The doctor was in a high anxiety.

'Lieutenant Trimm is *dead*, Captain.' Moribund wrung his hands. 'He never came out of the fever.'

'Ah no! . . . Poor fellow.' Captain Elijah sighed. 'I thought he was hanging on?'

'So did I. But his symptoms got worse. Like he had the flux.' Moribund paused. 'One of the men is down too, with a fever.'

'I feel bad about Lieutenant Trimm.' Indeed there was a new cramp in his guts.

'Shall we delay our departure?'

'No. We'll bury him upriver.'

*

On the forecastle deck Captain Elijah summoned Lieutenant Sploon to give him news of his promotion. Both men were overheating in their uniforms, blotching under the hot sky.

'Now we are only twelve. Does that improve our chances?' asked Captain Elijah.

'No, sir.' Sploon puffed out his already fat cheeks.

❧

On Flagstaff Hill, behind the gallows, a leering figure in a broken dray appeared. The ghastly horse and the waving rag revealed an awful face, a suppurating nose and dark red eyes. A crowd of spectators had gathered for the execution, but the ghost failed to excite their interest.

'Bloody Batman!'

The crowd cheered as the dray they had been expecting arrived, with the two condemned men perched atop their own coffins. They were Aboriginal men, Bob and Jack, who had admitted to cruel crimes.

Their executioner, John Davies, was a first-timer.

He dangled them a couple of times but the fall did not break their necks. Clearly the ropes were too short. John Davies gave a nervous little laugh as he stepped off the platform, leaving the prisoners to slowly strangle.

Edwin Robins found Pierre in the usual place. The others were gone, and Pierre looked oddly forlorn in his morning coat and dungarees.

'Ready?'

'Yep, I'm coming,' said Pierre.

They had to hurry. Edwin had no watch but he could see the sun had already arced past noon. They reached the river above the brickfields and worked their way along the bank past a couple of settlers' huts. Soon enough they had a view of the river harbour. *Bright Planet* was still there, docked at the wharf, gangplanks down.

William Watts ran a punt across the Yarra. Back and forth all day. The ferryman charged a penny a passenger, and looked so much like Charon in his crazy boat that the journey often took on a fearful air. He was resting on the left bank when Edwin and Pierre happened past. He had no passengers, they were all up at Flagstaff Hill, so he was eating an apple in the shade.

'Is that your rowboat?' Edwin asked him, pointing to an upturned dinghy on the bank.

'Yup,' replied Watts. He used it to commute down river to work from his hut in Jolimont.

It was a pleasant hijack. Edwin was still dreamy from his forest tryst with Charlotte Angliss. He may have been quick to rage but he was an idealist in love. Pierre was chattering now, as they approached the ship from the starboard side and William Watts steered them towards the prow where there was a rope they could reach. Edwin did not even bother with a parting threat for the ferryman, the man had been so amiable, as he followed Pierre up the rope.

Once they were aboard Edwin knew where to go. Down through the first hatch on the gun deck, past the crew's quarters, around the forward mast, and down again to the lower storerooms. Here, tucked in the prow, they would take their chances until the ship was well away. There was plenty of food nearby. Edwin made himself comfortable in the gloom. Pierre killed a rat with his oversize shoe.

❦

Giles remained in his cabin until quarter to two, then emerged sheepishly on the quarterdeck to watch the sailors at work. Above him, Captain Elijah bellowed orders from the steering position. The mooring ropes were untied, leaving only painters fore and aft. A single rat ran the length of the forward painter back to the wharf, then scurried under the riverbank.

Soon *Bright Planet* was in the middle of the river, carrying square sails on the fore and main masts and fore-and-aft sails on the mizzen. She moved slowly past the east end of Bareheep to the Falls, where a channel to the right gave them passage. There was no farewell party. They were away.

The river swept around headlands and ran quickly, circuitously through the landscape. The banks were lined with stands of blue and grey trees, and thick foliage folded out over the water, picturesque, water, tree, and sky. *Bright Planet* sailed a smooth line through the channels. In the crow's nest the smallest boy watched for signs on the surface, signs of change in the topography beneath.

Captain Elijah spent the first afternoon on deck chatting amiably with Sploon and Dr Moribund, while the ship progressed prettily with only a couple of sails and plenty of reach to manoeuvre.

How quickly the day passed. After little more than an hour's sail up the river *Bright Planet* came across a settlement of Scotsmen. Their huts were dotted over a cleared hillside, small domes of irregular height and circumference. Clumps of sheep roamed the bright green. The settlers themselves were not visible immediately to the party on the boat. Their camouflage clothes melded them into the acclivity they lay upon. Giles saw through his eyeglass that they were dozing, snoozing in groups beneath the trees they had neglected to remove, or draped in tartans across the pasture.

The water gurgled behind the ship as it coursed through the middle channel. The river was wide here. Captain Elijah called for soundings, as he eased toward the shore. The Scotsmen had built a landing deck there, to which canoes were tied, and he hoped the water would be deep enough to hold his ship's draught.

Basin made himself useful in the prow, dropping the lead every five yards.

'Five fathoms,' he called, reaching for the red bunting on the line. Then, 'Four fathoms now!', as the white cloth emerged.

This set off the Captain.

He delivered a volley of oaths and a series of commands that echoed around the ship. All sails were drawn, and the helmsman tried to bring the stern around.

They were close to shore, too close, for as the keel worked through the mud on the river floor, the stern swung late, splintering the jetty the Scots had made, and the ship docked directly into the river bank.

The crew erupted in one voice, a lofted oath that woke the sleepers on the hill, and scattered the sheep. The Scotsmen stood up in their kilts, and moved like lazy animals down the incline towards the ship.

Shortly a delegation arrived at the broken dock. Assessing the spectacle at close range, the Scotsmen remained dour. Bare-armed and bearded, they wore a harsh cloth, stretched over one shoulder and clasped with bright metal plates which reflected the spearing sunlight.

Before them *Bright Planet* leaned into the river bank, and the splintered planks of their jetty were splayed up like a set of bad teeth.

Captain Elijah observed the Scotsmen from his deck. He was in a fine stew. Red to his ears and muttering. He glared at the boards beneath him, trying to regain his purpose.

He hated the Scots.

'Sploon!' the Captain called out.

The first lieutenant squeezed up the gangway.

'Captain?'

'Take Lieutenant Trimm ashore. We'll bury him here.' The Captain paused. 'Moribund! Giles!'

These fellows strolled across the quarterdeck toward him.

'Gentlemen,' the Captain entreated, 'kindly greet the natives.'

Even while these two retreated he roared again.

'Carpenter!'

Several sailors had jumped ashore to assess the hull. They were followed by the ship's doctor and Mr Giles, who dangled from the gunwale before dropping feet first into the reedy shallows of the riverbank.

One of the Scotsmen stepped forward. He wore a familiar beard.

'What livestock are you carrying?' he asked.

'Dogs and goats,' replied Moribund, smiling warmly as he gained the shore.

'D'ye fancy a trade? Some mutton for yer men?' The Scotsman smiled broadly too, revealing the metal in his mouth. Behind him, his countrymen grinned.

'We are on an expedition, science, you know,' spoke Giles. 'And the ship is fully laden. We have no need for your sheep.'

'What about the wee jetty?' demanded another Scot. 'We didnae ask you to stop. D'ye have nae idea how to steer a boat?'

Into this riverside *détente* Sploon appeared with three crewmen labouring underneath Lieutenant Trimm's freshly made box. The burial party weaved through the assembled Scotsmen and proceeded south along the riverbank, as though they were giving the corpse some air.

'You'll not leave him here!' cried Angus, the negotiator. 'Oi!'

Sploon turned back, steadying the coffin with his hand,

but his face was too red to respond. The Captain had directed them towards a hill above the boiling-down station, and here they would wait. Already Basin was descending the ropes to the shore with a shovel in hand.

The negotiations fell apart. Moribund and Giles waited on the shore while the various Scots slipped away, back to the volley of wooden huts that formed the streets of their hamlet. Only Angus remained.

'What do you call this place?' Giles asked politely.

'Heidelberg.' His voice was affected.

'Why? Are there Germans among you?'

'Certainly not. Tha's the name of the git who was camped here afore us. He named it after hisself. He drowned in the river. But we done all the work. Macfarlands and Brutes we are, and Gregors.'

Meanwhile, Captain Elijah paced the quarterdeck. Every so often he scanned the hilltop with his eyeglass, awaiting the signal from Lieutenant Sploon. The Captain had watched the coffin's progress over the rising ground to the summit of the small mount. The outlanders had cleared the lower third of the hillside, leaving an incline of pocked earth, a graveyard of stumps through which the sailors bore their charge. They emerged from the remaining light forest onto a stony plateau. Lieutenant Sploon waited here while the sailors took turns to dig.

Captain Elijah watched him through the eyeglass, watched him mop his brow with a big red kerchief. A large number of birds were in the air behind Sploon, darting in and out of the Captain's view, a commotion in the yellow trees.

Finally Sploon waved his arm in the air, his kerchief flying splendidly, to signal that the hole was dug.

Captain Elijah refused to leave the ship.

In his stead Giles and Moribund stood alongside Lieutenant Sploon. They had ascended the hill together, both still a little out of breath as the three boys, Thom. Wickham, Denis De Louse, and Tom Collins, tipped the box into the hole. Lieutenant Trimm's coffin was now wedged at an awkward angle, the clay walls of the grave already grasping the wood. The sailors looked up contritely. Sploon nodded for them to stand to, then raised his red flag again. He waved solemnly at the distant ship.

On the quarterdeck the first mate raised a flag in reply. The Captain lowered his eyeglass and produced a prayer book from his inside pocket. His fingers brushed against the letter he kept in the same pocket. He began reading aloud the burial service while up on Poison Hill the ship's doctor began intoning from his own book.

Poison Hill, so named because here the settlers had fed poisoned meat to the indigenous men who gathered to observe the activities of the strangers, provided Giles with a superb panorama of the surrounding area, but for the moment he was awed by the facts of Lieutenant Trimm's circumstance and he stood with the others over the open grave, the awful accommodation, with his head bowed.

'We commit this body to the earth,' said Moribund.

'If flux don't get you, fevers must,' said the Captain.

Lieutenant Sploon raised his kerchief again.

On deck the first mate waited for his Captain's command.

'What the hell!' the old man cried. 'Two guns. Three volleys.'

The first mate repeated the order in a loud solemn tenor.

'Aye!' came the reply from the gun deck.

The first mate lofted his flag and waved to the party on the hill.

The first shots canyonned through the still afternoon. Across the river and into the trees.

Crows and cockatoos took to the air. One tree exploded into fire, while several others lost branches. Thomson and Slinkletter were firing the bow chasers. They fired both guns thrice, by which time the squall of birds in the air produced a deafening sound. A small headland on the opposite bank was ablaze.

Aboard *Bright Planet* and up on Poison Hill the naval officers saluted, and a wave of camaraderie passed among them, a kind of ennui.

❧

Almost directly beneath the two gunners' firing position, in the stifling place where Edwin and Pierre were sleeping, the explosions reverberated through the timber, the smell of cordite quick and heavy in the gloom.

The stowaways were rudely awakened, whispering with

their eyes wide, hearts abeat. Edwin looked around for anything that might act as a weapon, thinking, naturally enough, that the ship was under attack. That the disgruntled Scots he had earlier spied from the forward hatch were boarding *Bright Planet*.

But for a minute all was quiet.

Then Edwin heard the gunners, Slinkletter and Thomson, returning from their stations to the crew's quarters. He heard a rasping laughter echo as the sailors descended the companion way. Then a bout of coughing, a wretched cough.

'What's happen, man?' asked Pierre.

Edwin put his finger to his lips before disappearing into the passage. Pierre moved deeper into the shadows, settling against a crate of ship's biscuit, into which he occasionally dipped his right hand. For Pierre the experience had so far been less than he had imagined.

'Robins!'

Here was a familiar cry. The old boot, 'Jerker' Jenkin, the ambitionless first mate appeared in the prow.

But Edwin was gone. He was a quick rascal, he could hide anywhere. The first mate sniffed around, even looked over the bows for a dangling boy, before returning to the Captain's post.

'I seen you, boy,' he said as he walked away. 'Oh! My naughty boy.'

His voice boomed across the ship's deck, and in the ropes Edwin certainly heard him, perched as he was, thirty feet up. He saw everything clearly from there. The aching sky stretched too blue and too high, and the burning trees, burning silently across the river. The water was brown and cool.

Edwin saw too the party of explorers wandering across a hillside to the south, beyond the rough community of huts and the boiling-down works. While below him, on the river bank, Edwin observed the ship's carpenter, William Weed, already at work on the shattered jetty. All in all an agreeable tableau, but he could not linger. He was a criminal now and he had no wish to reveal his presence so soon.

❧

Quiet Giles strolled away from the grave site. He was still twitching from Sarah Jane, prickled with guilt and twinges of remembered lusts from their round of pleasure. He had spoken to no one of their warm morning in the cool library of Fawkner's Hotel. He had remained silent at lunch amid the heavy tales of whoring in Bareheep, but his body would not let him forget. Now, accompanied by the ship's doctor, he proceeded to mark some items of interest in the surrounding flora.

He retrieved a pine cone dropped from a nearby conifer.

'Notice the swirl of the pattern of scales, doctor, each layer of scales is the sum of the two layers beneath. Such a beautiful sequence.'

Moribund nodded.

Giles pointed to a distinctive grove of trees near the sandstone crest of the hill.

'Here of course are the banksia,' he said, moving towards the tangle of trees. Their trunks, a blood-red timber, were gnarled and twisted with bark, and their flowers, on closer inspection, consisted of golden spikes in neat parallel rows. Where the flowers had fallen a woody cone remained, host to seed cells which gaped like the open mouths of children.

Doctor Moribund was persuaded to indulge Mr Giles while the botanist collected samples for his flower press. The day was suddenly pleasant, after all. The forest they entered filled with all kinds of gumwood and birdsong, and the shade was most welcome.

Moreover, they both took the opportunity to answer a call of nature, for while Giles responded to his scientific responsibilities, Moribund retreated into the scrub to lower his trousers and evacuate his bowels. It was more dramatic than he would have liked, for although the doctor had experienced stomach pains all afternoon, he was not prepared for such a messy stool, or for so much blood to accompany it. He tried to clean himself with a clump of grass but there was little he could do. He wiped his bloating hands.

Giles followed this botanical interlude with another bout of loathing. He confessed his troubled mind to the bespattered Dr Moribund as they made their descent to the pastures of Heidelberg. Moribund was still winded from his recent cacation, but he was cheered somewhat by the idea of Giles and the milkmaid.

'I took my pleasure with the widow last night,' Moribund told Giles. 'I haven't felt well since.'

A noisy group of currawongs was circling over the wood-land; their distinctive ringing voice alarmed Giles, who identified them at once. He returned a jar of seeds to his satchel and hurried the doctor along.

'Come sir, we must depart.'

Under Captain Elijah's instructions William Weed, the carpenter, had taken an assistant and proceeded to refashion the jetty for the Scotsmen, a party of whom spent the afternoon watching Weed's progress and discoursing in Gaelic. He had worked quickly, stopping only to smoke a cheroot during the distant burial service, and by the time Quiet Giles and the demure doctor returned to the ship, he was standing athwart the new landing deck, rolling a second cheroot between his filthy palms. It had been a busy day for the carpenter, the morning spent fashioning a coffin for Lieutenant Trimm and the afternoon consumed with repairs to the damned jetty. It was somewhat smaller than the original, but William Weed had not wanted to waste his best wood.

'Nice job, William,' remarked Giles.

'It'll do, sir.'

'I must use the head,' Moribund interrupted, hissing through gritted teeth.

Quiet Giles and the carpenter watched the doctor's swelling form clamber up the ropes to the gangway. They looked at each other then followed him aboard.

'Ahoy!' The chorus of Scotsmen who had whiled the afternoon on the bank beside the boat came to life. 'Doona go sassoon!'

'Stay and feast!' cried Angus the spokesman. 'We'll eat a sheep.'

This brought forth a torrent of cursing from the quarter-deck.

'Stay and rot! You murderous swine!' Captain Elijah, whose face above his beard turned purple with the effort, bellowed out his message, then spoke calmly to his assembling crew. None of whom were disposed to linger amongst the hairy Dougals.

'We'll just anchor anywhere,' said the Captain.

It was still a sunny afternoon, the blue sky stretched to a pale horizon. There were a few high clouds, a breeze from the south. Captain Elijah looked sullenly over the lightly forested river plain and listened to Jenkin's report. The first mate had been ashore to glean information.

'Squatters for fifty miles, they say. There's a drover's track follows the river, but none o' these Scots ever been over that hill.' 'Jerker' Jenkin pointed to a low peak less than a mile to the north-east. 'These regions are well travelled.'

'Of course they are, Jenkin. We've hardly left Bareheep.'

'Yes, sir.'

Captain Elijah struggled with his clothing, unbuttoning his formal jacket with his hot red fingers. So hot, prickly hot.

'I had hoped we'd get further today.'

At four-thirty, by Mr Giles's watch, *Bright Planet* disengaged from the riverbank and was towed into mid-stream by two sailors in the rowboat. The Captain ordered a farewell gun salute as the sails were unfurled. Bombing a grove of Heidelberg trees, as if delivering a broadside to a passing corvette. The expedition was resumed, and with all hands on deck they cruised upriver to find a picturesque spot where they might spend the night.

❦

Dinner at the Captain's table, prepared this night by the Frenchman, De Louse, was a pleasant affair. De Louse had been unexpectedly seconded to the galley after William Weed could not be roused. The ship bobbed gently, at anchor in a deep lagoon some miles upstream. All personnel were relieved to be *en voyage*, relieved too that the stew was so heavily spiced, enough to disguise its ingredients. The ship's officers and the scientists shared several bottles of Constantia wine that Mr Cormac had provided. There was a discussion of natural philosophy, led by Giles, too tedious to relate. But there followed a good-humoured exchange about man's very first state.

'What are the laws of nature for a naked man with no property?' asked Cormac.

'To seek a naked woman to house him,' replied Captain Elijah.

'Very droll,' Moribund snorted.

'Are you unwell, doctor? You seem a little green about the gills.'

'My stomach has been poor all day. It seems to have swelled in the heat.' Moribund pulled aside his brocade dinner jacket to reveal his waistcoat, a garment so taut that the mere touch of his puffy forefinger sent the top button flying.

The doctor looked uncomfortable indeed, though he raised his glass to the Captain. There was an element of drunkenness in the merriment of the party. Although the redness of their faces was in some part due to the scratching of insect bites. Clouds of mosquitoes had arrived at sunset, forcing them to consume the first course of their meal under the relative safety of a mosquito net.

'Another drink, Moribund?'

A smile broke over the doctor's features, he nodded and turned to Giles's assistants.

'Where were you boys this afternoon? I didn't see you ashore at Heidelberg.'

Cormac demurred.

'My cousin was working on his drawings,' piped Angel.

Captain Elijah uncorked a bottle of Madeira and asked Lieutenant Sploon to call Midshipman Forte to attend his table.

When Sploon arrived with Forte, the Captain passed each of them a glass.

'Sploon! You are my first lieutenant,' he said to the florid officer – 'And Mister Forte here shall be your second.'

Forte was a tall man of about twenty years. He stooped in the doorway of the Captain's dining room.

'At what age did you go to sea, Mr Forte?'

'Fifteen, sir.'

'From now on you dine at my table.' Captain Elijah drained his glass and turned to address the cramped diners in a sweaty whisper. He was sweltering in the close quarters.

'Thus we rise through the ranks. So it was for me. My father was a clergyman and I was his third son. I had no prospect but the sea.'

There followed an appreciative silence.

'What about Jenkin, sir?' inquired Lieutenant Sploon. 'He's next in line.'

'Shut up, Sploon.'

Captain Elijah disappeared to his cabin briefly. He left the door to his room ajar, through which breach the pigeon-holed wall of his cabin was visible, crammed with sheaves of paper and rolled-up charts, and through which the sounds of his heaving and coughing were clearly audible. He returned carrying a uniform jacket, a slim brocaded frock coat with gold valance on the cuffs. It had belonged to the former Lieutenant Trimm, whose body had been too bloated to fit into the uniform and so was buried in his underwear, with his gold-tipped cane for company.

The Captain presented the garment to the botanist, Mr Giles, noting that it would hardly fit either of these recently promoted men.

Soon enough, the clutch of explorers thanked Captain Elijah for his indulgence and retired to their cabins. The Captain bid his subordinates and guests goodnight, closed the door and spewed again. The local stew was a powerful ejective.

Back in his own cabin Giles opened his diary and unpacked his pens.

JANUARY 13 1842

This day our journey interior has begun with fond farewells to the city of Bareheep. Nothing could have prepared me for the melancholy premonition I felt at departure from this outpost, a place we had known for a bare fortnight. I forced myself out of my cabin to watch the town slip behind, while before us the brown river beckoned.

I breakfasted again at Fawkner's Hotel and whiled an hour in the library. Afterwards I walked the streets of the town for the last time. Here came upon me the melancholy. A mysterious feeling. The colony is too eager for attention, its streets too willing to please. I felt aghast, as at the appearance of another's soul, that awful tenderest core of need. As ever, a result of too much introspection, I find myself unable to embrace such vulnerableness, and instead recoil. A feeling not unlike the small dismay one feels upon spending.

Giles continued making notes well into the night, cataloguing samples, and consuming small draughts of laudanum, though he was careful in this regard for he wanted to conserve his thinking. The ship slept while he worked, though he heard the animals bleating in the hold, and wild dogs barking.

Ship's Log

H.	K.	F.	Courses.	Winds.	Remarks,&c.
12			E..	s.se	livestock penned
2			NE.	S	Departure after noon fine weather
					Lt Trimm died a.m.
4			N	S	Burial at Heidelberg 12m NE Bareheep
					Ship's draught sufficient in most parts
					Regular soundings reveal deep channels
					Anchored 16 miles upriver

Day Twenty-One

It had been a week of swell evenings and portions for all, but it was another shabby morning for the Captain. The burnt smell of coffee rising from his mug hardly stirred him as he brooded in the great cabin. He had been sleeping badly and most mornings he remained here amending his log, estimating the distances travelled and nursing his headache. Once again he smoothed out the letter on the desk before him. This was the moment he relished, the moment of most sadness.

Generally speaking, love had been kind to Captain Elijah. The vagaries of his desire allowed him to play truant to many women, and indeed he was uncommonly skilled in the arts of physical love. Socially too, the Captain was a gracious man, and this combination of grace and ardour secured him many invitations. For his part, Captain Elijah exchanged bawdy tales with the merry gentlemen, and made *rendez-vous* with their wives. A satisfying arrangement for all parties.

But when the crisis had come, in the form of Clara Lacey, he realised too late that his ability for romance had been overreached.

Clara was presented to him by her father, Admiral Lacey, and Captain Elijah had seduced the lovely daughter in the usual manner. He, Elijah, was a lustful man with handsome cheeks, a trimmed beard; he fed her champagne and they danced under the chandeliers. The pair spent happy hours intoxicated with themselves, and there, without warning, amid the bright gaiety of London's ballrooms, the Captain fell in love.

How she could tire of him at the exact moment he had elevated her above desire was beyond his comprehension. What rumour had she heard that might cool her heart so suddenly? His mind had passed over these events too quickly. He dared not dwell. Enough that he was vanquished, like an old salt, banished to the waves.

Innocently he had taken the next post Admiralty could provide; hoping the pain of separation could kill him. But his heart would not beat still and his chest failed to explode.

So it was Clara's letter, received too late, and pored over daily, which kept him both in turmoil and emotional torpor. Clara had changed her mind. She would fly to Plymouth by Thursday's coach, notwithstanding her mother's health, there to greet him, or if he would not forgive her, to 'at least farewell his gentle soul'.

The constant ache that wore the lining of his stomach thin, the seeping interior life that poisoned; these he could live with. Though he accepted his life would be shorter. But the base torments his mind delivered, the ridicule to which he subjected himself, the ridicule of his own soul, would send him mad. He had a consuming dread of the past, and the torturous reliving of that landscape made him fearful of even closing his eyes at night. Rather, by force of will, he would concentrate on the present and the desolate circumstance of his ship.

Bright Planet had negotiated the courses of the river for a week without greater incident than the discovery of the stowaways. On the fifth day the river forked, and following nothing more than chance, the officers and scientists agreed, the boat took the passage left, and here the river flowed stronger and, indeed, flowed away from the sea. The crew realised at once the significance, and because the stream was wider here they thought nothing of the Captain's order for more sail. Half a day passed with feasting and early wine. Sailors trailed hooks into the water from the stern, reeling in carp and redfins. The carp they threw back, but the rest were fried nice and happy in the pan.

The river was full of fish. Again this morning the sailors were dropping lines and dangling them in the wake of the ship. Mr Basin, in particular, showed great alacrity for the sport and pulled in redfin by the dozen. William Weed waited in the galley for the morning catch with the fires stoked and his hair ablaze. Edwin Robins had stoked the fire too generously and now the galley was in uproar.

'You miserable whelp!' The cook batted at the flames with an oven cloth and kicked the boy. He kicked him hard but Edwin was curled up tight and the blows were largely ineffective.

'Your day is coming,' said the cook. He growled in pain as he wiped his brow, then hurled the smouldering cloth at

Pierre, who was wedging himself into the flour cupboard, unnerved by the close quarters he was being forced to keep. The stowaways were assigned to the galley for all meals. Their presence was tolerated on deck only when Mr Giles wished to ask questions of the native boy, or when First Mate Jenkin wished them to scrub.

❦

Bright Planet's deck gleamed in the dappled sunlight that speared through the riverside gums. To the east, over the purple plains, the sun arced above a range of low mountains. The ship's deck was washed and the fish were fried before Captain Elijah surfaced on the quarterdeck.

He was greeted by Mr Giles who had been taking his coffee on deck. The Captain cast his stare over the sailors camped out on the forecastle deck, eating their breakfast al fresco. Each of them gazing into the brown waters of the river. There was a coolness to the air that everyone enjoyed before the heat to come.

'I've been thinking, Captain,' Giles began.

'Good work, Mr Giles.'

The Captain assessed the trim of the sail, felt for the wind, and sprang up the stairs to the steering position.

The ship had been on the move for over an hour, cruising through the wide channels of the new river. Again she travelled under too much sail, or so the midshipmen thought. Basin was now perched in the prow, dropping the lead every couple of minutes. He, like the others, was aware of the dangers posed while Lieutenant Sploon was at the wheel. Although the river was wide here, about a quarter of a mile, Sploon had no eye for the perils hidden beneath the surface, and the crew remained on full alert until Captain Elijah appeared on deck. He did not take the wheel himself, but immediately directed his second lieutenant to replace Sploon at the helm.

'You must be tired, Sploon,' he said. 'How about some rum?'

'Yes, sir.'

'Fetch it for us, would you?'

The Captain turned to Giles. 'How is Slinkletter?'

'Worse, I gather.' Giles grimaced. 'I can no longer pass near the sick bay for fear the odours may infect me.'

The three men sipped their rum, contemplating the countryside as it slipped by. The river was flanked by flood plains spreading for several miles to the valley walls. The scrub was covered in the purple-grey down of wildflowers, and the soil was darker here than the country near Bare-heep. Small stands of stunted trees, small eucalypts, dotted the plains.

They were watching for movement. Animal or human. Half fearing the rustle of the breeze through the grass, they heard no sound from the land, no birdsong, no commotions.

Giles put his telescope to his eye, focused and unfo-cused, and pinned a small oasis of trees, high grass, a water hole. A flash beyond the trees, too quick for Giles who swung his eyepiece too far and caught only details of blue shining sky. He narrowed his eye again. The Captain watched the starboard side. Sploon wandered over to the railing, just in time to see the red check of the black boy's waistcoat disappearing down the gangway.

'You boy!' he shouted. 'Native – !'

'Shut up, Sploon,' Captain Elijah hissed.

'Sshhh,' Giles shushed.

The lieutenant stopped his cry. The three men listened, cocked their heads.

In a moment they resumed their scans. Again the land was quiet, only the sound of the river running through it.

Then the trumpeting began. First one, then a hundred birds took up the call.

Giles had not seen them immediately, their scarlet heads hidden in the reeds, but he saw them now as they took to the air. A riotous band of wings swarming into the sky. Several birds danced on the bank, rearing, holding out their wings and performing the high step. They too took flight.

'Brolgas.'

'Fucking brolgas.'

❧

Messrs Cormac and Angel prowled the forecastle deck with their blond heads bowed deep in conversation. Cormac's untrained curls gave him a girlish appearance, an impression confirmed by his high forehead and sensitive skin. The same could not, of course, be said of Angel, whose bulk was too overtly masculine to be tempered by the clumps of flaxen hair sprouting from his dome. Dr Moribund approached them with a wave. Moribund, whose alarming expansion had paused for the moment, was an indiscreet ally. He baritoned a greeting to the young men. They disengaged. Their expressions fell neutral.

'Any whispers, lads?' the doctor asked. 'Any news?'

'Nothing,' said Angel. 'I'm supposed to count trees. And Cormac's doing sketches.'

Moribund's newfound girth and floridity had hindered his movements about the ship, and indeed he had taken to his cabin for days at a stretch. He had missed the previous evening's meal at the Captain's table.

'No talk of turning back, then?'

'The Captain sees no reason,' stated Angel. 'Mr Giles will not hear of it.'

'We could run,' suggested Cormac, scratching the boil that had arisen overnight on his wrist.

'Shut up, Mac,' said Angel, as Second Lieutenant Forte approached.

'Good day, sir.'

'Doctor Moribund, may I have a word?'

The doctor pulled out his watch, as if to consult it, and flipped open the gold case to reveal a store of snuff. He took a pinch and regarded the young officer bleakly. The doctor's moods had not been improved by the swelling of his person.

'You must attend Slinkletter, sir,' Lieutenant Forte informed him. 'He is at his last.'

'He has been at his last for two days,' replied Moribund. 'He has disgorged his own entrails, for God's sake.' He paused to smooth his stained, brown moustache. 'How are the other men?'

'Fine, sir. Except for De Louse.'

'Oh?'

'I have taken him to the hospital, but he refuses to stay. He's feared of the stench.'

He paused.

'I took the liberty of strapping him in.'

Moribund examined his watch, then looked to the sky to confirm the co-incidence of the sun at midday.

Cormac and Angel took the opportunity to slink away.

Lieutenant Forte and Dr Moribund repaired below, past the animal pens – stifling quarters – to the doctor's makeshift hospital ward, cordoned off by three squares of canvas, behind which Midshipman Slinkletter and lately Seaman De Louse floundered on their fraying beds.

The olfactory assault of the hospital ward was indeed staggering. The fetor emanating from the sick beds had ruined the already private air. Dr Moribund's recoil was visible as he placed his hand on the forehead of the new arrival, a gentle touch, before crouching over Slinkletter's body.

The dying man opened his speckled mouth to speak. His tongue was thick and black, unable to negotiate the syllables, but the doctor nodded knowingly. He made a prayer with his fattened figures and bowed his head while Slinkletter continued his grave mumbling. At length he fell quiet. His eyes closed.

Moribund retreated one or two steps, ushering Lieutenant Forte back too, as if he knew what was to come.

Slinkletter's eyes opened, too blue, too far away, they gazed at the two black-coated men, a gaze that saw too much. Slinkletter saw the terror on their faces and kindly averted his terrible eyes. Shortly thereafter he took leave of his senses, emitting, through the nose, a large number of maggots.

❧

The ship slid past the flat lands. Still too much sail, thought Captain Elijah. The river was heavy here, swollen, unnamed. It ate through the purple land. Again the officers and gentlemen regarded the banks. A sheep had been spotted, a grey sheep, feeding on the purple grass. Soon enough, after a bend in the river where sweeps of *Eucalyptus mannifera* stood waist deep in the running water, they came upon a flock of the grey beasts.

The animals paused to regard the passing vessel. There was a camp nearby, a squatter's hut, with bark walls and a swinging door. A dog lay adjacent, unmoving. Also a grey mare, apparently stiff, in the dirt, legs in the air.

'Don't want to stop, do you?' asked the Captain.

'No, sir,' Giles replied. 'There is nothing here.'

'I don't like the look of it, Captain,' offered Sploon.

'Though I have a sailor to bury.'

'Let's give him a sea burial,' Sploon suggested.

Captain Elijah felt crapulous.

'Get the corpse prepared!' he shouted. 'Thomson to the bow chasers!'

In this manner he diverted the ship's attention, the

sailors sprang to, leaving only Basin in the bow, taking soundings with the lead. Sploon fetched the doctor. Giles peered through his eyeglass, scanning the squatter's camp for signs of life.

The Captain looked green. The Captain looked ill. The Captain turned a full swivel.

'Watchunder!' he cried as the vomit splashed on the deck below.

Two sailors traversing the orlop deck jumped in alarm.

Giles swung his telescope to view the right bank. Once again he was struck by the beauty of the spectacle. For a week now he had been recording the sights, the flora and fauna, the glittering surrounds. Generally, the riverside was punctuated by Aboriginal camps and fishing parties, but he had seen none today. Only the deserted squatter's outpost.

Bright Planet had passed many such barracks, most commonly housing two or three gentlemen whose appearance had taken on the wildness of the new land. These squatters, third sons and hairy priests, sought their fortunes in difficult climes, and most of them kept wives, native women, sprawled about their camps, to ease the loneliness of their situation.

The presence of these shepherds annoyed Giles, and he was pleased to think the expedition was nearing virgin country. He trained his telescope on the lands ahead. The valley was narrowing. The topography was changing slowly, the ground rising and the wood cover increasing.

*

The guns sounded. Slinkletter's body splashed and was gone.

'There is death,' said the Captain, pocketing his prayer book.

Several trees exploded in flames on the starboard shore, followed by shrieks from the bow. The assembled crew heard Thomson yelling at his new assistant, Master Wickham.

'Pull yer finger out!' Thomson roared.

Obviously the match had been lit.

This time the trees exploded to port. A plume of sulphur-crested cockatoos resultant.

The gun echoed through the air, a low growl beneath the complaining wildlife. Meanwhile, Septimus Slinkletter was looking through Davy Jones's peepers, dead at twenty-two.

❦

It was late in the afternoon when Giles came bounding across the planks. He had spied something on the shore. Giles and the Captain conferred.

'Captain,' he was flushed, 'we must stop here for the night. I wish to explore the shoreline before we proceed any farther.'

'It looks no different to anywhere else we've passed, Mr Giles. Do you insist?'

'I do, sir,' Giles replied.

Captain Elijah shrugged. He was in no hurry now. He called out to Lieutenant Forte who called in turn to the mate, and all along the ship the command was relayed.

Lieutenant Sploon was at the wheel. The sailors climbed the ropes and began to furl the canvasses.

The boat glided on until Sploon identified a suitable landing place, a scalloped beach overhung with old trees. Captain Elijah took the wheel himself. The anchors were thrown at once and the Captain steered *Bright Planet* out of the channel.

'Bring her in, Sploon,' he said, handing the wheel back to his eager lieutenant.

The first snag scraped against the hull noisily as the ship passed over. But the second log, the submerged branch of a fallen tree, impaled the boat below the waterline, and stopped the vessel dead.

On deck the ship's personnel tumbled forward, grazing arms and banging foreheads. Down below, Cormac and Angel, engaged in their own tumble, were propelled roughly forward, *in situ*, into the bulkhead, where they continued their play with Cormac on top this time.

The hole was taking water and *Bright Planet* began listing a dozen yards from the riverbank.

Lieutenants Forte and Sploon lowered the rowboat into the river and paddled around the ship to inspect the damage. Using oars and feet they managed to push the boat off the branch, wrenching the log out and making the hole somewhat bigger in the process.

Bright Planet regained some buoyancy and bobbed up in the water, causing cheers on deck and coinciding with Cormac's climax. This time he did hurt his head as Angel shoved him to the floor.

*

The anchors were recalled and ropes thrown to Sploon so that the little boat could tow the ship to rest in the shallows of the sandy beach. The carpenters began work at once, using the remaining hours of daylight to patch the planks.

Giles chose a site for his tent. His assistants set to the task with enthusiasm, though neither had pitched a camp before. He left them to it and waded through the sun-browned shallows back to the ship. *Bright Planet* lay on her side, her flank exposed. It was barely possible to clamber up the deck, which slanted at such a tilt that it was now necessary to haul oneself over the distance with ropes, like mountaineers.

Amidst all the commotion Giles had forgotten to inform the Captain of what he had seen on the shore. He found Captain Elijah in the great cabin. He had pinned a map to the table and stood now at an acute angle, regarding it. Giles adopted the appropriate lean in the doorway, everything tilted severely to port.

'I saw something, Captain,' he began. 'We must have our guns ready.'

'Guns!'

'Yes, sir.' Giles was agitated. His call to halt the ship, and their subsequent misfortune, had displeased nearly everyone. 'I saw natives, signalling, signalling to us.' His voice missed an octave. 'They mean harm, sir.'

'Well why the fucken blazes did you want to stop?'

Both men steadied their tilts.

'They were carrying our flag.'

The sight that had so alarmed the botanist was stark in his memory. Two dark men atop a small hillock – perhaps half a mile away. Giles had pulled the glass on them. The men were grinning, waving, laughing. One of them held a spear. Giles made out his nakedness. The other held up a bloody flag. He wore britches and braces. This second man was in hysterics, flashing his white teeth.

The sight had appalled Giles, he felt an immediate anxiety in his bowels.

'Yes, Mr Giles, very odd,' said Captain Elijah now, 'but most likely harmless. Find our little stowaway. We may need a go-between.'

'Exactly my thoughts, sir,' Giles replied. 'Do you have a pistol?'

Giles could not have known, of course, but the stowaway was at the heart of these developments. Pierre's progress upriver had been monitored by his family for the past eight days. Messages had been relayed down the long miles of riverfront, through the lands of neighbouring tribes, back to Pierre's cousins. *Bright Planet* was able to travel peacefully forth. It soon became apparent to the native observers that the ship was intent on exploring deep into the continent. Action was decided.

A delegation was elected to retrieve Pierre before the ship reached the nether lands. His cousins arrived on this day, 21st January, 1842, and had now temporarily derailed the expedition to a greater degree than they had expected. Indeed the two animated souls Quiet Giles had seen were none other than Prince Albert and Sneaky Pete, waving their Union Jack.

Quiet Giles sought out Pierre immediately. But he and the truant boy were ashore without permission. William Weed had booted them out of his kitchen and the first mate had been too slow to detain them while the ship was landing.

'Those monkeys are gone, Mr Giles,' said Jenkin. 'Someone saw Robins in the fo'c'sle after we came to shore, but they're not here now.'

'No one saw them go ashore?'

'No sir, but there's plenty of ways to fall off a ship.'

'Do you have a weapon, Jenkin? A pistol?'

'Yes, sir. I picked up a Regulator in Bareheep. D'you want me to shoot the scalawags?'

❧

Edwin Robins and his Australian companion were well away. The summer sky had turned pale, late afternoon, and all around the thin trees a cooler air moved easterly.

They retreated inland away from the trio of poorly pitched tents that marked the voyagers' camp. It was a precious freedom for Pierre. He had taken an increasing dislike to life on the water and he was a callow youth. He did not like the food or the company, though he had enjoyed several conversations with Mr Giles. With the flash tongue of a neologist Pierre had translated the land for the tall man, who studiously copied down the words.

Edwin trotted alongside Pierre. He was strangely happy, brushing the soot from his hair and shrugging the ship from his bones. He began to whistle a London air.

'Ssshh!' The black boy's eyes were wide.

Pierre cocked his ear, holding Edwin mid-stride while the breeze came through. Only a moment passed but Pierre looked satisfied. They continued over the light ground to the south, roughly following the course of the river, though out of sight of the water.

'Where are we going?' asked Edwin.

'Going home, brother.' Pierre laughed. 'This place is too far away.'

'I can't go back.' Edwin grasped Pierre's arm. 'They'll hang me.'

'All right, Jack?' someone called. Edwin spun around. Here were Prince Albert and Sneaky Pete, painted up like carny savages with spears and shields. Blood welled from a wound in Prince Albert's shoulder, his flesh peeled back like black and pink petals. Edwin began to feel uneasy, a turn of the stomach, and a violent flush passed across his white cheeks as the cousins embraced. He smiled too, but his circumstances had been reduced.

They rested about two miles downstream from the lamed ship. Pierre and his rescuers jabbered for a long time while Edwin lay staring up at the sky.

❦

Giles sent out two parties. Basin and Tom Collins took the Captain's dogs, two greyhounds the ship had acquired in Bareheep, and started their explorations with a series of sweeps to the west. Giles and his assistants covered the area south of their fresh camp. Giles wore a rucksack;

he packed his jars and his butterfly net. Both Cormac and Angel carried firearms.

They fanned out in front of the botanist, leaving him room to roam among the plants. The terrain was moderately wooded with a good soil. There was plenty for Giles to enjoy, birds and insects everywhere, cocoons in the leaves and spiders' nests. He had developed a special fondness for the eucalypts, for the forests of ironbark and blackbutt he had seen, their misshapen majesty adapted to every variance of their situation. At the present latitude stringybarks and spotted gums had proliferated, though many other varieties were evident.

They had only an hour until dusk. The first grey clouds appeared in the west and the wind freshened on their cheeks.

Cormac and Angel waited for their superior. Giles was examining spoor and dung, chasing a beetle with a stick. He had lost his first take of butterflies, half a dozen black and red queens, after Angel had fired his weapon inadvertently, whereupon a bear fell out of the trees, dislodged by the blast from Angel's gun. The bear took one look at the explorers and scrambled back up to the canopy. It so startled Giles that he had dropped a jar, and he was now determined to improve his collection before they lost the light.

Meanwhile Tom Collins and Basin sauntered through the glades to the south. They had found no sign of the boys, the dogs had hauled them in every direction following the scents of various local fauna. Basin let them off their leashes and the dogs immediately dashed in converging circles around the sailors, before trotting off towards the river. A spiky creature ran across their path, then stopped abruptly and rolled itself into a defensive ball. The dogs sniffed the creature, whose quills stiffened as they pierced the soft flesh of the greyhounds' noses. They yelped as they ran away, spearing off at full speed through the trees. The little hedgehog unrolled and continued on its way.

Sneaky Pete watched the sailors charge off in pursuit of the dogs. He was nervous about the dogs. He did not know the land, this was not his place. They had waited two days here for the ship to arrive. He had not expected the ship to land, of course, and now the rambling Englishmen were bothering his conscience. There had already been some trouble and Sneaky Pete was keen to decamp.

'Mr Giles!'

Cormac's voice carried from the other side of the hill. There was a shrillness to the call. It was the cry Giles had been expecting all afternoon, ever since sighting the two boys on the shore.

'Angel!'

This time Cormac's voice cracked with fear.

Giles hurried to the crest of the hill. Angel ran in from the west.

Cormac called again. From his new vantage Giles looked down on a lightly cleared area between two small hills, a nook in the landscape. A shanty had been built in the gap, a fireplace, a few items on the ground outside. Cormac stood a few paces from the door, which was no more than an open wall partially covered with hessian flaps.

Cormac was sweating, listening, and gripping his gun hard. Giles approached slowly.

'He's dead, Mr Giles,' Cormac spoke quickly, without air. 'Spear in the chest. Very recently.'

There was movement in the bush below them. Both men froze. Someone was trampling the shrubs.

'Who's there?' demanded Cormac.

'Easy, Mac,' said Angel as he appeared from behind the hut, all swagger and pout. 'I want to be able to eat my dinner tonight.'

'Take a look in there,' said Cormac. 'Then see if you want your dinner.'

Cormac stood guard while Mr Giles and Angel inspected the scene. The hut was large enough, one room with a wooden floor, but the dead man took up much of the space, spreadeagled as he was, as if the force of the spear-thrust had sent him stumbling backwards into the room. He had fallen with both arms behind him, one wrist was snapped, but it was the tip of the spear, having passed all the way through, that supported his body, so that his torso hovered a few inches above the floor, causing the blood to settle in a deep pool at his groin. He was a hairy man too, and barefoot.

The room contained a bed, with a neat ticker mattress. Some pages torn from books were pasted to the wall above it. Supplies had been stacked at the foot of the bed. Twenty tins of toothpaste and a large box of tea. A set of leg irons under the bed. A spoon was hung from a nail, alongside a framed picture of the Virgin. A trestle table ran the length of the opposite wall, and it was here that Giles's attention was drawn. The dead man and the six-foot spear made a graphic diorama, but it was the collection on the table that concerned Quiet Giles now.

The late sun still warmed the room and the brown dust which coated the surfaces lifted in the light. They heard the dogs barking to the south-west. The smallest movement, Giles's lightest touch, resulted in great shoals of shining motes which settled again over the floor and over the dead man. The dust lined the creases of his already dirty face and his mortification was complete. His spirit lost to the mystery of this desperate locale.

Giles handled every item. Mounting boards with insects and spiders, pinned in excellent style. Small reptiles swimming in brine. At the far end of the bench was a large jar, covered in grime and dust. It was sealed, Giles now saw, and he began wiping the glass, making terrible smears with his kerchief. But in the end the jar was clear enough for Giles to see what was there to see. An awful sight, but thrilling, to see one's first gorilla, even if it was small and pickled in rum.

Giles then regarded the dead man more closely, looking for clues in his face, looking for something that might explain the treasures stored here, in this wrong place. Meanwhile, Angel turned the mattress over, revealing stocks of flour and sugar. Empty biscuit tins and jam. He checked the tins, certain the dead man must have kept a trove of trinkets.

Cormac stood glumly outside while Angel and the botanist riffled through the contents of the hut. He heard shouting, at some distance, and the dogs started again. Cormac's heart sank.

Giles was single-minded now. He was concerned about the failing light and would brook no delay.

'Let's get this stuff back to the ship.'

'What about him?' Angel indicated the spear victim.

'We must protect the collection . . . How could we have come by such a store?'

It was a rhetoric Giles used to quell his own fears: already his mind had catalogued the mystery of the convict collector as an unanswerable enigma, and consigned the question to an empty lobe. He led Cormac and Angel away from the site. His rucksack overflowed and he carried several frames under his arm, squares of hessian stretched tight over wood to make mounting boards, suitable, Giles thought, for his own lively butterflies. Angel carried the gorilla. He cradled the jar under his left arm, leaving his right hand free to wield his single-shot musket. Cormac brought up the rear, emitting nervous hiccoughs and peering in every direction. He muttered a prayer in the growing gloom.

❧

The greyhounds had found the second man. He had been beaten with a rock, a sharp piece of limestone which had crumbled a little on impact, leaving fragments of rock in his bloody temple. (It was Prince Albert who had smashed him.) The man was no longer in chains but he wore his convict duds – a runaway for certain. He groaned soundlessly at the pain and the hot breath of the dogs upon him. They had licked his wounds clean and now sniffed the rest of him before continuing on their way.

The man discovered he was not dead, rather he was hallucinating. After a long time, during which he imagined that he had risen from his crumpled lie and was already making his way back to the hut, the runaway stirred. He felt for his rifle and folded his hand around its still warm barrel. The movement seared his temple. The pain ran jaggedly through his head and throbbed in his chest before shooting through his fingertips. He put a hand to his head, gently dabbing at the soft flesh that no longer concealed his skull.

By the time the ship's men came upon him he was sitting upright. Basin and Collins were still whistling occasionally for the dogs while rambling through the bush, uncertain of their whereabouts in any case. The sight of a man resting awkwardly against a tree quickened their pace. They raised the alarm with a shout and the wounded man turned to the sailors, revealing the white gash in his head and a pair of pale eyes. Eyes that recoiled from the approaching sailors and closed.

❧

The Captain listened in turn to his subordinates. One by one they stood at the entrance to the largest tent and delivered their reports to Captain Elijah, who sat awkwardly on a camp bed inside. He saluted each man as they arrived then resumed his slump while they spoke. In this manner he collected the available facts. By the time Giles arrived with his sweaty crew to add his disquieting tale to the officers' litany, Captain Elijah knew enough to be sure they had landed at a wrong place. He ordered a council over supper then called William Weed to his tent, proceeding to implore the cook to prepare something agreeable.

'But, Captain, there is little hope of using the galley.' The old man wiped some sweat from his eyes. 'Not with the ship at that angle. And we won't finish patching her till tomorrow.'

'I appreciate the double onus we have placed upon you, Master Weed,' replied the Captain, 'but surely you could roast a bird?'

William Weed looked tired.

'Not fish!' the Captain growled as the craggy carpenter decamped.

His guts had given him grief all day. He blamed it on the scaly fish that the crew hauled in each morning, though he knew the cause to be greater. The doctor had reported another man down with the flux, and Moribund himself exhibited symptoms of renewed expansion. The man was short of breath and popping bubbles of snot at his nostril. Numbers were becoming a concern.

The Captain strolled through the camp to the water's edge. He made out the shapes on the distant bank. He looked out over the black water and listened to the moan of its passing. There was a lantern on the boat, and a sailor perched on its tilted stern. Four-hour watches were scheduled till morning, but Captain Elijah held no fear for his ship tonight. Rather he expected simply to be murdered in his tent. He had posted Basin on watch at the campsite as his first penance for losing the dogs, with orders to swap with Collins through the night. Captain Elijah felt harried by events, foolishness and misfortune, and unable to quell the nausea rising through his frame.

The Captain needed the light of the campfire to guide him back from the waterfront, for there was no moon. He was greeted by the ship's doctor, whose pallor had improved markedly in the firelight, aided no doubt by the wine he swilled from his goblet.

A table had been laid for dinner in the open foyer of Captain Elijah's tent. His officers and the gentlemen awaited him there.

'Where is our injured colonial?' he demanded at once.

A quick conference between Sploon and Forte revealed that the man was unconscious again, curled in a fever and labouring to breathe.

'Has he been interrogated?'

'No, sir.'

'And the stowaways?'

'No sign, sir,' answered Lieutenant Sploon. 'Any chance of finding them was lost with the dogs.'

Despite the air of trepidation hanging over the meal a few pleasantries between the gentlemen enabled the diners to relax somewhat; glasses were refilled and the conversation moved along amiably enough. Soon the long-beaked mosquitoes made their way up from the river, causing the diners to punctuate their talk with furious slapping.

'I've been thinking of names for the river,' said Quiet Giles between insects.

'Who do you seek to please at home?' asked Moribund.

'Sir John Barrow, of course.'

'But the man's a laughing stock! We can't lend his name to such a miraculous waterway.'

'Barrow River, eh? Very dull.'

'I thought we were on the Yarra,' Angel remarked.

'This ain't the Yarra, mate,' said William Weed, a plated bird in each hand. 'It's the fucken Mississippi.'

'I was thinking of honouring Sir Robert Peel,' said Giles. 'My wife is acquainted with his daughter.'

'I'll be damned if we sail one mile farther up a river you name after that man!' Captain Elijah proclaimed from the head of the table. 'I, too, am acquainted with his daughter.'

William Weed returned with an armload of hot potatoes, and then pulled up a stool himself. The table fell quiet as Lieutenant Sploon struggled to his feet, *ahem*, before leading the prayer.

The food was excellent under the stars. The mariners picked clean the roasted birds then tossed the bones into the night. They sat in the dark now, in the porch of Captain Elijah's tent. A thin moon appeared through high cloud-cover but the only light came from the coals of the campfire where the sailors slept. The diners made drowsy movements themselves, stretching in their canvas chairs while the Captain fetched some cheese and dried fruit from his personal chest. Moribund poured out the port.

Mr Cormac sparked alarm with a sudden screech as he spilled his glass and rose unmelodiously, a moth in his ear, stamping his feet and flicking wildly at the flapping bug now caught in the ruffles of his shirt.

'Damn butterflies!' he said, resuming his seat.

'Are none of you fearful of our plight?' The Captain was vexed by his complacent fellows.

'I am most perturbed, sir, at the state of our expedition,' Giles replied. 'Although our circumstance is easily explained. There is an unwritten law of nature that holds good in any environment. It is the Law of Embuggerance, and suddenly, gentlemen, we find ourselves under its thrall.'

Giles, who was, it must be remembered, more than a dabbler in science, became reflective, pursing his lips and rubbing his forefingers against his unshaven chin.

'Entropy can only increase,' he said. 'Things can only become more complex. And wherever order exists chaos will follow.'

As usual the botanist's reflections tended to sombre the table.

Doctor Moribund sighed loudly as he released the top button from his trouser fly.

'Oooh!' he moaned. 'I just ate . . . Hic . . . fart . . . tHup . . . too much.'

Giles catalogued samples in the safari tent. By lamplight he recorded the collection he had so gruesomely discovered that afternoon. The dead collector had obvious tastes, arachnids and frogs, but his collection showed a charming eccentricity, as evidenced by the gorilla jar, which Giles balanced on the uneven ground beside his camp bed. He paused to prepare himself a draught then lay back on the stretcher while his heavy eyes watched the tricks of the flickering lamplight.

He tried to remember her unclothed, the line of her belly and the particular fold of her features. The light down on her buttock-cheeks. The pulse of a vein in her neck. Or the slight tang of her skin there, in the nuzzled neck. But Mary would not appear for him, or at least she would not disrobe, and he was forced to cool his heels in the drawing room while she chatted merrily with her friends and family.

Increasingly, his interior life sought to occupy the space of his former existence, and Giles's opiated consciousness recreated so entirely the narrative of his wife's London salons that he found himself forced to endure at large the sort of insincere evenings he so despised when he was at home.

He roused himself to make a brief entry in his journal. The tent was full of insects, midges and bugs, leaping over the oil lamp and swarming the light. He scraped a dry nib over the page, just some remarks on the variety of acacias he had noted during the voyage, but it was enough to soothe his intellect. He took a moment to glance at the previous entry.

*

JANUARY 20TH 1842

No occasion to stop or forestall today. There is no staying the operation now, we have watered once or twice and stretched our legs, but today we covered thirty miles. I stood with the Captain this afternoon while he tested the port side guns. He fired six cannons into the forest. We could see opossums and bears falling out of the trees. (A remark about the platypus. Ornithorhynchus anatinus everywhere. A creature I first encountered in Vienna fourteen years ago, in the Emperor's collection. Today I saw colonies of the amphibious mole all along the shoreline, occupying the dams formed by fallen trees.)

Tho' the some of the crew are sickly . . .

Quiet Giles doused the lamp and took his sleep greedily.

Seaman Tom Collins shook Basin awake and took over the watch. He squatted down by the fire and poked at the coals, sparking a little flame which blazed briefly in the new air then died, leaving the sailor to the dark night. Tom Collins listened.

Behind him high-pitched shrieks carried through the bush, followed by the moans of the patrolling bats and owls. Other animals scraped and rustled through the nearby forest floor. As the sounds came closer, the unmistakable rhythm of footfalls on the earth, his hackles rose and his heart jumped, and by the time the sprawling figure came down, thumping the dirt beside him, Tom Collins was almost stiff with fright.

'*Oooph!*' cried Edwin.

The boy had been returned.

'Captain!' cried Tom Collins, the sailor at full pace through the sleeping camp. He called out again as he reached his master's door.

'Keep your voice down, man.'

Captain Elijah drew back a tarpaulin flap and peered out. He was fully dressed, though mostly unbuttoned. Tom Collins released his grip on the prisoner and Edwin Robins fell to the ground.

For Captain Elijah the sight of the lunatic at his door confirmed the day's voodoo. Edwin arrived with blackened face and wild blond hair. His eyes were sullen and his grin was thin, but he represented no immediate danger.

'Give him to Lieutenant Sploon and return to your watch.' The Captain paused. 'No sign of the dogs?' he asked.

'No, sir.'

He closed the entrance flap and restored himself at his table. Some wax was spilt as he set down the candle, sealing by accident the pages of his log. He ignored this inconvenience and finished preparing his *chillum*. For the Captain, opium helped concentrate his mind.

He kept two inkbottles. One with a red stopper, the other black.

For the log tonight, he chose the red ink, to match the tired fever of his temper.

Ship's Log

H.	K.	F.	Courses.	Winds.	Remarks,&c.
12			NE..	SE	Fine weather
2			NE.	SE	Again made good progress in the morning – covered 25 mls But run of luck has ended with a disastrous landing at 4 pm. stopped for repairs at 143°56' long. 36°12' lat.
4			NE	SE	expect 2-3 days delay scientists will make good use of the time with botanical exploration. 2 men in sick bay nb. ship to be de-fumed

Day Thirty-Four

Mr Bonney's wound had closed. The ragged ends of flesh had joined in a livid scar above his right eye. His long grey hair was bound in a ponytail, his beard combed to a point. Every so often he moved a hand to his eye, his bad eye, as if by rubbing the vision might be restored. He made do with one eye, calculating his own perspective.

'How far from the shore do you reckon, Mr Giles?'

Giles lifted his eyes from the page he was reading but did not reply.

It was another bright morning, another royal blue sky. Quiet Giles and Mr William Bonney were basking in the gloriousness of the weather, the sun on their faces, an early breeze on their forearms. The ship cruised at a good pace while the crew all relaxed. Edwin Robins was dropping the lead from the prow. Basin was atop the forward mast, singing too lustfully for the hour and reciting odes. Two of his mates were gathered at the stern, minding the bathing ropes, which were stretched taut by the weight of Lieutenant Sploon.

The lieutenant was bathing in the net, his pink skin bobbing up and down in the wake of the ship. He had taken to the river each morning of late, scrubbing-brush in hand, determined to remove the dirt of disease from his person, but was yet to master the activity. He struggled against the rope to right his body, the unusual shape of which had caused him to roll upside down. The cool stream was harsh in his nose as he fought to breathe. Lieutenant Sploon was a mysterious amphibian, as alien to the water as he was to the land.

Tom Collins and Seaman Wickham hauled him in. The sight of their lieutenant spreadeagled across the ropes, his large bottom clenched, cheered them entirely. He came out of the water shining, slipping over the stern and landing like a dead dog on the deck. He dressed quickly, fresh shirt and cotton trousers. His jacket was stiff from the sun. He had dried it high in the sails, away from the vapours that shrouded the lower decks of the ship. He buttoned it over his belly and proceeded along the gangway to the forecastle deck where Quiet Giles and Mr Bonney sat with their legs outstretched, watching the boy sound the channel.

'Five fathoms,' he said softly.

'Christ!' said Lieutenant Sploon. 'Drop it again, boy.'

Edwin tossed the lead out in front of the ship, counted the seconds until it touched bottom then reeled it swiftly in.

'Four and a half, sir.' Edwin showed the officer the black silt dredged up by the lead cap. He grinned. 'Better call the Captain.'

Lieutenant Sploon met the Captain on the steps to the quarterdeck.

'A sieve for a ship!' Captain Elijah complained loudly. 'Blast the Admiralty and God damn Lacey. They've given me a crock!'

'Indeed, sir.' Sploon's voice quavered between registers. 'We are moving into shallower parts, five fathoms, but there is a bend ahead, and not much tide.'

'Jenkin!'

The Captain called the mate.

A cry issued from the back of the boat, and soon the first mate was hurrying along the gangway towards the officers.

More than usually grubby, 'Jerker' Jenkin growled a greeting.

'Send the boy below with some pitch,' the Captain told him. 'Water is pissing into the hold. Tell Mr Weed to move the animals, then get back up here. I want those sails down.'

On the forecastle deck all hands awaited Captain Elijah's command. He stood at the wheel, passing an impassive gaze over his charges. His displeasure was not unexpected. Any disruption over the last days had seemed to rouse his ire, and his temperament took a particular pique when executing the manoeuvre that now confronted them. Too often now the barque had been forced to back and fill when negotiating bends in the river, sliding sideways into the turn and maintaining position in the deep part of the channel.

'Now, Mr Jenkin, now,' the Captain said quietly.

Then the shouts came, first the raucous cries from the wet throat of 'Jerker' Jenkin, then the corresponding calls from Sploon, and finally the exploding tones of the Captain as he wrenched the wheel to starboard. In the rigging the sails came down, furled quickly by the three monkeys in the ropes, and the ship began to slide.

William Bonney cleaned his gun during the mánoeuvre. He chatted to Giles about affairs in Lancaster and Grimsby, though none of his information was current, and Giles, for his part, knew nothing of these locales. Bonney recounted a youthful episode in London, boots flying in the brewery, and laughed with both hands on his belly.

He prided himself on his memory, but with most of the recent past wiped from his mind he was forced now to engage with such early exploits.

'Have you perhaps been to Lincoln Cathedral?' he asked, turning to his companion. Giles had taken to wearing Lieutenant Trimm's jacket, though the garment was too warm for the season. He enjoyed the extra status the stripes gave him, imaginary or no. This far upriver and Giles was beginning to tire of the crew. The diversions of the enigmatic convict beside him were welcome enough.

'The statues are all fucked about,' said Bonney. 'Most of them had their heads pulled off in the Civil Wars. When finally they came to be restored in the last century the restorer put the heads of the male bishops on the bodies of female statues. A most amusing sight.'

Giles smiled at this. But he was alert for disaster as the ship, travelling at right angles to the shore, approached the headland.

As it happened, *Bright Planet* rounded the bend easily, and soon found herself in wider water. The right bank of the river veered away and a lake of grand proportions opened up before them. An expanse of calm water more than two miles wide.

The ship hugged the shore for several minutes before venturing away from the dense thickets that lined the bank. These low trees, their olive hue strangely dark in the sunshine, covered the shoreline in every direction. Giles did not immediately recognise the stunted trees. He drew a quick sketch of the riverbank and made a note to himself. He remained with the curious Mr Bonney on the forward deck.

They both felt an unexpected sense of relief as the ship ploughed through the gentle water. She was running at half sail again. William Bonney watched the play of wind on the water's surface. It came in all directions, great shadows loomed across the water, advancing and retreating.

Captain Elijah found his spirits lifted marginally by the new vistas, but the state of the ship was a pressing concern. He was looking for an inlet where they might repair the leaking hull. His lieutenants stood at his rear while he scanned the unnamed lake.

'Is this it?' asked Sploon. 'Sir?'

'Shut up, Sploon!'

Lieutenant Forte drew out his own eyeglass, another of poor Lieutenant Trimm's involuntary bequests. He found it difficult to focus the instrument at all, but he enjoyed the affectation. He spied a blur of blue and grey, and further blurs at each corner of the compass.

Below deck Edwin Robins was knee deep in water. He waded through the powder room, restoring the barrels to higher shelves. The rats scampered past him, headed for the food stores he had rescued from the hold. It was dark and humid in these quarters and several chickens were floating around him. The noise they made was quite excruciating to his ears. He fumbled along the curve of the inside hull, feeling for the hole in the unpleasant gloom.

There were in fact three holes. An underwater snag had split a plank the previous day and the pitch could no longer hold out the water. Edwin held both hands to the leak, but the river was rushing through his fingers. He cursed to himself, alone in the bowels, and wiped his eyes on his sleeve. It was difficult to inconvenience Edwin Robins, but this voyage was affecting him. He left the leaking wall and waded back to the gangway, wiped his eyes again and called for the cook.

❧

The inlet they chose to make their repairs was hidden by a rocky promontory. A series of granite ledges jutted out over the lake, one of which bore the signs of a recent fire. Indeed, the point provided an excellent lookout, and most certainly their approach had been espied. The lieutenants had their glasses trained on the silent forests around them. There was no movement, no sound, just the stillness echoing through the air.

Giles had remained in the bow with Mr Bonney. He was taking particular interest in the forest itself, the rather ghostly wood that covered the low hills above the inlet. Sheets of white bark hung in long pale strips from the slender trees. It was a wonderful sight, and for a few moments Giles gazed in fascination, before producing his notebook.

He rested the book on his knee and began sketching the trees. His hand was not as fine as Cormac's, but Giles was able to produce a serviceable representation. And in Cormac's absence, with his other assistant inconsolable, Giles was bound to double his workload. He was determined that his journal of the voyage should be fully illustrated with every example of the exotic they had discovered.

The ship glided into a brownish shallow beach, dragging along the riverbed until the keel finally caught and she tipped of her own accord onto the sand, where once again she lay with her hull exposed, like an animal baring its belly. Cries and shouts erupted from the deck as the sailors lost their footing and the officers tumbled sideways. Mr Giles and Mr Bonney found themselves entangled and pinned to the bulkhead by the weight of young Basin. The confusion of their limbs was made worse by Giles's frantic effort to stow his book inside his jacket. In the midst of this ripe co-mingling he made a mental note to find a waterproof case for his books.

The rest of the crew were quick to scramble ashore. They waited on the narrow beach for William Weed to emerge with the tools. He had been below deck when the ship was capsized and most likely was nursing a sore temper.

Captain Elijah sent Tom Collins into the forest for firewood, and while Collins was normally an obedient servant, on this occasion his shoulders slumped and he shot a surly glance at the Captain.

Collins was sober. There had been no rum this morning, on account of Wickham's behaviour at Cormac's burial, and Collins's reluctance was genuine. Nonetheless he trudged off over the sand to the woods, whereupon he turned inland and skirted the trees, following the line of the inlet. The other unfortunates below deck – Edwin and the remaining animals – were tending their knocked knees and could be heard bleating sad bleats.

There was a strip of rotten planks on *Bright Planet*'s underside. They had been pierced and splintered by the snag and it was clear that the ship had been lucky to remain afloat. The carpenter was at work, looking as feverish and grimy with hammer and nail as he did in the kitchen. Edwin was assisting, moving nimbly over the hull with a tin of pitch, while on the white beach the officers conferred. It was clear they were laid up for the afternoon, and Giles had suggested pitching tents, but the Captain was firm, he wanted to be back on the water by nightfall.

'I'd like to take a closer look at these trees, Captain,' said Giles. 'Can you spare Mr Basin? I am without an assistant for the moment.'

'As you wish, Mr Giles. But please do not take long, and if you see Collins slouching about smoking a pipe, kick him up the arse for me.' The Captain turned to Lieutenant Forte.

'You better send Wickham for wood, lieutenant. And don't let him out of your sight.'

Giles took his leave. He had no desire to tarry too long in this place, but the strangeness of the forest was also compelling. He invited Mr Bonney to accompany them, if he would like to admire the fauna, then he sent Basin to fetch a musket, a knapsack and some collecting jars.

The birds began again. After a long period of silence the forest awoke around them. First came the cawing and shrieking, then the yellow-beaked fuckers that Dr Moribund so disliked appeared in numbers on the ship, hopping across the tilt of the unmanned deck, picking off the trail of oats Edwin Robins had spilled earlier in the day.

Moribund's health now required him to lie on the sand. He fashioned an umbrella for himself with a piece of hemp and two spars, and was able to recline with a mug of rum the Captain brought him. Captain Elijah sat with the doctor a while, together they slapped at the flies, but the odours Dr Moribund was regularly producing drove him off.

The sailors made a fire without the benefit of Tom Collins's wood. Though the atmosphere in the camp cooled as Collins's absence grew less and less plausible.

A search party was required, but there were already four men away, the doctor was no use, Weed needed one man to help him, Mr Angel was confined, and the Captain had few men at his disposal. He decided to leave his lieutenants with the boat, and set off himself with Gunner Thomson in the footsteps of the previous parties.

It was cool among the trees. An iridescent light softened the air and a hush of wind smoothed the ghostly bark. The sound of their own clumsy footfalls drowned out Giles's thinking. He knew they were announcing their arrival to anyone who might care. He stopped.

Mr Bonney halted too, rifle raised. Basin felt the changed atmosphere, and froze also.

The three men peered into the forest. A cloying fear gnawed at their bowels, blood pounded through their ears, and each of them seemed a dull distance from the others.

Moments passed. Giles was not unused to such sudden paranoia, first cousin to his customary *cafard*, but the other two were surely not subject to the same imaginings.

'We'll go back to the waterline,' said Giles. 'These trees have eyes.'

Basin resumed the lead and, apparently jaunty, quick-marched north toward the inlet. 'I'll warrant we are being watched,' William Bonney said to Quiet Giles. 'Whichever way we go.'

'We'll be all right,' replied Giles. 'I just wish they'd show themselves.' He looked at Mr Bonney's ragged visage.

'You can still shoot, can't you? With one eye?'

The explorers emerged from the trees, shielding their faces from the sudden piercing light, and picked their way down to the water. The inlet had narrowed here. It was an easy swim across. Basin dropped his satchel and unbuttoned his flies. He urinated with a ferocity befitting the scaly nature of his organ. A stream of unnatural yellow flowed brightly downstream.

'*Oooh!*' he said, returning his fat penis to his trousers. 'Excuse me, gentlemen. Just draining the trouser python.'

'How long have we been walking, Mr Bonney?'

Bonney consulted his fancy watch.

'Twenty minutes,' he said, closing the instrument and returning it to his waistcoat pocket.

Giles was on the point of returning to the ship. He would have turned back right then if the Captain had not appeared.

Now they were a party of five, and Captain Elijah was determined to recover his wandering crewman. They marched in single file, following the inlet, clambering up and over fallen logs, scrambling through heavy vegetation, and clinging to the roots that protruded from the muddy banks. The air buzzed with flies, insects large and small leapt upon the Englishmen, blackening their lips and crawling into the corners of their eyes.

Soon the water began to look darker and the banks of the inlet widened into a lagoon, leaving a green island, a good stand of trees, entirely circled by the old channels. It was here Giles and his companions surprised some Aboriginals fishing in the lagoon. They were dragging a net, and from the quantity of bream lying on the bank they appeared to have had good sport. The group comprised three mature males, a boy, and two mature females. At first they were displeased by the intrusion of the Englishmen, but Giles was all smiles, warmly greeting the fishing party, then producing gifts of one sort or another, handkerchiefs and spoons.

The eldest male spoke in a quick tongue, pushing the boy forward, and lifted his spear. His face and chest bore many pockmarks, dark scars on his already black skin. He was stark naked, as were they all, and stinking, as were they all, totally unashamed of their natural state. The naked boy crawled forward to retrieve the trinkets.

The group set off along the lagoon. Captain Elijah took this as a signal to follow, but the elder male shook his spear at the ship's men, urging them back.

'Easy, fella,' said Mr Bonney, sighting his rifle.

No one wanted a confrontation.

The fishing party continued across the marshy ground. The two women carried the fish in strips of the ghost bark, the three men followed, chattering loudly. The boy was gone, lost in the long grass or already in the trees. The intruders kept a discreet distance. They were in the rushes, listening to the wind and sniffing the air, hoping for a warning of what lay beyond. Through the eyeglass Giles watched the natives approach a small rise where the forest began, watched as they filed over the embankment and into the trees. He could see a path worn out of the earth where the natives had climbed.

'See, Captain! There might be a path.'

Giles handed him the glasses.

There was indeed a track through the early part of the forest, where the soil was damp and black – in fact there were two. One wound away to the north, the other led directly ahead. Captain Elijah asked for a coin.

'Heads we go right. Tails straight ahead.'

He flipped a florin and let it land on the path. The Queen's rough head stared back at him.

'Best of three,' said the Captain, as he retrieved the coin and flipped a second time.

Victoria's head again. Captain Elijah examined the florin before handing it back to Foretopman Basin, who returned it to his striped silk purse.

'I won that last night,' grinned the sailor. 'Off Tom Collins, as it happens.'

'It's a sign,' said Gunner Thomson.

'It's not a sign,' said Basin. 'Is it?'

Such an eerie place. Giles had already made a mental note to record a suitable name for it on their charts.

The ground beneath them sweated sour suspicious smells. The trees on every side inched closer. The air temperature dropped abruptly. No one wanted to continue, it was as if they had been sapped of their initiative, and it was with the greatest reluctance they pushed ahead, straight ahead. The Captain was rather brazenly pushing his luck, the sailors thought, by ignoring an oracle such as Tom Collins's own florin, but they followed him, of course. Giles found himself in the lead, a situation he corrected by stopping to examine a sapling, thereby allowing Mr Bonney and his rifle to go ahead. In this manner the search party travelled, single file through the green afternoon light of a shady wood.

Stately plump Septimus Sploon took the opportunity to shave. He stood in the shallows with his trousers rolled. Wickham held a mirror for him. The sailor was much more sedate than he had lately been, since his rum had been taken away, and this quaint subordinacy was completely out of character. Sploon shaped his ginger chops. They reached to his jowls and formed a wedge of bristles either side of his plump chin. He asked Wickham to sing him a tune while he applied the razor to his pink reflection.

The inconsolable Angel remained aboard. He had refused to leave his cabin since Cormac's burial, and he entertained only the tedious 'Jerker' Jenkin, whose brutal coupling Angel found diverting. Twice a day the mate knocked on the cabin door with some hotcakes or coffee, but Angel would not eat any more. He drank the laudanum Giles had given him. He drank the laudanum and curled himself on Cormac's bunk. He wore his dead cousin's boots – Angel had pulled them from the corpse himself – and buried his face in the dead man's pillow. Angel made no effort to temper his grief. His opiated tears permanently dampened his skin, and the gnashing and wailing emanating from his cabin reverberated at all hours through the decks. It was ridiculous, Cormac's untimely demise, simple, stupid, and many other things besides. Angel had seen Cormac fall, watched him helplessly from above. They had been skylarking in the rigging of the mizzenmast, clambering up the spars, and enjoying the sun on their shoulders. Cormac shrieked as he slipped. His canvas right heel missed the topmast housing. Unbalanced so, he reached out to steady himself on the topgallant yard, but missed that too.

Suddenly Cormac was airborne, his blond curls flying in the breeze.

'Mac!' cried Angel.

'*Whoah!*' cried the falling man.

Those on deck looked up in time to see Cormac tumble head first into the rope net amidships, where his progress was halted all too suddenly. His neck snapped loudly as the ropes broke his fall and left him swinging just a few feet above the quarterdeck, where William Bonney and Mr Giles were conversing. No one looked more surprised than poor Cormac himself. He was not so far from Tyburn after all. His eyes bulged and his tongue protruded, and his body spun clockwise two or three times, before spinning out again.

High above, Angel began to howl.

❦

Doctor Moribund, who had not been denied liquor, slept through the afternoon under his nomad's tent. His head was wrapped in a cloth to further block the sun, and his labouring snorts came irregularly as he struggled for breath. The others kept their distance. Lieutenant Forte stood the perimeters, unwilling to socialise with either Sploon or Moribund. Edwin was banging nails for William Weed while the carpenter shared a beverage with Lieutenant Forte. The lieutenant admired Weed's wiry frame. Brown as a burnt berry pie.

'D'ye reckon the doctor is going to die there?' asked Lieutenant Forte.

'Soon enough,' replied Mr Weed. 'It is an unhealthy ship.'

'I wonder if there was some contagion we picked up in Bareheep.'

'I'd say we wus cursed,' opined the carpenter.

'None of us wants to be here.'

'No.'

They sat on a crescent of sand overlooking the inlet. On the far side of the water the forest stepped up the rocky slope. It was a tranquil afternoon, warm and lazy. Before them lay the beached ship, her hull gleaming. Edwin had washed her clean. He climbed down now, finally able to earn a few moments in the sunshine. He lay flat out on the sand and squinted, his eyes playing with the brilliant sunlight. He had thought of running away, but he disliked the spook of the forest. He knew there were better lands to come.

'The ship is ready, lieutenant.' said William Weed.

'We must refloat her at once,' Lieutenant Forte replied, but he made no move to rise.

Together they finished a flask.

The Aboriginal encampment was spread over rocky ground. Situated at the top of a rise, its triangulated position, should anybody have bothered to make the calculations, would have revealed the site to be almost exactly equidistant from the two other hilltops visible from this vantage point. The camp consisted of bark huts and lean-tos made of sticks and blankets. Three separate fireplaces operated in the centre of this village. One acted as an underground oven; indeed the air was heavy with the spice of roasting flesh. Nearby a freshly speared emu lay on the ground awaiting the pan, its neck twisted awkwardly. On another fire, two black cook pots were stood in the coals, and all around were signs of domestic activity.

Into this scene the explorers stumbled. They had climbed the steep forest hill in the hope of finding just such a coign of vantage. They had been walking for over an hour and their shirts were sodden with a sweaty mix of fear and perspiration. They could smell themselves as they stood at the edge of the camp, breathing.

'Now, I don't like this,' said William Bonney. 'Where is everyone?'

The camp was deserted.

'Prepare for ambush, lads,' said Captain Elijah, drawing his musket.

He had used the ghost-ship ruse himself, playing doggo on the high seas in the face of a black flag. The curious pirates then were lured aboard and ambushed from below. A good fight always ensued and within half an hour they had burned the blackguards' ship to the waterline.

Today, though, he was in strange country and there was no language for their predicament, no rules of engagement. He was tired. He almost laughed at the tickle of the gun on his thigh. He felt light-headed and went down on one knee. His upturned face with its medieval beard had the look of prayer, or so thought Giles before he turned away. Slowly regarding the members of his party, the Captain blanched. For an instant he was gone, unregarded, and weightless. As if in pure clarity he realised that it was possible to die – that he need not bother with the trouble of being. The notion brightened him.

Giles, though, wished for patience. This constant adventure was driving him to distraction. There was simply too much information to record, and the frequent episodes of emotional excitement upset his powers of observation. He needed calm air and placid companions.

'Should we turn back, Captain?' he asked. 'Make a run for it?'

'Give him a musket, Basin,' the Captain replied, as he set off through the native bivouac. 'And stick together!'

Liberated by his new fatalism, Captain Elijah walked with a reckless gait, scanning the surrounding trees for movement. The forest was thinner here. Shady trees with blackened trunks towered over the site, but there was little undergrowth. Fire had worked through the area recently, creating an avenue between the trees, along which the rest of the company followed the Captain. They marched through the camp quickly, barely stopping to examine the emu, a huge bird not unlike the ostriches encountered at the Cape. Giles poked the cast-iron cook pot with a stick. An animal was stewing. The presence of blankets, too, indicated that these forest dwellers were not unfamiliar with the European. A conclusion which did little to combat the explorers' uneasiness, for despite the deserted scene, no one doubted that the missing natives were close by.

A plaintive cry came through the trees. It was a wailing bird, a raven's cry, a series of slow notes tolling through the forest, like tones from a grey priest, with a strangled, dying finish. Giles recognised the call at once. He knew the *Corvus* family well – he even pictured the throat hackles fanning into a black beard as the bird sang – but there was something amiss here, a resonance too strong, or an insistent note.

The cry was repeated and Giles listened again. Suddenly a reply sang out, then another. These were not birds that he was familiar with. Calls and crows, songs of all kinds, filled the air.

The search party stopped at the edge of the camp to assess their position. They stood under a hail of black bush flies, waving their arms frantically to keep the bugs at bay. The men were forced to press on.

They followed a path along the ridge of the hill. The soil was flinty and the trees were smaller along this exposed track. The sky was blank above. Still the carry-on of the birds disturbed their thoughts. The rocky path led to a scar of rock, a stony crag that Mr Bonney scaled quickly. He was more nimble than his appearance suggested and was soon atop the rusty boulder, surveying the land beyond.

'God's Blood!' Bonney whispered.

He looked back at Captain Elijah and his crew curiously. He was trying to determine their capacity for battle, for he had little appetite himself.

'We found them, Captain.'

Beneath the rocks that Mr Bonney was balanced upon lay a gentle slope covered with dry grass. Here was a natural amphitheatre, bounded by tall silvertops to the east and the west, an amphitheatre dominated not by a stage but by a huge, rather majestic tree. Its white trunk shed the same ghostly strips as the forest trees beyond, but it stood alone, as if to emphasise its extravagance. Its branches spread out over the grasses below, where there were upward of a hundred souls sitting in its significant shade.

A naked man stood before them. He unleashed a cry as the explorers watched from above. The assembled tribe responded with one voice, and here, again, was the Caw Caw Birdsong that had been haunting Quiet Giles. The naked shaman called again and hopped from leg to leg, dancing over the figure at his feet, the pitiful figure of Seaman Tom Collins. When he had completed the moves the congregation stood and moved slowly into the clearing of afternoon light. Tom Collins was manhandled to his feet and dragged to the big tree. He offered no resistance. He leaned heavily against the trunk, limp with fear, or so Giles supposed. From a distance it was difficult to tell.

The ship's men had no choice but to move in.

They were halfway down the rocky slope to the clearing before they were spotted. A dozen men approached, daubed with white paint and a menacing air. Bonney fired a shot and the men halted. Bonney loaded and fired again, over their heads, and waited for their retreat.

The explorers marched across the clearing, five abreast, with weapons drawn. The black magus wore a broad smile, unnerving the Europeans. They stopped a short distance away, close enough to see the strange details of his skin. The man was covered in welts and bumps, mutilations and glistening scars. The patterns of scarification on his chest and arms were quite beautiful, but many pockmarks had ruined the silk of his skin, and his face, especially marked, was a twisted map of tortured flesh. The man had had the pox. He stared out of this landscape with searing eyes. No one wished to return his gaze.

*

Giles began the negotiation. He produced gifts for the natives, specimen jars and a magnifying glass, and ceremoniously proffered them. The tribe moved in to regard the offerings. Giles called a young man forward, a thin young man whose skin was also heavily pocked. Giles held the magnifying glass an inch above the lad's arm. The sailors were smiling and the boy acted pleased. But after a few moments the sunlight spearing through the glass began burning the young man's skin and he yelped, wrenching his arm from the botanist's grip.

Giles beamed a most civil countenance and presented his gift to the scowling boy, who took the glass and grabbed Giles's arm.

'No. No.' Giles recoiled. 'It's for examining.' He retrieved the gift from the boy's hand and aimed the glass at a leaf on the ground. 'You see. It magnifies.'

The boy gripped the glass and peered through. The leaf was lanceolate, dark green, with moderately dense reticulation. It was covered with numerous intersectional oil glands. The detail surprised the young Aboriginal and a look of concentration came over his face.

Captain Elijah slipped away. He took advantage of the distraction and hurried across to the tree where his crewman Tom Collins was tethered, bound like a goat and moaning unfamiliar nouns. Close up he was a ragged sight, his eyes were bloodshot and his face was scored with bleeding scratches. His shirt was gone, his trousers were bunched at his ankles, and the rope he used for a belt now secured his hands. Another length of twine cut into his hairless belly and wrapped twice around the pale trunk.

Brown ants ran in regiments up the tree, coursing in and out of the bark, running also through the sailor's hair, over his brows and onto his cheeks where the blood was flowing.

Captain Elijah untied him. The knots were poor, any fool could have escaped, but Collins appeared entranced. He leered a peculiar prayer in the Captain's ear as his commander lifted him free. Captain Elijah threw him over his shoulder and carried him out. The magus regarded them curiously, as did the rest of the ship's party.

'Come on, then,' Captain Elijah entreated. 'Back to the ship!'

The summit was concluded. The Europeans backed away, ignored by the natives. The shaman, the scarred man, had turned his attention to the flames licking at his feet.

The magnifying glass was being used to ignite the grass and two spot-fires were already gathering pace, to the great amusement of the young men who were lighting them. The rest of the tribe moved back to the shade of the big gum. Giles was disappointed to leave this way, without a chance to study the lofty eucalypt. He would have liked to measure its girth, maybe strike his initials in the wood.

They sailed again with the sun late in the sky. *Bright Planet* turned smoothly into the lake and followed the left bank north-west. The forest along the shoreline thinned, to reveal miles of low scrub, stunted colours and muted terrain.

The last hours of daylight passed without emotional incident though there was a mood of unease as the collective stresses resonated about the vessel. Giles wore Lieutenant Trimm's smart jacket. He had changed his soiled attire in anticipation of an early dinner, and now paced the quarterdeck while the sailors enjoyed the freshening breeze. The ship picked up a couple of knots, and soon she was fairly skating across the white-capped water.

Giles gripped the rails. There was time for a brief storm. A white shudder passed through him. It was as though the mist had arrived by force rather than stealth.

The dense air rolled in and what had been a cloudless day grew dark. Then came the buffeting wind. He braced against it, feeling the sting in his cheeks. His hair was blown in all directions. Amidst the confusion Foretopman Basin and Seaman Wickham greeted Mr Giles cheerfully as they passed him on their way to the foremast. The sailors quickly furled the fore bonnet, but by the time they reached the topgallant yard, the storm had passed.

The mist began to disperse and Giles walked carefully across the slippery deck. He was sodden from the cloud, but his spirits were good and he was suddenly eager for work. He knocked on the Captain's door.

Captain Elijah was poring over his measurements. He was a competent cartographer, though he oftentimes relied on memory. He was mapping the lake onto his chart of the river. Four paperweights, four solid mandalas, held down the corners of the chart while the Captain drew. He wore shirtsleeves and stockings, surprising Giles with his undress.

'Long day, eh Giles?' he greeted the scientist. 'Has it been raining?'

'A cloud passed over,' replied Giles, pulling up a chair to better view the Captain's chart. He viewed also, by chance, the Captain's unusual toe as it wriggled through a hole in the hose, a buckled and warped digit indeed.

'What shall we name the lake, then?' Captain Elijah turned to his companion. 'Lake Giles?'

'How very kind, sir.' The botanist smiled. 'Lake Giles.'

Captain Elijah laughed. 'I shall mark it now.'

'And the inlet?' asked Giles. 'Could it be called Kidnap Cove?'

'I've already named it Pox Point.'

Giles enjoyed the naming process. It reminded him of his purpose, for it was the mandate of this voyage to know the unknown. By naming the lands they were able to bring them into being. He looked at the Captain's unfinished map and imagined where a colony might settle, though these were not his concerns; he was merely an agent of empire and had more pressing matters at hand.

'What about the river, sir? I have a –'

He was interrupted by a knock at the door. Lieutenant Forte arrived with a bowl of warm water for the Captain to soak his wretched feet, and the news that dinner was to be delayed, unfortunately, due to the commotion below decks.

Mr Weed had found kittens in the pantry. One of the cats had crawled into a bag of oats and given birth to six blind nubs. Mr Weed refused to touch them. He refused to cook until they had been removed. He shouted for Edwin, who was at the head and most inconvenienced to be summoned at this time. His red bottom was itching still as he carried the kittens below in a tea cloth. The cook demanded he drown them but Edwin had other plans. He liked cats and in any case there were plenty of rats that needed catching. He hurried past the crew's quarters and dropped into the hold, cooing to the baby kittens as he crawled into the forward storeroom. The mother cat had run away, screaming appallingly, but unwilling to risk another swipe from Mr Weed's boot. Edwin cradled the kittens inside his shirt as he squeezed between barrels to his secret sleeping place amongst the big mice and the sacks of grain. Here too was his stash of secret food and the possessions he had pilfered. He hoped the mother would find the kittens here, sniff them out or come looking for food.

Edwin stole five moments to lie with the hopeless creatures. He ate a piece of cheese, though he knew the cook would be calling out his name by now, cursing and juggling burning pans on the stove. Calling for his precious tomboy.

In the stinking dark Edwin blinked.

They sailed past a forest of dead trees. Still a mile distant from the eastern shore, their pale trunks rose high out of the water and sadly splayed their hollow white branches, stark against the last cloud on the horizon. Here were hundreds of trees, drowned long ago, that once lined the banks of the great brown water. The sight confirmed what Giles already suspected, i.e., that the lake, Lake Giles, was not a lake at all, merely a wide section of the river they had been following for the last seventeen days.

He was a relieved man as he sauntered around the quarterdeck, chastened too, by the fates that deemed this voyage would continue. His journal could not have borne the anti-climax had the voyage ended here. He told as much to Foretopman Basin who strolled with Giles while Lieutenant Forte brought the ship towards a cove where they would moor for the night.

At dusk a troop of bats came past. A group of ten or twelve, then two more rounded the bend, then another and another. Mr Giles smoked a cigarette on the quarterdeck while he waited for dinner to be announced. He and Fore-topman Basin watched the purple sky. The black procession continued for half an hour, more than a thousand beasts flew past, beating their silent wings into the dark night.

'Goodnight, Mr Giles.'

'Goodnight, Basin.'

Basin took the port gangway to the forward decks, past the longboat and the guns, then descended the steps to the orlop deck, where already the crew's quarters were thick with tallow smoke. He stood, only slightly stooped (for he was a small man) waiting for his eyes to accustom to the gloom. He could hear the cries of the cook through the deck above his head, coming from the forecastle where the galley stoves were firing. William Weed's frustrated vocals had a reassuring effect on the men below, who lay fanned out on hammocks, waiting for their stew to boil.

Basin stepped over the low table they used for cards and climbed into his own six-foot sheet. Their quarters were less cramped since the departure of Slinkletter and De Louse, and though none of his companions had spoken of it, would shortly become roomier given the state of Tom Collins up in sick bay.

'No creature eats the mosquito. She has no predators save the human hand and the occasional swat of a horse's tail.'

'I think there are many creatures who might eat the mosquito, birds or fish for instance.'

'Quite so,' said Giles. 'But no creature relies on the mosquito as a primary food source. The mosquito is not essential, as such, she serves no purpose.'

Mr Bonney did not pursue the matter. He swirled the wine in his glass, examining its colour before downing a good mouthful. It was a sweet Madeira wine, too innocent for his taste, but he did not bother to comment on this either, simply posting a piece of Mr Weed's hot bread into his mouth to soak up the sugar. His cheek muscles tugged unpleasantly at the scar around his eye as he chewed.

The Captain's table was an unusual place for a convict, but William Bonney was an educated felon. He had proved his value to the expedition through his willingness to provide Mr Giles with information about the local country, its flora and fauna, particularly its human inhabitants. It was his, Bonney's, own collection that Giles had confiscated from the runaways' hut, and although, with the exception of the gorilla, the entire collection was previously owned by a gentleman of Mr Bonney's minor acquaintance, in sooth it was Bonney who was the connoisseur. He had also shown an enthusiasm for the workings of the ship. He enjoyed very much the operations and calculations of the sextant, an interest which pleased the Captain, who, ever conscious of the crew's dwindling numbers, decreed that Mr Bonney be given one of the cabins allocated for scientific staff.

'Did you obtain any samples today?' A polite inquiry from Lieutenant Sploon.

Giles regarded the red-scrubbed cheeks of the lieutenant, suspecting him of irony or some lame form of humour.

'I miss the opera,' he said, by way of reply. 'There is a fine establishment in St Martin's Lane where Mary and I often take supper after the performance. The Pelican.'

'There is an opera called The Pelican?' asked Sploon.

'No, a restaurant,' Giles answered slowly. 'The Pelican Dining Room.'

His reminiscence was interrupted by the arrival of the ship's doctor, who made difficult work of his entrance, an awkward hop across the threshold then the impossible squeeze between Sploon and the cabin wall.

As usual Doctor Moribund had restored himself for the evening meal. In fact, since re-commencing their voyage that afternoon the doctor had shown a marked improvement, particularly in his bung leg, enabling him to occupy some of his duties. He had smoked some hashish in his room and changed into his black frock coat before attending Thomson's fundament. The poor man had aggravated his piles during the long afternoon ashore, and his bum had become a caked and bloody mess. Moribund had looked in on Tom Collins too, but the coma continued. The doctor dipped a cloth in a bowl of water, wiped the man's brow and squeezed a few drops of moisture across his lips, then buttoned his frock coat and hobbled aft to the Captain's dining table, where he now gave an account of his efforts.

'Will he live?' asked Captain Elijah. 'Is he under a thrall, doctor?'

The Captain spoke sharply. He was impatient with the manginess of the ship, a condition he could not help associating with his own infirmity.

'I cannot say, sir,' Moribund replied. 'He has mutterings from time to time, but the matter remains in the Lord's hands.'

'I shall look in on him directly,' said the Captain, leaning back in his chair to allow William Weed to serve the vegetable, which was tonight, as usual, burnt onion.

Moribund consumed his food warily, not trusting his own digestion.

After the meal Giles produced a volume of lyric poems.

'How the day drags.' This was Lieutenant Forte's first contribution.

Giles overlooked the comment. 'I think I have found a satisfactory solution to the problem of naming our river.' He brandished the book. 'Wordsworth.'

Sniggers and a snort from the Captain.

Giles read.

> *And is this – Yarrow?– This the stream*
> *of which my fancy cherish'd . . .'*

He beamed at the table. 'Don't you see?! The Yarrow! It

hearkens to both Sir John Barrow and the Yarra Yarra, which is its offshoot. But it is also the name of Wordsworth's ideal waterway.'

'I fancy, Mr Giles, that William Wordsworth's ideal is more likely a babbling brook. But, very well, we sail upon the River Yarrow.' The Captain raised his glass.

'What's a yarrow?' asked Forte.

'A turnip?'

Like Percy Shelley in his sailboat, Quiet Giles prowled the gangway, seeking the moonlight after a torpid meal. He carried a vial for poor Mr Angel, whose grief required sleep, but he tarried along the railing to admire the heavens. Points of light were scattered in every direction and scrawled in every pattern, stars both distant and near, compelling the scientist, as usual, to wonder. He felt a pang of the loneliness that plagued him so far from home. Such moments inspired a humility in Giles. His inability to comprehend the immensity of the globe they floated upon, let alone the mysteries of the celestial sphere, had been the reason he was so quick to agree to the voyage. Yet he had never imagined such distances or counted so much time. For, despite all his travels, London, and more particularly, St James Terrace, where his wife resided, remained at the centre of his universe, and his mind lurked there while he looked at the stars.

Captain Elijah appeared on the gangway.

He was likewise eager to breathe the late evening air. He slapped Giles on the back.

'The River Yarrow, eh?'

'Yes, sir.' Giles smiled, relieved by the interruption. 'The Yarrow River.'

'And we shall unlock its secrets, Mr Giles. You and I.' He held a hand to his stomach.

Such optimism was unusual for Captain Elijah, but his good humour was genuine. He had breached an impasse that afternoon. He was unburdened now by his own existence, his life was a trifle, dispensable and unessential. He felt ready, for the first time, to undertake the journey. His mind was free of the black doom that had so lately surrounded it.

The Captain's body, though, was still complaining. He sweated in the night air and gripped his side. He had consumed several glasses of wine over dinner, but he had only picked at the food and so had confidence that the episode would be brief. He leant over the ship's railing alongside Mr Giles and together they gazed at the black shore of the lake and the dark void beyond. The apparent silence was disturbed by the sounds of scuffling, which carried across the water from shore. The muffled cries of the animals seemed to be amplified in the desolation.

'The chipmunks are noisy tonight, Mr Giles,' the Captain remarked.

'Jerker' Jenkin emerged from Angel's cabin with a red flush on his skin. The boiling complexion of the mate was an everyday sight, but tonight his visage was surprisingly scarlet. With embarrassment, Giles thought, as the two men collided outside the scientists' quarters. But the lamp-light was good enough for Giles to notice the man's beetroot ears and his foaming mouth. His greasy hair had been pulled out in clumps, and Giles thought he saw in the sweaty face an instance of hydrophobia; certainly this was the flush of disease on his skin.

The first mate grinned, revealing a horrid set of teeth, and brushed past Mr Giles in the tight corridor, leaving the door to Angel's cabin ajar. Giles froze in the doorway.

His assistant lay half-clothed on his bed. A lamp beside the bunk illuminated the young man's face. His skin was fulvous and waxen, framed by a wig of tawny hair. He was as thin as a girl. Angel struggled out of his recline and his eyes met Giles's gaze, exchanging an awkward truth. He reached for the vial Giles was holding and prised it from his grip. Giles managed a weak smile before retreating to his own neighbouring quarters.

Once inside, Giles lumed his lamp and lit the two candles on his desk. They flickered a jaundiced shadow across the open page of his journal. He opened his wicker case and unstopped a quart of laudanum. This was bottle number seven. His stocks had been in greater demand than he had anticipated, and Giles allowed himself the sorry realisation that there would come an inevitable evening when this supply was finally exhausted.

He measured a large draught and downed it quickly, before turning to his journal. He read with his forehead in his hands, smoothing his black locks with his fingers. He could feel a dampness in the ends of his hair, still wet from the soaking he had received that afternoon, and played with them idly while he re-read his opening line: *'In the future people will be able to read of me, a description of how I lived and died.'*

A bold beginning, he thought; indeed Giles was convinced that this document would confer upon himself a greater status than he currently enjoyed, and that the expedition would, in time, become renowned for its discoveries.

I became impressed as a very young man with the workings of science after a visit to the Linnean Society of London whose collection consisted of 19,000 sheets of pressed plants, 3,200 insects, 1,500 shells, and 3,000 books, including all of Linnaeus's immaculate correspondence. These are all kept at Burlington House where my father took me in 1828 as part of my education. A process which also took us across Europe to see the personal museum of Kaiser Franz at the Hofburg in Vienna. The Emperor himself showed us through the fauna collection. Primates and simians of all kinds were cased in cabinets along the walls of a grand ballroom. His wife's personal taxidermist had mounted them in all manner of poses. My father and I examined each exhibit carefully. The chimpanzees were especially impressive, snarling and rearing up inside their glass boxes. My father complimented the Emperor on the taxidermist's skill.

'How I tire of monkeys!' Kaiser Franz replied, and with a sweep of his hand led us to a display at the far end of the hall.

It was a splendid diorama, like none I had seen before. A group of Australian kangaroos were stood around a water feature – depicted in their natural setting, their intelligent eyes regarded the middle distance, and I was struck at once by their unusual serenity. In the foreground, at the edge of the water, a curious creature was curled, half beaver, half duck. Ornithorhynchus anatinus. Known as the platypus, this animal embodied a most unusual disorder, and, as my father pointed out to me, its jumbled features were emblematic of the upside down world of the Antipodes.

Giles was fond of this reminiscence. Of course by now he knew that the platypus was ubiquitous in the new land, but its presence in the Hofburg so many years ago had sparked his first curiosity about the unexplored lands he now inhabited. He was fond of the memory of his father too, imperious as he was then, bearded and confident. A man of substance who carried a cane. It was in this image of his father, severe and tall-hatted, that the young Master Giles had seen his own future. He saw that it was his destiny to be a serious man.

He inked his nib and turned the pages of his journal, pausing to read the occasional passage, ready to scratch out any dull or inappropriate remarks. His description of the scenery around Bareheep had particularly troubled him.

Batman's Hill is a gentle slope covered with verdant natural lawns which run down to a pretty lake with white swans, surrounded by she-oaks, giving the whole the appearance of an English Park.

He crossed out this sentence, then rewrote it in the margin unchanged.

*

Captain Elijah spent the late evening alone, wearing only his shirt and clutching his aching blue balls. Desires sometimes overwhelmed him and, unfucked, unfulfilled as he was tonight, he dispatched reason to the frontal lobe and searched for release in the memory of Clara Lacey. He had drunk enough over the course of the day to warrant sleep, but his mind would not go away. He stroked his groin, several quick strokes, and though his member responded briefly to his disaffected ministrations, he could not bear to think of her this way.

He gripped his balls again and turned his attention to the ship's log. He read over the previous few days, notes on the burials and the quarrels between Sploon and Lieutenant Forte. The Captain despaired for the health of the crew, for there was disease aboard. The Old World pathogens, which the Europeans carried in their blood and bile, were infecting them anew with the inconstant symptoms of the flux, something between an infectious fever and a lethargy. Already three had died, and now Tom Collins was sick with a charm. It was not a subject he wished to dwell upon, so Captain Elijah took up his pen and entered the date on a clean page of his log. He wrote with an economical hand, a neat schoolboy script, and kept his entries brief.

Ship's Log

H.	K.	F.	Courses.	Winds.	Remarks,&c.
12			NE..	SE	The river changed direction
4			E.NE.	SW	easterly before widening into a
					large basin we have named
					Lake Giles, after the ship's
					botanist.
					Hull repaired again – most of
					the afternoon lost
					the land heavily wooded Many
					natives in the area
					Mr Giles made some exchanges
					Seaman Tom Collins showed
					bravery in an unpleasant
					instance ashore and remains in
					sick bay where I am hopeful he
					will recover

Day Fifty-Five

Captain Elijah remained in his cabin, as he had these last mornings, until well after nine. William Weed contrived to bring him flapjacks and coffee, but these the Captain left largely untouched. He was preoccupied, and in any case he preferred his flask. He pushed the tray to one side and cleared some papers from his desk. He sat in his dressing gown, thankful for the coolness of the cabin, and wrote sorrowful letters to the families of his fallen crew. He signed them with his full name and sealed them with two blobs of wax. The letters, though identical, were moving and heartfelt. Indeed, Captain Elijah proved to have some facility for the genre, tapping into the wellsprings of his own grief to produce the obituaries. He bundled the letters together with a length of string and stored them, along with the rest of his unsent correspondence, inside a water-proofed leather pouch that he kept in his strongbox. The movement made him listless and he slumped back in the chair to catch his thoughts. He toyed with the idea of returning to his bed, but decided, once more, to face the day. He undid his dressing gown, stepped out of his shorts and picked up a ladle.

There was a knock at the door.

'Captain?' Lieutenant Sploon's voice quavered.

He knocked again, before entering the big cabin.

Sploon discovered his Captain taking a bath. Captain Elijah ladled water from a wooden pail, trailing the spoon over the back of his neck and letting the cold juice run down his back. Water dripped from his beard onto the floor and streamed from his ears. He looked up at his well-scrubbed lieutenant.

'What is it Sploon? Why haven't we weighed?'

'We're still waiting for Lieutenant Forte, Captain. He has taken two of the men ashore for water and wood.'

'How long have they been gone?' The Captain wiped his face with a grey towel, and cocked an irritated eye at Lieutenant Sploon, who had remained in the doorway, conscious of the Captain's dishabille.

'Nearly two hours,' the Lieutenant replied meekly.

'God's Balls!' Captain Elijah threw the towel to the floor and reached for a shirt.

William Bonney was fishing from the stern, catching the sun on his face and closing his good eye in a squint. His face was brown – the deep pores of his skin just soaked up the sun. He wore a patch to cover the mangled ruin of his wounded eye, and cut a convincing figure as he lurched through the gangways on his restless way about the ship. His presence aboard was the subject of some debate. In the Captain's mind it was a rescue, but Mr Bonney thought of it more as a kidnap. He opened his eye now and looked back with some dismay at the lands spreading away to the east, country that he feared they would never pass again. The ship had covered many miles of river, but even this far inland there were squatters' camps. Only the previous morning they had passed two wild men on the shore. Their appearance was distasteful and their language foul, but they represented a link, however remote, to a civilisation Mr Bonney had once known. The squatters' presence here was, he knew, an imperial imperative. It divided the unknown from the known. William Bonney, who was obliged to roam at the fringes of the universe, courtesy of the outstanding charges against him, wondered now at the wisdom of hitching his luck to *Bright Planet* and her crew, particularly as the voyagers seemed determined still to tramp indefinitely on, at their continuing peril, into the interior of the continent. Mr Bonney's fishing line screamed taut against his palm and he let out some slack. At least he would be frying fish for morning tea.

The shore party had not returned. Those left on board *Bright Planet* circled the decks, eyeing the riverbanks uneasily. Giles paced the length of the quarterdeck. He wore Trimm's brocade jacket over a ruffled shirt and scraped the heels of his best boots as he walked. He had woken early from an opiated sleep, refreshed and, for the first time in a week, eager to be under sail. His predictable frustration at the procrastinations of the rest of the personnel – the endless ablutions of Lieutenant Sploon in particular – had been compounded by the delayed return of the shore party. He checked the time, raising his watch and making a tic with his mouth, like a man kept from an appointment. He climbed up to the poop, greeted Mr Bonney as he reeled in a redfin, and gazed at the shoreline. *Bright Planet* was moored only twenty yards off the river-bank but Giles saw no signs of activity ashore. The ship's dinghy was tied to a tree where Lieutenant Forte and his men had landed, close to a creek, which the party would have followed inland to collect clean water. He scanned the tree line, squinting through his eyeglass at the blur of green and grey, listening too, as invisible birds sang the hour. The forest was thick, so dense that Giles was reminded of some African locales he had seen. Soon enough his concern at the delay turned to apprehension for the welfare of the missing men. He waited now for the trees to expel them.

Poor water had been blamed for the deaths of Mr Angel and the first mate, though their symptoms had much in common with the flux, and the ship's doctor's subsequent request that fresh water be obtained at every opportunity was the precise reason Lieutenant Forte had taken his men ashore this morning.

Dr Moribund himself refused to drink any standing water at all, secreting his own supply in flasks about the ship. His digestion, flawed for weeks now, had become so slow that his bowel movements were almost non-existent. Today he had been half an hour at the head, evacuating nothing more than air, before deciding that a clyster would be required. Puffing and blowing, he ruminated how ignominious an end it would be, how simple it would be, to die this way, straining at stool, his bung leg extended, and his immaculate dress starting to fray.

Instead he produced a pump and a length of rubber tubing from his Gladstone and proceeded to administer himself an enema.

'Blast! Damn! Dang!'

The levels of invective on board were rising.

'The Devil take it!' The Captain swore at himself this time. The buttons of his piss-stained pants flew off in protest as he hitched them over his hairy belly. He was forced to use a cummerbund to belt himself in. It was not that Captain Elijah had gained weight (rather, the opposite was true) but the absence of a cabin boy had led to a serious disrepair in the Captain's wardrobe. He hoped the doctor had a sewing kit – although, in truth, his appearance was of small consequence to either himself or the crew. All of them, excluding Lieutenant Sploon, were stained, unshaven and red-eyed. Even Mr Giles was beginning to exhibit some shabbiness in his grooming.

Nevertheless, Captain Elijah took particular care with a ribbon for the mane at the nape of his neck. He brushed his thick hair back from his forehead, perched his black hat on the resultant quiff and stepped out into the day.

The Captain found Lieutenant Sploon on the quarter-deck. His face was spotted with moisture and there were blotches of perspiration on his stiff white collar. The heat felt distinctly equatorial.

'Still no movement, sir.' Sploon stood briefly to attention.

The morning sun had pinkened the lieutenant's face, and the Captain felt compelled to admonish him.

'Fetch your hat, Sploon!' he growled. 'That sun will send you mad.'

'Yes, sir.' Sploon pressed at his nose with two pudgy fingers, testing for tenderness.

He smiled queerly at Captain Elijah and marched quickly off, trousers chafing, to the gun deck. The Captain was left to survey the scene. The pretty cove where the shore party had landed seemed impossibly benign. The cool river swept slowly past. The Captain raised his eyes to the sky, and there too, the outlook was fine.

Alone on deck, Captain Elijah enjoyed a few moments of silence, marvelling at the clarity of the light, the agonising shine of the air that breezed around them. He liked to appreciate the beauty of the lands they passed. But as usual this pastime was short-lived.

Behind him a cry came from the poop and Quiet Giles leapt to the gangway, and certainly the day was alive with foreboding.

The spear had passed through Gunner Thomson's shoulder, and each step they took sent a shudder of pain through his frame. Lieutenant Forte supported his right side while Seaman Wickham gripped the spear just above the entry wound. Together they lowered the grimacing man into the dinghy. It took precious time to manoeuvre the rangy sailor into a position that would enable the other two men to row. Eventually Lieutenant Forte cast off with his foot and the boat zigzagged towards *Bright Planet*. Their attackers remained invisible behind the tree line, but their proximity was made evident by the frantic motions of the rowers.

Lieutenant Forte rowed with one arm, loading the musket between his knees with the other. He fired blindly into the trees hoping the discharge would stay the marauders for long enough for the dinghy to reach the ship.

Captain Elijah and the remaining shipmates monitored the shore party's progress from the quarterdeck. There were cries of encouragement, urging the dinghy on, and even the Captain submitted to the collective fear, the danger so much greater for being unseen. He sent Edwin Robins for the ship's doctor.

When the dinghy finally pulled alongside the ship and Wickham accepted the line Mr Giles was dangling, the grisly extent of Gunner Thomson's wound became clear. The agony he suffered during his rough transfer from the dinghy caused him to pass in and out of sense.

Mr Bonney and William Weed dragged him to the gangway before realising that the spear, jutting from his shoulder, front and back, would have to be removed before they could get him past the stairs. Moribund would have to operate on deck.

Moribund was still at the head, puffing and blowing, muttering in untender language the Hippocratic oath. The splatter he produced was extravagant to say the least. He breathed heavily, aching with relief, and hitched his trousers up. He made a token effort to wash the wood but the black rinse underfoot was unyielding. A sudden cramp doubled him over and he feared that it was beginning again, but the fart passed through him quickly, a burpy blast that tickled his scrotum on the way past.

It was in this condition that Edwin Robins found him, the boy's unfortunate timing forcing him to submit to one of Moribund's ancillary farts before retreating.

The doctor hurried along behind Edwin, bag in hand, to the quarterdeck. Gunner Thomson was surrounded by his shipmates, propped up in an awkward pose to protect his left side. His face was grimed with his own blood and his eyes were heavy with pain. He spoke a number of times but his voice became too breathy, causing him to cough, and triggering a spasm so severe he passed out again.

Dr Moribund performed well, considering his personal tribulations and the chaos of frightened men jostling around the injured man.

He collected his wits as quickly as he could. He experienced a rush of excitement in his bowels at the sight of the emergency, but was able to contain himself and began ordering the men away. Boiled water, bandages, a saw, blankets, and a bucket. He pointed to each man in turn as he assigned the tasks, then assessed more carefully the state of the gunner's wounds.

With Mr Bonney's help he positioned Thomson so that he lay resting on his right arm. The spear protruded from his back at the shoulder to a length of three inches – enough to grip, enough for Moribund to pull the spear through.

*

Gunner Thomson woke from his daze to find himself straddled rather gracelessly by the ship's doctor, who was sawing through the shaft of the spear with apparent abandon. Wood clogged in the teeth of the saw and the spear shuddered in the wound. Gunner Thomson closed his eyes. He knew worse was to come, and when it did he passed out once more.

Four men held him still while Dr Moribund wrenched the sawed-off spear from his back. It brought with it a gush of blood so red and hearty that Moribund thought the man had died. But Gunner Thomson still gasped against the deck and they were able, after a while, to staunch the blood and wrap his chest with cloth and gauze before carrying him down to the sick bay in a blanket.

Captain Elijah watched them carry the lad away. He stood with his lieutenants, all slightly queased by Moribund's crude spectacle.

He felt a sudden, keen loneliness for England's shores, and the life he might have led. It took all his concentration to wipe the image of Clara Lacey from his mind. In her place the craggy white visage of her father appeared, unnerving him further. He sought refuge in the operation of command, for if he was no longer master of his own existence, at least the ship was under his control, and the situation demanded something decisive from him.

The Captain began issuing rapid instructions. Only the pitch of his voice betrayed his anxiety.

'Weigh anchor as soon as the men return, Forte.' He wet his forefinger to test the breeze. 'Send Basin and Wickham to the rigging, and ask Mr Giles and Mr Bonney to operate the capstans. I want full rigging.'

He turned to his other lieutenant.

'Do you know how to fire the guns, Sploon?'

'I think so, sir,' the lieutenant replied warily.

'Take the bow chaser. I'll run the ship close to shore and you may fire at will.'

'Fire at what, sir?'

'The shore, Sploon! The shore.'

The Captain wiped his neck with a kerchief.

Lieutenant Forte's report had been brief, an unembellished account of the ambush. A group of Indians had confronted the sailors as they walked along the creek. Their faces were painted white – laughing white. They taunted the Europeans with threats and raised spears. Lieutenant Forte reported that his party had not provoked the natives. Nevertheless, clearly, a spear had been thrown.

Captain Elijah's response was both inept and impressive. Inept because Sploon's bombardments had no particular target, but impressive to the unknown numbers on the shore, whose experience presumably had not thus far extended to gunpowder and fireworks. The ship ran at a quick heel, the sailors working hard to keep the wind, while the bow chaser roared at irregular intervals, firing grapeshot high into the Downsteepy hills.

The Captain saw Edwin Robins lurking near the gangway. The boy had been released to general duties – necessity had demanded it – but he had not resumed normal relations with the crew. Given the run of the ship, he still chose to curl up in his dank corner of the hold. He liked to keep to himself.

This morning however there was too much excitement to ignore, and he was particularly enjoying Lieutenant Sploon's display. Captain Elijah summoned him.

'Clean up this mess, would you mind, boy?' The Captain pointed at the bloody deck where Gunner Thomson had lain.

'Yes, Captain.' Edwin bowed his head in exaggerated deference. Not for the first time he felt a hot impulse. He managed to contain the flush but it was clear to Captain Elijah that the boy's behaviour had begun to deteriorate.

❦

Bright Planet sailed through the hot afternoon.

The terrain they passed had changed over the course of the day. Steep ochre hills closed in now from the west and the river itself narrowed as they approached a series of gorges. The brown water was turning decidedly black, signifying deeper channels in the middle of the river, which allowed the ship a safe passage between the outcropped walls of the first gorge.

Quiet Giles and Mr Bonney were down on the gun deck, out of the sun, but sweltering in a bath of humidity as they went over the collection. Together they had pressed three books of flowers and catalogued several dozen jars of insects and arachnids. Despite Giles's superior education, William Bonney's natural talent for the art proved a most useful tool when identifying species. They had also kept the skeletons of several larger animals, and a platypus bottled in brine. Only two days ago they had caught a species of kangaroo they had never before seen or tasted. The smell of its meat, still rotting in shreds along the bones, offended in rank blasts issuing irregularly from the corner where it lay, blackened by a swarm of flies. This was the easiest way to clean the bones.

Mr Bonney had managed to reclaim the collection he had carried from Bareheep and, save for the baby gorilla, it was now restored in one of the empty officers' cabins. Large parts of the collection suffered from moth and vermin, also damp, but it remained an impressive display, and when coupled with Giles's accumulated specimens, the scientific output of the voyage was more than satisfactory.

'My father will be proud when he sees all this, you know,' Giles told Bonney. 'Yes, he had high hopes that this expedition would make my reputation.' Giles smiled. 'As did I,' he added.

'I shall be thankful merely to be returned alive,' replied William Bonney, already disgruntled by the humid conversation. 'I have a bad feeling about this river . . . How many of your crew have been lost to it?'

He didn't wait for a reply. He produced a thermometer, tapped the glass twice and held it for Mr Giles to read.

'One hundred and five degrees!' Bonney's voice cracked with incredulity. 'It's too fucken hot!'

Giles appraised the sweating man before him, his lank grey hair, his one pale eye, the contortions of his ravaged face. Clearly Mr Bonney's mind was not on collecting.

'You're right, of course,' said Giles. 'Let's take a stroll on deck. Our work is done for today.' He patted Mr Bonney on the shoulder, hoping this reassurance would comfort him.

The orange cliffs rose high on both sides, shading the river from the fierceness of the sun. A pleasant breeze cooled Mr Bonney's cheeks, a moment of relief he had not expected. He shared the deck with Giles and the ship's officers. Together they admired the ravine and the black water they sailed narrowly through. The æons had carved a majestic gorge out of the rock, a silent channel between one place and the next. It was a dangerous and lonely fall in the landscape. The geological strata were plainly visible in the walls of rock. Trees clung where they could, but for the most part the rock was bare, and the many ledges and overhangs were like so many steps up to a giant's lair. In which ancient place, amongst the boulders, the timekeepers knelt.

High above, unseen from the river, a dozen black men watched the white boat sail past.

Bright Planet navigated the passage slowly. Basin stood in the prow with a long oar, pushing off from the rocks when she sailed too close. The Captain took the wheel and displayed his helmsmanship as the ship rode the faster water between the cliffs. In the suddenly cool space on deck, Mr Giles braved a smile. Once again this river, the Yarrow River, had proved to be a most impressive beast. The ancient gorge, heavy with foreboding, was nothing short of a natural wonder. Giles beamed as a plume of birds took flight, river martins no doubt, rising from crevices in the rock. They swarmed in unison and twisted through the canyon. The bird life in these reaches of the continent was not as colourful as Giles would prefer, swifts and swallows mainly, but the martins were beautiful to watch. He said as much to William Bonney.

'And they really are the most superb example of the group mind.'

His words hung expectantly between them, but Mr Bonney did not reply.

He and the two lieutenants had ducked instinctively as the missiles hit the ship. It was an unexpected attack, and they found themselves in the open and vulnerable from above. The first stone hit the deck and ricocheted behind the officers. The next two smacked into sail and fell back to the deck. There was time for Sploon to cry out his warning before he joined the dash to the gangway. Captain Elijah was alone at the wheel.

'Sploon, to the guns!' he ordered.

Mr Giles and Mr Bonney were the last to turn. A hail of rocks pelted into the deck, splintering the wood behind them. Mr Bonney glanced up at the cliffs.

The late afternoon sun cast the gorge in shade and Bonney did not see the stone fly out of the shadow. It struck him full in the face. The force depressed his cheekbone while a sharp point put his remaining eye out and sent him to the deck.

Giles, who had skipped ahead, turned to see his friend clutching his bloody face and rolling in some agony amongst the ropes he had fallen into.

'Mr Bonney!' he cried. 'Captain! A man is down.'

Giles covered Mr Bonney's hands with his own.

'We must get below, sir. We must get below at once.'

More stones were landing around them, pitching and clattering across the deck.

'Basin!' the captain's voice boomed.

'Captain!' replied the sailor from the forecastle. He had wedged himself under the lip of the gunwale and, in truth, was reluctant to move.

'To the bow chasers, lad,' the Captain yelled across the quarterdeck. 'Tell Lieutenant Sploon to start firing!'

The steering position afforded Captain Elijah some protection from the attack, but he remained the only target on deck.

He had seen Mr Bonney go down, and watched now as Mr Giles carried him limply across the deck. At the gangway Bonney regained his feet and, shrugging off the attentions of his companion, raised his arms to the sky and raged, as if he were railing at the recalcitrant gods who brutalised him so.

Giles edged the injured man downstairs.

The Captain steered his ship right. He was an excellent sailor and he worked the tight spaces until, fortuitously, the ravine widened. The attacks continued sporadically for five hundred yards. There were snipers high in the rocks pelting the boat with stones. He had spied natives running along the top of the gorge. He saw several more perched on a ledge. He saw them take aim and hurl their yonnies as *Bright Planet* slipped past.

The Captain was at some disadvantage. He knew nothing of his attackers save their advantage over him. His best hope was to outrun the varmints and make a lot of noise as he went.

Lieutenant Forte was called to the deck. In turn he called Wickham and Basin. The sailors sprang to the masts and clambered up to let the canvas out. The wind caught immediately, Captain Elijah responded at the wheel. The ravine acted as a wind tunnel and *Bright Planet* started to race.

'Fire!' yelled the Captain.

Below deck, Lieutenant Sploon had primed the guns and was waiting for William Weed to spy a target.

'I canna see anything,' growled the carpenter.

'Fire!' yelled the Captain again.

Sploon lit the cannon. High up on the port side an explosion and a pile of rocks came tumbling down to the river.

'Are you an imbecile, sir?' William Weed had a poor temper. 'You have to aim first.'

Sploon did not take this advice kindly, but fell short of disciplining his subordinate. These were anxious moments, after all. Instead he ran to the starboard gun, aimed high and lit the fuse.

Bright Planet lumbered in the fast water. The sight of her in full sail, at high speed through the rocky gorge, and guns ablaze, must have been impressive, though no one saw. The local people had departed after the first cannon burst into the cliff face, wisely adjudging that the battle had been fought.

In the sick bay, Quiet Giles lowered William Bonney onto the vacant stretcher. The other two beds were occupied by the injured Gunner, who had not woken all afternoon, and Dr Moribund himself, who was trying to avoid an episode at the head. He had lain perfectly still for an hour, distracted by the hashish, and was unaware of the buffoonery upstairs until Mr Giles arrived with another patient.

Dr Moribund raised himself stiffly, forced his jacket back over his stomach with one hand, and restored his hair with the other. He shuffled past Gunner Thomson and knelt beside Mr Bonney's sorry figure.

'I'm blinded,' said Bonney, his hand still covering the wound.

'Let's see,' said Moribund, prising Bonney's hand away.

Mr Bonney's face was now in total ruin. His good eye had been dislodged from the socket and his cheek had been opened in a cruel line.

Dr Moribund gave the patient a huge suck of rum before pressing the wayward eye back into its socket with his thumb. Mr Bonney gagged with pain, then socked back more rum. He submitted to the ordeal, deferring all responsibility to the gods who had abandoned him, and pondered his dark future. While Dr Moribund sewed his cheek, Mr Bonney was thinking about murder.

❧

A state of vigilance gripped the boat as she glided through the dark water of the canyon. All hands scanned the cliff tops, searching the shadows for movement, fearful still that their attackers were laying ambush. There had been no sightings for half an hour, but the men were sore with fright and beginning to snipe at one another. Even as the gorge widened and their danger was lessened, the two lieutenants could be seen in heated debate by the mizzenmast.

Lieutenant Sploon had abandoned his post at the guns, refusing to waste any more shot on the impervious ochre rocks, and fed up with the attitude of William Weed, his blunt-faced assistant. He registered his displeasure to Lieutenant Forte, whose agitation was exhibited in a series of grimaces as he struggled to speak. The mutinous tones of his stammering echoed around the ship.

They left the gorge behind and passed through old country. Flood plains now stretched across the valley to the old cliffs, which diverged to the west and disappeared into the land. The river snaked across the red valley floor. Penetrating the land, or passing through it, the foredoomed expedition inched ahead, all through the long, mistrustful afternoon.

Giles took a break in his cabin. It had been a disheartening day. The two attacks had signified to Giles that the new territory they were entering was indeed virgin country. The anticipation of unfound riches ahead, usually such a spur to men of adventure, was tempered by the evident danger of passage through the new lands. The attacks had unsettled several men on board, particularly Lieutenant Forte and

Seaman Wickham, who had witnessed the events ashore. Their brains had become clouded with fear, and Giles had been forced to quell their insubordinate suggestions before they reached Captain Elijah's ears. He lectured both of them, in separate speeches, exhorting the spirit of exploration and reminding them of the rewards that so surely lay ahead.

But Giles could not dissuade the men of their fear and the quiet talks continued around the ship. Even Edwin Robins, usually so unobtrusive, contributed his ha'porth to a conversation between William Weed and Seaman Wickham in the galley. He told them that he was considering jumping anyway, taking his chances alone.

'It's a long way back, lad,' the carpenter told him. 'If yer on shanks' pony.'

'Besides,' said Wickham, 'the blackfellas are fucken savage around here.'

Edwin was peeling green potatoes. He threw a handful in the pot.

Captain Elijah had remained at the wheel ever since the afternoon attack. He was aware of the mood on board but he was unmoved. There was no turning back. He had led them out of danger with a decisiveness and fearlessness that belied his increasingly hollow self. He had shown remarkable nerve in the twisting canyons of Thomson Gorge, already named – after the man injured that morning – in the Captain's head, and impressed even the most disinclined of the crew with his display.

He was exhausted by the time he called for Basin to drop the anchor. The light was failing at the edges of the pale sky and a heavy moon was already risen. The river was not wide at all here, and running swiftly. It had been difficult to find any shelter so they anchored as close to the red starboard bank as possible.

The current gripped the keel immediately and swung the ship around, pointing her stern downstream. Captain Elijah retired to his quarters and closed the door behind him.

At dusk the officers and gentlemen assembled in the Captain's dining room. Each one of them had spent the previous hour restoring their temperaments with medicinal draughts of rum, except Mr Giles who chose laudanum and spent the hour dreaming of his wife. He transported himself to a cold afternoon in London and joined the throngs in Oxford Street. Returning home from the office, he was tired and only fit to lie on the sofa and be made much of.

He had roused himself with a sherry and dressed for dinner.

Two of his dining companions were already drunk. Mr Bonney, who should have remained below, had consumed so much grog during Moribund's surgery on him that he was now in a most garrulous state. His head was bandaged thoroughly and he was finally blind. His nose flared as he took in air.

'Some of you fellows are beginning to smell 'orrible.' He complained. His tone was amiable. 'When I was a lad I worked down the mines. There was a blind man they fetched sometimes when they needed a canary. They used him to sniff out new tunnels for gas. His sense of smell was very good, you see. One time he did smell some bad gas, yes, fell down where he stood.'

Mr Bonney bared his teeth and flared his nostrils. He listened intently for a response.

'Do you understand!' he barked. 'That's all he was good for!'

'I knew a blind man once,' piped Lieutenant Sploon. 'He lived near me mam.'

'And?'

'And nothing.' Sploon inched a finger behind his ear. 'He had a stick.'

'Of course!' cried William Bonney. 'I'll need a stick.'

The second inebriate was the Captain himself. He was in a fine mood. He had uncorked his best wine and already two bottles were empty. He filled his officers' glasses from a third bottle and toasted all with *bonhomie*. He was in an extremely personable state. For three weeks now he had been able, at difficult moments, to detach his self from proceedings. It was a pact he had made with his own demons. If he would merely relinquish himself to his own fate then the pain might be lessened. And so it was this newfound ability, to engage with and operate in the world, without actually being there, that saved him any embarrassment at his table this evening.

William Weed arrived with the stew. He placed a tureen

on the sideboard and ladled out six portions. Six steaming soups.

'God's Teeth! Are you trying to poison me?' gasped Captain Elijah as he sniffed his bowl. 'I hope there's bread,' he snarled. 'I'm starving.'

'There's bread too,' William Weed reassured him. 'Though I had bare enough time to prepare a soup . . .' He cast a look at Lieutenant Forte. 'With all the goings on.'

'Will you taste it for us, Mr Bonney?' the Captain laughed.

Mr Bonney could not even find his mouth with a spoon. Denied the ability to glare, he frowned, silent again with his murderous thoughts.

'Yes, Captain,' he said eventually. 'For though we are all dead men on this ship, it will not be the soup that kills us.'

The rest of the party watched Mr Bonney's mouth and whiskers as he spoke. Now that he had no eyes to meet, they watched the way he chewed his words.

Hunger overcame any distaste for the texture of the meal. Captain Elijah gulped his wine to wash it down. He regarded his companions, as he regarded himself, from afar, from the distant place he had abdicated to. They were, except for Mr Bonney, happily engaged. The food was warm in their bellies and the wine was doing its work. Bonney hoped someone *was* trying to poison the old man. His voluble pre-prandial state had given way to a more sombre drunkenness. He lamented the day.

*

In the close air of the cabin, between the wood walls and the officers, the subject turned to women. Only Quiet Giles was married. The others, Sploon, Forte, Moribund, Bonney, and the Captain of course, were all more or less hoary bachelors. A breathy reminiscence was always appreciated, for it would often provide material for fresh fantasy, and at this stage of a journey such as theirs, imagination was a salutary gift.

Tonight's conversation was fertile indeed, in this regard, for it was Captain Elijah doing most of the regaling. His story of the pearl was a most entertaining debauch, completely captivating the inebriates around his table. Lieutenant Forte, who had been silent for most of the evening, showed a keen interest in the oriental anatomy of Captain Elijah's heroine. His face beamed somewhat like a puppy.

'What happened to the Nubian girl?' he asked.

'She's in every port from Aden to Cape Town, my boy!' The Captain gave him a friendly pat on the shoulder. 'We'll visit her on the way home.'

After dinner Captain Elijah persuaded his guests to stay for a round of cards. He opened a fresh bottle of wine, a Tenerife tokay, and they played a hand of gin rummy while the room rolled with the movement of the river. Dr Moribund and his patient, Mr Bonney, did not join in the cards but remained at table in the interests of conviviality, although in Bonney's case it was the wine that held his interest. Bonney's head ached. He sulked beneath his bandages, and, with his mouth set in a pugilist's sneer, delivered his recriminatory remarks to no one in particular. His world had been removed from him, a fact that had slowly settled over his disbelief, and in his cups he derided all about him.

'Damn you! What is this game you are playing?' Bonney demanded. 'Is it cribbage?'

'It's rummy, man!' Captain Elijah. 'A cruel game, too,' he said, laying down all four jacks. 'Gin!'

'Mr Bonney, it may be time to rest,' said Dr Moribund. 'You must take care of yourself, you know.' The doctor was eating a stale cake, one of a dozen petrified buns that Lieutenant Sploon had produced from his own store, and reaching for the tokay. 'I'll take you down myself.'

William Bonney glowered unconvincingly. He knew he was sick. The sad blackness he gazed into gazed blackly back, and when he closed his eyes a giddy nausea came over him. He waved his hand.

'I say, Giles, my good man!' He had difficulty with the vowels. 'Did you ever meet Mr Darwin? Or anyone in the Admiralty?'

Everyone looked at Bonney's bandaged face.

'I mean to ask,' Bonney continued, speaking in no one's direction, 'does anyone in England know about this expedition? Are you acting under any authority? Or is this some private folly?'

'Are you quite mad?' Quiet Giles blustered. He had heretofore been enjoying a pleasant evening, a certain relaxation at least. 'I have met Mr Darwin on more than one occasion. I have even had cause to visit him at his house in Kent where he keeps his fancy pigeons. And I can assure you that not only he, but all the members of the Royal Geographical Society are aware of our journey!'

Giles's look of affronted dignity was lost on the blind man.

'In addition, it was the Admiralty who appointed Captain Blood to take command.'

'Admiral Lacey, indeed,' Captain Elijah confirmed.

All of a sudden – the men had been drinking steadily and the sweat was dripping down the walls – Lieutenant Sploon held his hand up for silence, and then spoke himself.

'My spirit guide is here,' he said.

Sploon's hand remained aloft while an exultant flush passed through him.

'What are his instructions?' asked the Captain earnestly.

Moribund snorted. Even Mr Bonney gave a quick laugh. But Lieutenant Sploon remained entranced. His body had come alive with skin conditions. Welts appeared on his forearms and swirling rashes raced underneath his shirt, patterns like lace formed on his heavy neck.

'Lieutenant?' Giles inquired politely. 'Are you feeling all right?'

The man was shuddering, wide-eyed, his fine hair plastered over his skull.

His response was drowned out by the shout from the man seated beside him. 'Jesus Christ!'

Lieutenant Forte recoiled from the table as a black spider ran past his glass, dropped over the table's edge to the floor and dashed the short distance to the wall. It remained about halfway up the starboard cabin wall.

'That's a very big spider,' the Captain noted. 'Lieutenant? What do you say?'

'It's a very big spider, sir.'

'Perhaps you might remove it for us, lieutenant.'

'Yes, sir.'

'No!' Mr Giles protested. 'Let me fetch a jar.'

Some kind of tarantula, he thought, and edged around the table to get a closer look.

Lieutenant Forte was quick, however, his shoe was in his hand and in an instant the creature was a creamy smear on the cabin wall.

'Can't be too careful, Mr Giles,' he said soberly.

'What was it, Giles?' asked William Bonney, who had remained rigid during the tense moments. 'Something fine, no doubt.'

'I'm not sure. It was as big as your hand, though. Furry.'

Lieutenant Sploon was ill. A sudden reaction, no doubt, to the unknown leavings in William Weed's stew. He stood up with difficulty and Dr Moribund was obliged to help him below, to the sick bay where he could administer something for the nausea and perhaps some unguent to mollify his skin. Giles watched their clumsy exit and could not help wondering if the curious circumstance of the officer was related to the black spider spread upon the wall and on the underside of Lieutenant Forte's shoe.

❦

Giles helped Bonney to his cabin. An awkward walk conducted in silence and very unpleasant air, due to the stench in the gangway. The ship was ripe with vomit. Lieutenant Sploon had spewed several times on the way downstairs, leaving pools of his greenish bile on the steps. It was particularly trying for William Bonney with his newfound olfactory ability, and it was with some relief that he felt his way into his cabin and lay down, head throbbing, on his bunk. He searched for an itchy blanket to protect himself from the mosquitoes, which had never been more annoying. He slept almost immediately, still fully dressed, and with his boots on.

Giles had continued to his own cabin. He lit two candles and settled himself at the desk, his knees bunched close to his chest. He was not sleepy, though his bones ached from too much wine. He spent some time turning the pages of his diary, re-reading the details of the long days that had led him here. It was an interesting document, he thought again, definitely one that deserved a wider audience; and the compulsion to continue, to reach the sea, was fuelled equally by his desire for discovery, and by the need for a grand ending to his account of the journey. Failed expeditions were only deemed heroic by the London press if the protagonists died in the attempt. Above all, Giles wished to return home alive. To greet his loving wife at Deptford and together take the long carriage ride to Kensington. Giles imagined himself, homecome, Mary by his side in the back of the Clarence, administering little kisses all over his body, while the horses pulled them through the familiar streets to St James's Terrace.

*

Dr Moribund took leave of his patients in the sick bay. Both Sploon and Thomson were sleeping. He had spent twenty minutes preparing a pipe and smoking it while Sploon drifted into unconsciousness. He smoked a mix of hashish and tobacco and the heavy smoke charred the back of his throat. He had never, during all his terrible bout of bloat, felt so poorly. His stomach ached with cramps. He was foolish to have eaten at all.

Dr Moribund placed wet cloths over the foreheads of both men and returned to the head, the scene of such discomfiture earlier in the day.

Inside his cabin Giles heard the water slapping against the hull, and the clink of iron in the rigging. He found the sounds soothing. He had taken a draught of laudanum and its irresistible calm made him dreamy.

He looked up from his journal and spent some blank moments regarding the gorilla kept now on the corner shelf. Giles had become fond of the pickled ape and in the interests of its greater safety had transferred it to his own cabin.

He turned back to his journal.

FEBRUARY 6
The sickness on board was surely an untimely omen. The bodies we tipped overboard would not sink. Though they be wrapped in chains. The bloat caused them to rise after only a short time – sometimes they surfaced ahead of us, having played in the currents beneath our boat, then floated towards the banks, where they were caught in the great roots of the

eucalypts, or snared by fallen boughs, grounded shallow in clumps of reeds.

Giles was developing a boil on his nose. He dabbed its tender point with a wet handkerchief, wet with his own spit, and resolved to visit Moribund directly for some cream. First, though, he embarked on another letter to his wife.

My dearest Mary, [he wrote,]
A wife so comely and rich deserves a husband by her side. It is my greatest ambition to fulfil that role as soon as practicable. We have sailed for six weeks the length of the uncharted river, and now find ourselves deep in the country. It is a lonely land, but surely our goal is near! How I think of you, my love, abroad in the streets of the metropolis. Retiring home at day's end I imagine your undress, the sweet state of your cunny . . .

Giles stopped. The sudden deterioration in his tone was due in part to his opiated state, but also to the sense of futility he often felt when corresponding. He had written many letters. Letters that would not be read for a year, or read not at all. They were bundled in packets inside his sea chest. He returned to his boudoir scene. He spoke his wife's name as she lay down for him, tracing his thumb across the tiny puckers of her belly, and all manner of venery flowed from his pen. It was a goatish romp he would have tonight.

*

Afterwards, Giles thought suddenly of tomatoes, and how he liked them fried with eggs.

He scratched his nose, disengaged from the desk with difficulty, and went in search of Doctor Moribund.

The Earth was wobbling on its axis, surrounded on all hemispheres by millions of stars. Moribund gazed upwards at the southern constellations. The mysterious operations of the stars had fated him here, god forsaken, horizontal on the wooden deck and clinging to life itself. His breeches were bunched at his ankles. The pain had gone and he took heaving breaths in the frightening air of his toilet. His head fell back onto the cold planks and he lay there, his face awash with perspiration, contemplating the sky. A few precious cool moments before they came again. A series of vivid convulsions ratcheting through his frame. In a few minutes he began expelling his insides, a watery paste that included the lining of his stomach. And in this manner Dr Moribund met his maker.

Captain Elijah slipped down to the sick bay himself, hoping to find something in the doctor's bag. He pulled aside the blanket that served to screen off the area and was surprised to find a burglar already at work. Between the two silent figures – Lieutenant Sploon and Gunner Thomson on their sick beds – a third frame was looking through the doctor's leather bag by the light of a match. Its flame illuminated the face of Edwin Robins as he turned to regard the intruder. He smiled.

The two men regarded each other, the burglar and the thief. The match went out.

'Captain?' came a voice behind him. 'Is something wrong?'

It was Quiet Giles. He peered over the Captain's shoulder into the dark sick bay.

Captain Elijah lit a match of his own. Edwin shuffled forward.

'I couldn't find the doctor,' he bleated, aware of his compromised position. 'I needed some medicine, sir.'

'Find a candle, boy.' The Captain swayed slightly on his feet. 'I need some morphine myself.'

'Where is Doctor Moribund?' asked Quiet Giles. 'He was not in his cabin. I have just come from there.'

Edwin struck another match to light the candle he found between the beds. He held it up to the Captain, who grasped it clumsily and spilled the first wax on his fingers. He stepped closer to the beds and waved the yellow light across the faces of the sleeping men. Neither of them looked well, but the slackness of Lieutenant Sploon's skin gave him the look of a dead man, though he breathed through an open mouth. The injured gunner lay still.

'Go and find Doctor Moribund.' Captain Elijah addressed Edwin Robins. 'Tell him he is needed at once.' He paused, squinting at the boy with his sorry eyes. 'Tomorrow you will report to Lieutenant Forte for extra duties.'

Captain Elijah did not wait for a reply. He picked up Moribund's bag and set it on the bench, where he was better able to examine its contents. Edwin wiped his hands on his shirt and squeezed past the Captain. He nodded to Mr Giles before scampering away on his second grisly mission for the day.

'You may go also, Mr Giles,' the Captain said.

Ship's Log

H.	K.	F.	Courses.	Winds.	Remarks,&c.
					Lt. Forte's Shore party attacked a.m.
12			N	S	One sailor injured – party returned without wood or water.
4			NE	S	Modt breezes and clowdy afternoon.
					Escaped unorthodox attack from natives through Thomson Gorge. A Particularly dangerous passage.
					The ship sleeps with two corpses tonight.

Day Eighty-Nine

Captain Elijah smoothed out the letter again. He was at his desk early, having slept briefly, and was working on his charts. As always, the temptation gnawed away at him and he soon abandoned the maps in favour of Clara Lacey's letter. He had to be more careful now, the paper was weak along its grubby folds and dry as old parchment since his unfortunate dunking. The ink had run but the text remained true. He smoothed out the page with his hand, as if attracting by magnetism whatever residues of her might remain there.

He sat in his dressing gown staring at a map pinned to the cabin wall, his hand still resting on the open letter and his mind elsewhere. He believed that their expedition was over. There had been no progress for seven days, and there would be none today. He had not surfaced from his cabin this morning, and had spoken to no one save William Weed, who had already supplied him with coffee and biscuit, but the Captain knew there had been no change in *Bright Planet*'s circumstance. Torrential rains would be required for the river to rise enough for the ship to clear the sand-banks that thwarted their way.

Captain Elijah felt disinclined to move from his desk. He added up the days since he had left Plymouth. Three hundred and eighteen. Then he calculated the time he had spent on the waves over his career, the long hauls, the Mediterranean runs, two years in the Indies. The result was sobering, a fetid collection of days which, unravelled, form a life. He doodled with his red ink around the numbers. He was considering how long he might wait for the rains to come. He had no knowledge of the weather here, but he could safely assume they were too far south for a monsoon, and in all likelihood there would be no rain at all. The skies had been clear for a fortnight. The plains on each side of the river were dry fields of long brown grass. A few thin trees. The only sign of water was a little creek, which barely burbled over the pebbles onto the southern sandbar. The ship took its drinking water here, and indeed this creek was the only piece of fortune keeping the expedition from turning back immediately. For as long as they had fresh water they could afford to wait.

Bright Planet was anchored some hundred yards from the first of the sandbars, which stretched across the whole river at a depth of four or five feet. Downstream there were further sandbars clearly visible and it was obvious to the men on the forecastle deck that there would be no passage through this stretch of water. William Weed cleared his throat, hawked, and spat an arcing gob over the side of the ship. He and Basin sat on the deck with an upturned tea chest between them.

'What have ye got, lad?' He spoke softly, with a gravelly edge to his words. 'Show us, then.'

Slowly, Basin laid down his cards. He had a pair of twos and a pair of queens. It was his best hand for the morning and he had staked his remaining crown on the strength of it.

'Ahh,' William Weed sighed. 'The lamb comes creeping in to the butcher.'

He laid out his own hand and looked up at his companion through his craggy grey eyes. With a twist of the lips he smiled, as he revealed his three sixes, and swiftly pocketed the coins. He rolled them in a sock and they swung heavily in his dungarees as he got to his feet.

He liked the feel of money, the weight of it against his leg as he sauntered along the gangway. He waved to Lieutenant Sploon, who was pacing the quarterdeck around the prone figure of Mr Bonney.

Bonney lay flat on his back with his face turned to the sun. He liked the burning feeling behind his eyes, as if there was light there. His face had become more ravaged with scars after his second wounding, but it had achieved a symmetry that was in some way pleasing. His grey hair spread across the deck. He had brushed it out, stroke after stroke, like a lady would, and it shone now in the clear sunlight.

In general, Bonney's hygiene had improved markedly since he lost his sight. He spent many hours each day scouring the crevices of his body with whatever cleaning agents his fellows would supply. The deodorisation of his person had become paramount due to his vastly improved olfactory powers, for he could no longer stand the slightest smell of mould or scurf.

Mr Bonney's hearing had also improved and he could hear quite distinctly the mutterings of Lieutenant Sploon as he paced the deck. Sploon smelled of river water and fish. The smell of fish was pervasive across the deck since young Basin had produced another haul for breakfast. Mr Bonney had happily eaten his share, but the smell of blood and entrails was now clinging to his nasal passages, and in every direction the remnants of the graveolent creatures hung in the air. Barely a breath of wind and already it was another hot day.

'Why does he not appear?' asked Lieutenant Sploon.

The lieutenant wore full regalia. A navy blue jacket and black woollen trousers over white spats. His buttons were gleaming and the badges on his epaulets glinted like minia-ture suns. He produced a tub of toffee and popped a square into his mouth.

'Why does he spurn our company?' Lieutenant Sploon spoke to Mr Bonney, but it was a rhetorical speech. 'We need to stay strong in our convictions, dear man, we must take the situation in hand. We must convince the Captain to turn back.'

Sploon smacked his lips and the sweet smell of toffee rose into the general fetor of the ship.

When Captain Elijah did appear, hopping down the wheel-house steps, well after ten, he found his lieutenant in an agitated state. Sploon hurried across the deck towards the Captain with the expression of a lunatic on his face.

'Sir!' He caught his breath. 'Good morning, sir.'

'Yes, lieutenant,' he replied with a smile. 'All's well, no doubt.'

Captain Elijah waited. His feet hurt and Lieutenant Sploon was blocking his path. He could see the words burbling in Lieutenant Sploon's throat before the torrent came.

'Turn us back, sir. Before we are all dead. Lieutenant Forte was healthy a week ago, and where is he now? Under a tree with no cross.'

'Agreed, but that may not have been the flux. He went so quickly, poor boy. It may well have been the berries he ate. The ones Mr Giles brought back.' The Captain frowned. 'Unless we have an agent aboard employing the infernal Italian practice.'

'Sir?'

'Poison. Unless it was poison.'

Lieutenant Sploon was taken aback.

'You don't suspect a poisoner?' His voice trilled like a child's. 'Do you, sir?'

'We have no medical opinions available, but I suspect what happened to Lieutenant Forte was that he got sick and died.'

'That is my fear for all of us.' Lieutenant Sploon tried to take a stronger tone. 'We could make it back to Bareheep within a month, Captain. Do you not think that the safer course?'

Captain Elijah laughed.

'We have been abroad for seventy-six days, lieutenant,

and we must travel against the current to return. Be assured it will take more than a month.' The Captain shifted his weight, wincing, then continued in a reasoned tone. 'Besides, we must wait for Mr Giles.'

The Captain's feet were bad. He had cut the toe-leather away from his left boot, leaving his enlarged digits to the daylight. An alarming sight, the Captain was aware, but he was grateful for the small consolation the air provided. He walked with a stick to ease the burden on his tender toes. This slowed his progress and he lagged behind the figure of William Weed striding lazily through the grass.

Captain Elijah had elected to accompany the cook ashore on his hunting trip, rather than face more whining and insolence from Lieutenant Sploon. They passed the tree that marked Lieutenant Forte's final resting place and picked their way over uneven ground, following the creek bed.

'What do you think his chances are, William?' the Captain asked.

They had stopped to survey the undulating plain before them.

'Mr Giles, you mean?'

The Captain nodded.

'Well, sir, I don't think much of them.'

Mr Giles was overdue. He had been gone four nights and he was still half a day's sail upriver from *Bright Planet*, crouched as he was, against the clay bank of the little cove where the skiff had beached the night before. He had told Captain Elijah that he would bivouac one night only and return to the ship the next day. But he had sailed for two and a half days, Giles and the boy in the little skiff. Only a rapids had prevented him from continuing even farther, for Giles felt the lure of the sea. The river seemed so certain, and despite the inconvenience of a small craft Giles too was certain. The Yarrow River flowed to the sea.

He waited by the river, watching the water stretch away. He had splashed his face and wet his hair, which hung half dry in bangs over his ears. Quiet Giles had been accused of coxcombry before, but his unkempt appearance gave him no mind today. He hunkered down with his journal on his knees, and waited for Edwin to return.

The sun arced over midday and burnt down. Giles recorded his thoughts, though he had few insights today. He had collected nothing for a week, for he had been confronted with the reality of a most anticlimactic end to their journey, and could think of little else. He had proved these last days that the river was indeed passable in a smaller craft, but the question of who might accompany him was vexing. It was entirely possible that no one would agree to make the journey with him, and Giles doubted he could make it alone.

With this in mind, Giles embarked on a letter to his wife.

My Dear Mary,
In the event you are reading this, you must know, ma chérie, that I have perished froid. At this moment I have my wits and

one remaining companion. We have left the ship aground and a bare crew, and are continuing interior in the skiff. Many are dead, under water or under ground. The miasmas rising off the water have a stupefying effect on Europeans, from which they succumb to their own pox.

A wonderful year of sickness and death. Nothing prepared me for such sights but somehow I have avoided the fevers.

How I think of you, my love, in your elegant wear. I torch my body. I have nothing left to reveal my soul already sundered beneath these cruel skies. I cannot worship Nature. My collection is with the ship. I carry only my drawings and some seeds, pressed flowers in my book, which I enclose in this parcel.

My companion is the ship's thief, Edwin Robins, a stowaway. He carries no more than a price on his head, but he has proved himself useful with the gun. He skins animals and cooks them up for our sustenance.

I imagine this makes distasteful reading at your breakfast table, still in your sleeping robes, still in the colour of your skin. Remember I have loved you, though I have forgotten the touch of your fingers, used only to the meditations of my own palm. I remember your regal bearing at the morning table. Let me imagine that inside your white slippers you are curling your toes. Let me imagine the down on your legs. What colour now your cheeks?

I am bedded down in the clay. My companion has gone missing with the gun. Each day he disappears longer, through the river country and into the hills, barking and calling, imitating the animals he has seen. At intervals the gun

discharges and I wish he would return. I pack some leaves for
my bed. I am forced to cover my skin from the burning sun;
already it is blackening to a most unusual shade.

Tomorrow we continue by sail, or as soon as the thief
returns.

I wonder at your skin, dear wife, its shades of white. I run
my hand through your curling hair. Was that a birthmark on
your neck, that rising flush I cannot remember?

How well you use your fingers.

Everything entwined. Let your guests – Is there someone
for tea? – hear you play.

Deliver my book to Messrs John Murray & Sons, and
keep my letters to yourself.

There was an element of exaggeration to his correspondence, but if it indeed proved to be his last epistle he
wanted more than poignancy. In any case it passed the
time.

Edwin, the stupid thief, was still missing with the gun.
Giles had intended to be well away by now, but the boy
was not reliable. He was reckless and also mean, but Giles
needed him for protection. He was a good shot for food
and had exhibited an uncanny ease in his dealings with
the native people. Though he had shown a violent temper
to many of the crew, Edwin was very friendly and quite
demure among the tribes that seemed to inhabit all parts of
the continent.

Giles leaned his head against the red clay of the riverbank and closed his eyes against the sun. He resolved to
wait one more hour.

Tom Basin remained the most agreeable sailor on board. His temperament rarely faltered. Again this afternoon he had a tune, despite the earlier indignity of losing his coins to the cook, and he happily loaded the dinghy for the short passage to shore.

Captain Elijah had built a good fire on the riverbank, and the ship's complement was headed ashore to watch William Weed roast their lunch. Lieutenant Sploon guided Mr Bonney to the gunwale and watched him climb down the ropes to the dinghy where Basin caught the blind man's feet.

Basin rowed the few strokes to the river's edge. He rolled a keg of Colonial Ale up the bank to the knoll where the Captain had lit his fire, beside a little grove of lemon-scented gum trees. Lieutenant Sploon carried a hammer and a handful of nails, and wedged under his arm were two slim lengths of oak. He had smashed a chair for the purpose.

Bonney clambered up behind him and stood uncertainly on the edge of the bank.

'Smell the trees!' he said loudly.

Lieutenant Sploon sniffed the air and put his closed hand to the small of Mr Bonney's back.

'This way,' said Lieutenant Sploon, nudging him forward.

William Weed had skinned a marsupial and was preparing to mount it on the spit. He and Captain Elijah lifted it over the fire and slotted the skewers into the mount. Flames licked up at the fat immediately. William Weed had built the device several weeks ago and they had since perfected its use as a means to barbecue. Soon the fat started spitting. The two men stood back from the fire and watched the meat start to cook. Tom Basin unplugged the barrel and everyone cheered. They shared their first beer in silence, watched the fire, and stood around.

Captain Elijah walked over to Mr Bonney, who noted that he still retained, after all this time, the smell of brine upon him. This did not overpower however the vapours emanating from his gaping boot.

'What is the landscape here?' William Bonney asked the Captain. Their relations had become more civil of late, for they were kindred spirits in one sense now, both forced to accept their fate.

'Oh! These are much drier lands than you have seen,' Captain Elijah replied. 'Low scrub everywhere. A few little hills and undulating land. There are some trees here and there but nothing big.' He looked around. 'It's very pleasant where we are here, though. Don't you think? Very jolly.'

Mr Bonney agreed. The smell of kangaroo flesh roasting on the spit thumped through his sinus and he was momentarily stricken with pleasure. He drank his ale and that too was good.

Lieutenant Sploon finished his second ale and moved away from the fire. He knelt on the ground and set to nailing his bits of wood together. He set a nail at their intersection, and bashed it with the hammer. It took three nails to fix it, but he had made a cross for Lieutenant Forte's grave.

He wandered over alone to the tree above the creek where Forte now lay. His cross slid easily into the freshly turned soil, and Lieutenant Sploon made a sign across his own chest. He waited a moment, sacrificed a moment for the dead who have none, then returned to the dinghy to retrieve a basket of bread.

They ate bread and meat, juicy red meat, and washed it down with flat beer.

'My compliments, William,' said Mr Bonney, licking the grease from his fingers.

'Hear! Hear!' Lieutenant Sploon seconded. He had a lot of grease to lick.

The picnickers sat under the grove of scented trees, and the lemon perfume proved a most delightful sedative. Each reclined with their back to a tree, forming a rough circle, across which the sailors traded affectionate jests. The round of barbs continued until Basin got up to fetch the keg closer and refresh their mugs.

'Here's to Thomas Wickham!' Basin lifted his jar and they all drank to Thomas Wickham.

'Poor lad,' said William Weed.

'Yes, it's a shame,' agreed Captain Elijah.

Spare a thought for Seaman Wickham, who fell overboard one afternoon a fortnight since. He was drunk that day and must have tripped over the gunwale. Various re-enactments by the crew proved such a debacle was possible. No one saw him go. No one noticed he was missing until nightfall. Next morning the ship turned around and retraced her passage for half a day but found no signs of him.

'What a way to go,' said Basin, for of course the water was the sailor's greatest fear.

'Many men 'a drowned before him.' William Weed was upbeat. 'They say it feels very peaceful at the end.'

'Who says?' asked Bonney.

'Well, them that nearly drowned,' replied William Weed. 'Who else?'

'I don't believe they would know. How near were they? To the end, I mean.'

'I don't know.'

'It might be very painful at the end.'

It was impossible to read the expression on William Bonney's face.

'I have heard the same thing,' Captain Elijah announced his support for the ship's cook. He raised his pewter mug. 'Let us drink now to our voyage. For as soon as Mr Giles returns we will begin our return.'

Cheers followed this most welcome disclosure, and another round of Colonial Ale to celebrate. They basked in the dappled shade of the trees and felt the kangaroo settle in their stomachs. To a man, they felt lucky to be alive, and Sploon most of all. Tears spilled from his eyes.

❧

Edwin Robins had been walking all morning. He carried a satchel and a gun. He had left Mr Giles before dawn, packed a few things and headed west. The botanist was snoring like a horse. Now Edwin marched along the low-slung spine of a cluster of hills, surveying the red lands stretching out below. He could no longer see the river to his east, only the dry plains he had been traversing. Edwin was looking for prey. He was hungry and his throat was caked dry with dust. The scrub he moved through provided good cover for the smaller beasts, but he preferred to shoot a kangaroo, and these animals were too big to hide. He had fired the rifle several times already, but each time the animal had been warned, and they were quick to run away.

He rested on the hilltop, under a small tree, and watched the plain below. The soil was reddish brown, blanketed with grey shrubs. The patches of colour were flowers and fruits. He was trying to see through the camouflage. Edwin sat with his satchel between his knees. Every so often he reached inside the pack to pat the ginger cat, which murmured at his touch. The cat had been his constant familiar since he had saved it from William Weed's kitchen – he had become overly fond of the tom – and now on his great adventure he carried him still, rather than leave him to the care of the untrustworthy fools on the ship. Edwin could use the company and, in any case, the cat could feed itself.

Edwin took off his shoes, sniffed them suspiciously, and set them aside. He had already removed his shirt. The sun had darkened his skin over the last month and bleached his hair, which he refused to cut, an improbable white. He struggled out of his blue trousers and stood naked by the trees, leafless in the shade, and the heat was prickling his shoulders. He was hungry still and now thirsty as well. He surveyed the land confronting him to the west, scanning the dense scrub. He knew, of course, that water lay to the east, but he was not going back that way. He rummaged past the cat for his flask and took a mouthful before setting off. Edwin strode away, in his natural state, protected only by the gun in his left hand and the satchel on his back. But he made just a few yards before turning back, appalled by his red genitalia, to retrieve the speckled trousers. He returned the frayed canvas shoes to his feet and stuffed the shirt in his pack.

Edwin's figure, his white hair sticking out at every angle, was visible from afar. He tracked slowly across the plain all afternoon. His head bobbed above the grey foliage, marking his position as he trudged along. His progress was easy to follow and all the creatures of the land kept their distance.

After an hour Edwin reached a small hill from the peak of which he saw the next hours stretch ahead. He rested among the saplings and, with his satchel between his knees, let the cat out of the bag. The ginger tom ran a few steps then stopped to sniff a pale flower. It looked back at Edwin before setting off, shoulders hunched, into the scrub. Edwin waited, listening to the raucous crickets, feeling a chill of solitariness, despite the heat of the day. He had expected to encounter someone by now, a hunting party, a camp, a wandering savage. These were empty lands, dun-coloured and unappealing. Edwin supposed that the natives thought as much and kept away. A distant line of hills to the north-west was the only break in the landscape. He was deciding to head for these when the moggy returned, growling softly. The cat was dragging an awkward lizard by the neck. It dragged the catch up the hill and presented it to Edwin. It was a fat lizard with a blue tongue and Edwin was pleased.

Giles waited more than an hour. He waited another twenty minutes, uncertain of the ethics. The boy had gone off and not come back and Giles could wait no longer. He was worried Captain Elijah had given him up for dead and lifted anchor. Giles reasoned that he was not leaving Edwin to die, because the boy had the rifle with him and, after all, he would be returning down river soon enough, and continuing all the way, God willing.

With that, Giles pushed off with his foot and jumped in the skiff with a splash. It was twenty past two in the afternoon. He tightened the mainsail, pulled on the jib and clenched the rope between his teeth as he had seen the boy do. He grasped the tiller and the boat lurched into the river. He had the wind behind him, what wind there was, and he steered as straight as he could.

It was nearing dusk before the crew returned to the ship. The shambles climbing the rope sent Basin onto his backside in the dinghy and Lieutenant Sploon into the water. He wore his best naval attire, his heaviest boots, and sank immediately. Basin reached in to retrieve him, and though he was laughing hard, pulled the struggling lieutenant to safety.

'Sorry, sir.'

'I should bloody well hope so,' said Lieutenant Sploon, struggling to his feet in the dinghy.

He was looking down river, past the sandbars.

'I say – !'

A sail appeared past the bulrushes and soon enough the skiff came into view. Sploon recognised the figure of Mr Giles, waving from the stern.

'Mr Giles is returned!' Lieutenant Sploon chimed triumphantly, as he sloshed up the side of the ship, Basin pushing him from behind.

Giles found the crew in high spirits. They had cheered his approach and loudly criticised his attempts to bring the little skiff alongside *Bright Planet*. Captain Elijah eventually threw him a line and Basin scampered down the nets to help transfer the missing botanist aboard. He was greeted warmly by all, gleefully even, and Giles wondered what could have caused this improvement in the collective mood. No one even asked about the boy. He wanted to debrief, but the Captain showed no inclination to detach himself from the boisterousness.

'Basin, fetch the rum!' Captain Elijah put a friendly arm around Giles's shoulder. 'Let us celebrate Mr Giles's safe return with a drink.' The Captain did not wait for Basin. He produced his own flask and offered it to Giles.

The sun had barely dipped below the horizon, yet they were as drunk as monkeys. Captain Elijah included. Giles was exhausted and his hands were sore from sailing. He saw no reason now not to follow suit, and took a heavy swig from the Captain's flask. He could not tell what it was but it burned all the way down. He swigged again and wiped his mouth with the back of his hand. He looked over their smiling faces.

'Where is Lieutenant Forte?' Giles asked.

A look of shame passed across Lieutenant Sploon's features, and one or two others adopted grave expressions, but no one answered his question, and then Basin had returned with the ship's rum. He passed out tumblers to each grinning man, and *Bright Planet*'s contingent stood on the deck in the gathering dark, holding their glasses in salute. They drank a toast to Mr Giles. They toasted the Captain. Then the cook. Mr Bonney for his bravery. Lieutenant Sploon for his considerable effort. And Basin for his looks.

'Well, he was in excellent health when I left here last Sunday,' said Giles, loading a plate for his companion.

'He died only two hours later,' Bonney told him. 'As soon as you were gone, the pains began. Captain says he ate some of those berries you found, the ones that smelled like camphor, though I can't see why he would have.'

'They were very pretty,' mused Giles, 'but hardly appetising. Would you like mustard?'

Mr Bonney nodded and Giles completed the sandwich. He set the plate down and Bonney searched with his hands.

'Not quite the tastiest meat we have known,' he announced, upon taking a mouthful, 'but perfectly acceptable.'

They were in the galley. Giles had surmised, correctly, that the celebrations on deck meant that the only way he was going to eat tonight was to feed himself. Mr Bonney was glad to accompany the botanist, and Giles, who had been alone all day, was glad of the company.

'I am determined to persist with my journey.' Giles spoke softly now, but with a forcefulness that was like a wind in William Bonney's ear. 'I have seen the river ahead. It is passable! It's wide and deep and I want to see where it goes.'

'You'll be going on yer own, then.'

'Why do you say that?'

'We're going home. The Captain said as soon as you returned we're on our way.'

'I need someone to go with me. In the little boat. I tell you, William, we're close.' Giles's vehemence was genuine. He bit into his sandwich and chewed.

William Weed lurked in the gangway. He watched Mr Bonney and Mr Giles eat their sandwiches, and eavesdropped a moment before entering the galley.

'Hello, William,' said Giles.

William Weed steadied himself against the doorway.

'Ev'nin', sir,' replied the cook. 'Have you had enough food? D'ye want me to open a tin o' soup?'

'No, thank you, William.' Giles smiled. His face was unused to it. He still felt poorly and the damper sandwich sat heavily in his rum-soaked belly.

'In that case, sir,' William Weed lurched towards the pantry, 'would you be offended, sir, if I asked the two of ye to leave my kitchen?' He wore an apologetic face. Strands of grey hair were plastered all over his forehead.

'Of course not,' said Giles, observing the man quizzically. He ushered Mr Bonney, sandwich in hand, to the gangway. Up on deck the laughter continued.

William Weed waited for them to go before diving to his knees and pulling open the bottom pantry. He reached in and manipulated a shelf to reveal a neat cavity. It was a booty hole, and here he duly stashed his coins. He reached into his trousers for the coin-heavy sock, which had been dangling inside his pants all day long, swinging like a second schlong. He transferred the coins to a strongbox that contained his fortune. He ran his fingers through the silver before returning the box to its hole. He kept his secrets in that hole, his best tools, his sweetheart stuff, and his secret fancy for a little house in Kent.

On the quarterdeck Tom Basin drank with the ship's two surviving officers, entertaining them with a saucy doggerel. A brassy laugh echoed through the warm evening. Lieutenant Sploon was a happy drunk indeed, and was insisting upon another song as Quiet Giles and William Bonney joined the merry group.

'It's very good to see you, Mr Giles,' said Tom Basin, affectionately clapping him on the shoulder. 'I've always liked you, sir, since you fixed my head that time, anyway.'

Quiet Giles smiled again, his face still uncomfortable.

'Thank you, Basin,' he replied. It was an effort to be convivial. He had tried to get drunk, and in fact accepted another swig now, from Captain Elijah's proffered flask, but the various climes of intoxication enjoyed by his shipmates were denied him.

'Yes, Mr Giles, we had begun to worry,' said Lieutenant Sploon. He sighed and adjusted his portly frame. 'But it is a happy day. And we are fortunate to see it.'

'Not I,' said William Bonney.

'Captain, I would like to deliver a report of my findings on the situation farther down river. It may cause you to rethink your decision.' Giles kept an even tone.

The Captain eyed him blearily.

'But, Mr Giles, it is obvious we cannot continue. The ship cannot pass.' He closed one eye. 'The decision is made for us.'

'The skiff can pass. It may only be a matter of a few days' sail. Come with me, Captain.' Giles implored. 'The two of us could make it.'

Captain Elijah pursed his lips, as if he were weighing up the ship's scientist's remarks. He was, rather, assessing the fitness of his limbs to make the climb to his cabin.

'Goodnight, men,' he said. 'I must make amends for a long day.'

'Captain, I must insist on a private conference.'

'Tomorrow, Giles! Tomorrow!'

The Captain had not meant to speak so harshly, but a sudden impatience had gripped him, and he shuffled off without another word.

Giles's indignance was further tested by the reappearance of William Weed on deck. The cook strutted across the quarterdeck piping a high tune on his stupid panpipe. How Giles hated the sound. He would waste no more time in the night air. He bid a polite goodnight and fended off an amorous sailor.

'No. I will not dance a jig!' Giles said forcefully, and beat a retreat to his cabin.

Once there, Quiet Giles lay down on his bunk and looked around his maudlin room. He felt a great relief to his bones as the laudanum surged through. His first taste in a week. The contents of his mind quickly cleared, leaving the empty space for his memory to fill. Of course Mary appeared, white-gloved and corseted, but it was an inexact version. He could not remember the detail of her face, and the reconstruction of his wife dissipated into another woman's image. A woman he did not recognise, but who would stand in for Mary for the purposes of his hallucination. Giles was too weary to object. In such small ways the mind decays, weakening by increments and unable to remember its failures.

So Giles amused himself, eyes closed and gritted teeth, and even dozed for a few moments. The loud songs of the sailors on the quarterdeck brought him back. They would sing old shanties all night, Giles was certain. There was no discipline any more. He rose from the bunk and carried a candle to his desk. He gathered his book together, many of its pages now loose-leaf, and was pleased to note that more than half the journal was filled with his own coppery hand. He needed to add the notes he had made while down river, but as always he wanted to go over his old entries, liking to polish here or there. He flipped backwards through his book.

JANUARY 3 1842

*I have spent the day ashore, enjoying the comforts of Bare-
heep, and coming to know one or two of its citizens.*

There was a gap in the page following this brief entry in
which Giles had drawn a good sketch of a female anatomy.

*How does love work? How many daily contempts can it tol-
erate? Clearly her decision was formal – her heart so full, her
eyes so tired and so unhappy. There she sits. Her cup rattling in
the saucer. Nothing could have been more surprising.*

Giles scratched out these remarks but left the drawing. He
made a mental note to improve the descriptions of his
movements on that day, although he could remember
nothing particular about January 3rd. He sought a more
recent entry.

MARCH 21ST

*The days I choose to write grow farther apart. I chide myself
for such inarticulateness, but these events are banal, the daily
routine, the unreasonableness of the journey. Today we travelled 21 miles through plains of the same description as yester-
day. It is the spring equinox, alas in this hemisphere it is
autumn. We are far from civilisation now. I have not seen
a squatter for weeks, only the natives that appear along the
river's banks. Today I observed a great horde of them. I was
relieved to find them quiet and orderly as we passed. They had
dozens of dogs with them, although many were sick and lame.
I do feel a sympathy for the savage tribes, whose tenure is
surely short. Several months ago the Colonial Parliament*

passed the *Pre-Emptive Act*, allowing any fortune seeker to settle lands prior to survey. Settlers will reach the lands we are now passing within a year.

It was satisfactory, no more, but the hour was getting late. Giles turned to a fresh page and wet his nib before commencing.

MARCH 30TH 1842

I have ventured 3 days beyond the sandbars that block Bright Planet's *passage. The river ahead is wide and strong. The terrain also is improved. Our prospects there are the opposite of discouraging yet Captain Blood is determined to turn the expedition back. I intend to convince him on the morrow that our destiny lies ahead. Only by continuing can we give value to our recent labours. I am resolved now to uncover the invisible geography of this continent and wish that my name should be remembered by after generations as the first to sail upon its interior lakes.*

The songs did not continue all night – the rum finally took its toll. Basin fell asleep first, boards for a pillow, followed by Lieutenant Sploon who slept upright, and William Weed whose fingers still gripped his pipe.

William Bonney eventually realised that his companions were aslumber and sought out his cabin without a guide. He sniffed his way forward and was soon kicking off his boots and laying down his embattled self. All the sounds of the night came alive in his head. He heard Mr Giles curse and an insect whirred away. He heard the water slapping against the hull, a fish splashed out in the river. Once again, Mr Bonney heard Captain Elijah at work. The scrape of his nib at minuit, while the crew is sleeping.

Ship's Log

H.	K.	F.	Courses.	Winds.	Remarks, &c.
					Mr Giles has returned from his reconnaissance.
					Ship's complement is now six – (the stowaway has been lost, presumably.)
					The warm weather continues and with no indication of a change our passage remains blocked. It is now my Strongest impulse to turn back the expedition.

Day One Hundred and Forty-Four

The skiff containing Mr Quiet Giles and Captain Elijah skated across a deep rapids and descended into a large lagoon, where it circled until the current resumed its tow.

The river had been widening for several days. Sandy islands marked the new channels as the river spread out, and baking upon these little beaches were the dry flotsam of fauna and the tangles of weeds the water had relinquished. The skiff piloted itself across the eddies and into a deep channel. It was caught now in a tidal flow and the boat moved swiftly despite its one remaining sail hanging useless from the mast. The two bodies were curled improbably in the open cockpit, already burning in the morning sun.

When Giles awoke, when consciousness returned, he delayed any movement, absorbing first the shock of the light on his features. High in the sky, those same black birds were circling in the too-blue air. Giles looked down at the Captain, whose folded form had shifted during the night.

Captain Elijah reclined in a pool of water that had settled against the bulkhead. He lay in his blue coat, half propped against the stern, with his right arm tied to the tiller. He moved like a dead man, to the tug of the rudder, as if his body was already under the sea. The gauze on his face could not conceal the ooze from the pores beneath.

Giles held a pistol. The flint was wet but it had fired successfully the previous afternoon when the dark birds had descended upon the explorers' craft. Again the botanist swivelled his eyes from side to side, as if he expected the receding banks to reveal their danger. He could not see beyond the starboard bank, but to the north a treeless pene-plane stretched towards a line of blunt ranges. Here the purple slopes climbed to a plateau. Giles shielded his eyes to scan this horizon.

The parched grey scrub provided obvious cover for the natives and the low animals that inhabited the continent's interior, the marauders who had dogged the expedition for weeks.

The morning slipped past. Giles made a meal from some rancid salt beef. He trailed his hand over the side and brought some water to his briny lips. He still wore the dead lieutenant's jacket, oversized and missing a sleeve, despite the impracticality of the latitude. He was hoping for a breeze to dissipate the steamy stench hovering around the tiny craft. Giles had no idea of the time. By day he watched the sun's arc, by night he observed the moon. Now, with the sun directly overhead, Giles installed himself in the stern alongside his friend. He produced a draught of poppyseed from his satchel and drank it with a grimace. At last he attended to the skiff, which had been navigating, aided by the weight of the Captain's arm, towards the lee bank where a series of sandbars now loomed. Giles untied the Captain's hand and negotiated the islets himself. The black birds circled lower.

The river's banks were less distinct now, the water merging into marshes and slobland, and even in his cups Giles recognised that this new vista was unmistakably estuarine. The edge of the sea always looks like the edge of the sea.

Giles raised his pistol in the air, firing it blindly, as if testing a proposition. He was too distant to disturb the birds.

'Now am I dead?' he asked. He spoke aloud, neither to the Captain nor himself.

For here, at length, after these many days, was a district of water they had barely dreamed of.

The skiff was already a mile from the shore and, looking back, Giles realised how opulent the river had become. At this distance the white sand of the lido glittered across the surface, and beneath the boat, surely, a trove of lacustrine creatures. At once, Quiet Giles, the botanist, reached into his satchel. He retrieved his journal while above him the birds worked through the air.

Acknowledgments

I owe a debt of gratitude to Robyn Annear for her marvellous work on the history of early Melbourne in *Bearbrass: Imagining Early Melbourne*. The ship *Bright Planet* first appeared here, as did the blue-speckled trousers of Edwin Robins.

Thomas W. Laqueur's essay, 'Amor veneris, rel Dulcedo Appeletur', was also invaluable on the 19th-Century idea of 'clitorisme'.

I thank the Australia Council for its support during the writing of this novel.